Taylor felt like Humphrey Bogart in *Casablanca*. Of all the psychologists and all the talk shows in all the world, why did he have to show up at this one?

Jonathan didn't respond to Katrina, instead focusing all of his considerable attention on Taylor, making her feel as if she were the most beautiful creature on the planet. He'd always been good at that trick, she reminded herself, even as she fell for it.

"Congratulations," he said, speaking for the first time, "on receiving your doctorate and your publications."

That voice. That liquid chocolate, come-to-bed-with-me and-I'll-make-you-touch-the-stars voice. Telling herself she was immune was one thing. Ignoring the sensation of bone-melting desire was another.

"Congratulations to you as well," she said, giving him her best smile and thanking God her bout with the flu the previous month had made her lose five pounds. "You always wanted to be the top in your field and you are. Dr. Jonathan Kirby, superstar."

"Thirty seconds, people."

Katrina raised an eyebrow. "You two know each other?"

"Of course," Taylor said, holding out her hand to the man who had once been the center of her universe.

Critical acclaim for best-selling author
Susan Mallery's
Sweet Success

"Susan Mallery makes a much anticipated mainstream debut with this gem. The humor, warmth, and rich characterizations make this a must read."

—*Romantic Times*

"Subtle touches of humor and interesting secondary characters carry this sweet tale from beginning to end. Readers who enjoy character-driven stories will find *Sweet Success* a delightful read."

—*Rendezvous*

"Susan Mallery has knocked herself out. *Sweet Success* has so much going for it. [An] exceptional book . . . filled with warmhearted laughter and wonderful relationships. . . . A delightful read with a luscious hero and a heroine to die for. Ms. Mallery is one writer I don't want to miss for the world."

—*The Belles and Beaux of Romance*

Also by Susan Mallery

Sweet Success

Available from Pocket Books

SUSAN MALLERY

Married
for a
Month

POCKET STAR BOOKS
New York   London   Toronto   Sydney   Singapore

This book is a work of fiction. Names, characters, places and incidents are products of the author's imagination or are used fictitiously. Any resemblance to actual events or locales or persons, living or dead, is entirely coincidental.

An *Original* Publication of POCKET BOOKS

A Pocket Star Book published by
POCKET BOOKS, a division of Simon & Schuster, Inc.
1230 Avenue of the Americas, New York, NY 10020

Copyright © 2001 by Susan Macias Redmond

ISBN: 0-7434-0596-X

First Pocket Books printing December 2001

10 9 8 7 6 5 4 3 2 1

POCKET STAR BOOKS and colophon are registered trademarks of Simon & Schuster, Inc.

For information regarding special discounts for bulk purchases, please contact Simon & Schuster Special Sales at 1-800-456-6798 or business@simonandschuster.com

Front cover illustration by Tom Hallman

Printed in the U.S.A.

*I have frequently thought that had I known where
I would end up, I would have prepared better.
This book is for those who face the unexpected
with grace and dignity.
You are an inspiration to us all.*

Author Acknowledgment

The town of Marriageville is my own creation and if you try to find it on a map, I fear you will only give yourself a headache. Marriageville is a compilation of what I learned over the three years I spent living in the Houston area and during several visits to Dallas–Ft.Worth, influenced by movies and books set in Texas. I have always been a fan of the Lone Star state. I suspect in real life Marriageville would be close to Austin.

As for the characters themselves, they are fabrications, although I have to admit that several of them have become quite real to me over time.

While the act of writing in and of itself is solitary, the process of writing is not . . . at least not in my world. I do have a fantasy of creating a perfect work of fiction in the privacy of my office—of never discussing it with a soul, and then turning it in to my editor, who will faint from the brilliance of my prose.

That has never happened to me.

So until it does, I owe a great debt of gratitude to several individuals who helped, encouraged, and simply listened when I felt an overwhelming desire to whine that this was all just too hard.

To Christina, Maureen, and Terry who offered advice and encouragement. To my editor, Amy Pierpont, who had wonderful ideas for making the story better. And to Callie and Jake, who brighten my day.

Finally, to Mike—who knew it was brilliant from the start.

Chapter 1

"We have a surprise for you, Taylor," Katrina Melon said in her oh-so-perky voice.

Taylor McGuire blinked at the fifty-something cable-show host and forced herself to speak, despite the fact that her throat was closing tight enough to snap steel. "No," she managed, then licked dry lips. "No surprises."

Katrina, in her too-pink Chanel suit, with her styled white-blond hair and perfectly made-up, taut features, leaned forward and patted her hand. "You'll be fine," she murmured soothingly.

Oh, yeah, right, Taylor thought, desperately searching for the humor in the situation. Her palms regularly went from damp to dripping, while her legs trembled—even though she was sitting down. If this was fine, she couldn't wait to experience anxious or even panicked. The good news was she could now say she'd had a near-death moment and survived. The bad news was that she was seconds away from making a complete fool of herself in front of millions of viewers, including her friends and family back home in Texas.

Katrina put down her notes and smiled again, sort of—with her tight skin it was hard to tell. "All set?"

Taylor didn't answer. What was the point? The plastic princess would dismiss any protests she made. Instead she concentrated on her breathing, trying to ignore the fact that *Psychology in the News* was a well-respected national cable show produced in New York. Professional cable, not badly done cable access with strange people and grainy pictures. Actual doctors and professors and cutting-edge psychologists watched the show, participated in the debates and wrote papers about subjects discussed. Taylor herself rarely missed the weekly broadcast.

Katrina's features relaxed slightly into an expression of sympathy. "I know we were going to bring you on the last two minutes of the show and talk about your theory. What was the title of your thesis again?"

"Compatibility as the Key to a Successful Marriage," she managed through clenched teeth.

"Right. But with Dr. Bill getting food poisoning last night and our show being live, we had to make some changes." Katrina patted her hand. "Think of the exposure. Maybe now you'll get a book contract."

"Maybe," Taylor murmured, thinking she would rather go home. Dreams of fame and fortune were way overrated, anyway. Right?

A man standing just outside the bright lights yelled something about ten seconds back to air.

Exposure for her theory, she reminded herself, repeating the phrase like a mantra. Exposure meant interest. Interest could mean a sale. A sale meant a lot of things—like the potential of financial stability, validation, and a chance to feel she'd accomplished her goals.

She'd been doing her darnedest to sell her book on compatibility, but so far no one had made an offer. Part of the problem was her lack of expertise. She was a single mom from a small town no one had ever heard of. Her doctorate was so new that in human terms, it was still a zygote and her entire publishing history consisted of exactly two professional articles. Hardly a body of work impressive enough to inspire excitement in the publishing world.

Or on cable television, she thought, wondering how she was supposed to fill thirty minutes of live TV.

"Five, four, three—"

Suddenly the lights got much brighter and Katrina turned her smooth face toward an invisible audience.

"We're back with Dr. Taylor McGuire, whose thesis, "Compatibility as the Key to a Successful Marriage" is stirring interest in the world of psychology. Tell us about your ideas, Dr. McGuire."

Taylor tried to remember the only yoga class she'd ever attended. She'd been unable to walk for nearly a week after because her body just plain didn't bend that way, but she did recall how wonderful the deep breathing had been. That's what she needed to do now. Keep breathing.

"I have a private practice," she said, hoping her voice wasn't shaking as badly as she feared. "Over the past few years the emphasis has been on marriage counseling and premarital seminars. I began to notice a pattern in successful relationships—not just marriages. From my observations I realized that the more people had in common, the more easily they could get along."

Katrina nodded. "You realize that there are those who don't agree with you."

"Of course." Taylor thought about saying they were wrong.

"One such person is a frequent and popular guest here on *Psychology in the News*. Dr. Jonathan Kirby. Dr. Kirby, as we all know, believes that opposites attract and make for the most exciting marriages. In fact, he's written several books on the subject. He's here now and I'm hoping that he and Dr. McGuire can enter into a spirited discussion on the matter."

The room might have been blurring before, but now it was positively spinning. Jonathan Kirby here? Now? It wasn't possible. No trick of fate could be that unkind.

Oh, but it could, she realized a heartbeat later when a tall, dark-haired man strolled out onto the set. He had a lean, yet powerful body, and moved with the grace of someone comfortable in front of a television camera. Or naked. Jonathan had always been completely unselfconscious in the buff. It was just one of oh, fifty million factoids that zipped through her brain. They flew through in a nanosecond, accompanied by a screaming voice reminding her that seventeen years ago, Dr. Jonathan Kirby had dumped her and walked away without a backward glance.

This is so unfair, she thought. Reminding herself that life was not fair didn't make her feel any better. She wasn't even surprised. This was so *her* life. Just when she thought she had it all together, a ghost from her past showed up to rip it all apart . . . on live cable, no less.

"And we're out," the disembodied voice from beyond the cameras called. "Back in a minute-thirty, people. Stay ready."

The intensity of lights faded some. Katrina rushed from behind her desk toward Jonathan.

"Thank you so much for coming," she purred, placing one long, slender hand on his upper arm. "When I heard that Dr. Bill was sick and our only other guest was Taylor here, I nearly died." Katrina flashed Taylor a smile. "No offense, dear, but no one has heard of you, and your ideas aren't exactly earth-shattering enough to fill up the entire half hour."

Taylor wasn't offended. She felt like Humphrey Bogart in *Casablanca*. Of all the psychologists and all the talk shows in all the world, why did he have to show up at this one?

Jonathan didn't respond to Katrina, instead focusing all of his considerable attention on Taylor, making her feel as if she were the most beautiful creature on the planet. He'd always been good at that trick, she reminded herself, even as she fell for it.

"Congratulations," he said, speaking for the first time, "on receiving your doctorate and your publications."

That voice. That liquid chocolate, come-to-bed-with-me-and-I'll-make-you-touch-the-stars voice. Telling herself she was immune was one thing. Ignoring the sensation of bone-melting desire was another.

"Congratulations to you as well," she said, giving him her best smile and thanking God her bout with the flu the previous month had made her lose five pounds. "You always wanted to be the top in your field and you are. Dr. Jonathan Kirby, superstar."

"Thirty seconds, people."

Katrina raised an eyebrow. "You two know each other?"

"Of course," Taylor said, holding out her hand to the man who had once been the center of her universe. The sudden flood of sexual attraction was a tad distracting but she was determined to be a grown-up about the situation.

She realized then that facing a blast from her past was the best medicine for overcoming her fear of being on television. The trembling had fled. In its place was a sense of purpose. She could debate Jonathan Kirby and win because she did it every time he was on the show. She paced in her living room, shot off witty responses, exposed his theories to the light of logic and soundly trounced him. She would ignore the fact that their one-sided conversations didn't give him the opportunity to answer back.

Jonathan took her hand in his and held it as they moved toward the seats.

"I'm looking forward to debating your theory," he said easily.

"I'm looking forward to winning," she said, settling next to him and removing her fingers from his, trying not to let anyone see that his touch had burned all the way down to her geez-I-haven't-had-sex-in-three-years soul.

"In five, four, three—"

The lights came up. "Welcome back," Katrina said, staring directly at the camera with the red light on top. "Dr. Kirby, what do you think of Dr. McGuire's theory of compatible couples having the best marriages?"

"I would say it's interesting, but not statistically sound. As I've said before, what makes a marriage work is just that—work. We've all seen couples whom everyone assumes will stay together for years divorce after a few months, and other couples who don't have a prayer of a happy relationship staying together for fifty years. A good portion of marital longevity comes from a willingness to stick it out through the tough times. Add in sexual compatibility and attraction, and you've got a winner."

Taylor found herself getting distracted by the reality of seeing Jonathan again after all these years. *Focus,* she told herself. *Deal with him later.* She had to concentrate on his theories and blast them into the ether.

Taylor leaned forward slightly and smiled at Jonathan. "Dr. Kirby is referring to anecdotal evidence," she said calmly. "Those great stories we all like to tell of people triumphing over nearly impossible odds. However, they are the exception, rather than the rule. Most people consciously and subconsciously seek a partner who is similar in most respects. Life is made more pleasant when our partner has the same fundamental value system, as well as a like expectation for future goals, such as wanting or not wanting children. I'm afraid Dr. Kirby is confusing good drama with real life."

Katrina glanced at her, surprise and the tiniest kernel of respect in her wide eyes. "Jonathan, how do you respond?"

He winked at Taylor. "I'd ask about sexual attraction. In my view, it's one of the most powerful forces around and far more important than compatibility. I would also remind my esteemed colleague that a traditional marriage is made up of two of the most fundamentally different creatures on the planet," he said. "A man and a woman. Talk about opposites attracting."

Katrina chuckled. "Excellent point." She reached over and patted Jonathan's arm.

Taylor resisted the urge to roll her eyes. Traditional marriages might be made up of men and women, but Katrina had more in common with a cat in heat. Of course women had always loved Jonathan, flocking to him everywhere he went.

"All the more reason to have them compatible," Taylor said crisply. "Growth and change are a natural part of a life cycle. If two people begin a journey together in relatively the same place, emotionally, and share the same experiences, the odds of them going in the same direction are much greater."

Jonathan shook his head. "Dr. McGuire, you couldn't be more wrong. If two people are in the same place when they start, you can bet they're going to end up in different places. It's not about starting in the same place, it's about the goal. We can be on opposite sides of a mountain, but if we both head for the peak, we'll end up standing on top. And if we have good sex along the way, all the better."

Taylor ignored that last comment. "Life is not a journey up a mountain. It's a road trip with no map.

People who are alike understand each other. They work together, each supporting the other."

"Or they get bored, fall asleep and drive into a ditch."

Katrina chuckled. "An excellent point, Dr. Kirby." Reluctantly, she turned her attention to Taylor. "Dr. McGuire, what does your thesis say about the boredom issue? If people are too alike, don't they get tired of each other?"

"Not at all. When two similar people build a life together, they have goals and want to achieve them. Who would you rather have on your side? Someone you understand and can depend upon, or an exciting, but unfamiliar wild card, who may not be there when times get tough?"

Jonathan grinned. "So you're admitting that similar couples are unexciting."

Taylor winced as she realized she'd neatly baited her own trap and stepped into it. "My point is, when times get tough, and they will, most people prefer to have a known entity on their side. For the initial thrill of the chase, someone different can be an interesting diversion, but in the long haul, we want a partner similar to ourselves."

He raised his eyebrows. "Want to bet?"

Taylor blinked at him. "Excuse me?"

"I am asking if you're willing to wager on your theory. You know. Put your money where your mouth is."

She glanced at Katrina. Was this a setup? But their pink-clad host looked as confused as she felt.

"Dr. Kirby?"

"Dr. McGuire and I are at opposite ends of the spectrum," he told the camera. "I thought it might be interesting to find out who's right. Let the people decide. I propose we set up a contest to test our respective theories."

"You're crazy," Taylor said without thinking.

Jonathan touched her arm, sending a river of sparks floating through her. "Dr. McGuire, you know we don't use words like that in our profession."

"All right," Taylor said twenty minutes later when they were off the air and standing in a conference room. "Maybe crazy was a bad choice of words, but there's something very wrong with you."

"Is that your professional opinion?" Jonathan asked, enjoying the temper flaring in her eyes and the way Taylor wouldn't look at him.

How long had it been since he'd last seen her? Ten years? Fifteen? She'd been all of eighteen when they'd gone their separate ways. He'd been nearly as young and just as foolish.

She placed her hands on her hips and sucked in a breath, the way she always had when she'd been preparing herself for battle. Funny how he could remember that. He could also remember what they'd been like together in bed—they'd created enough heat and energy to power a solar system.

"Don't toy with me, Jonathan," she told him. "You may be an incredibly popular media psychologist, but you don't impress me."

"You never were one to be impressed easily. I'm glad you got your degree, Taylor. I know that was important to you."

She glared at him. "You're not some doting aunt meeting me at a family reunion. Quit pretending you know anything about me."

"I used to know everything about you." His gaze settled on her neck and the sweet spot under her ear where she loved him to—

"Whatever you're thinking, stop it," she demanded. "I know I'm not in your professional league. As far as the world is concerned, you're the expert and I'm just some hick from a small town. Well, here's a news flash—I know I'm good at what I do. I don't spend my days being an expert guest on every talk show on the planet and I don't make a career out of publishing best sellers. I work with patients, and I understand what helps them and what doesn't. I see validation of my theories on a daily basis and I deeply resent your attempting to make a mockery of me and my ideas."

She practically breathed fire as she spoke. *So much energy,* he thought, enjoying her passion.

Had she always been beautiful, he wondered, watching her blue-gray eyes widen with indignation and the way her mouth trembled. Her shoulder-length hair was still the color of honey, and if he remembered correctly, as soft as silk.

He leaned against the wall and folded his arms over his chest. "When did you get so earnest?"

"When did you sell out?"

"When the money got good."

Before she could reply, Katrina burst into the room. She clutched a pad of paper to her chest. "The phones are going crazy. Legal's screaming about it, but who cares what they think." She hurried toward him and crowded close. "Jonathan, you're a genius. Do you know what this is going to do for the show's ratings and for your book sales? A contest based on your two opposing theories. It's brilliant."

"Thank you," he said modestly, watching Taylor instead of the talk-show host.

"I've already spoken with your publisher's publicity department," Katrina continued. "We think this can be big. And we came up with a brilliant idea. After all, people must be motivated to participate, right? So there's going to be prize money for some very lucky contestant! And a big boost to both your careers!"

She clasped her hands together. "Get this. By taking a small percentage of book sales, plus money from your publisher and our show, we think we can put together a million dollars."

"Quite a price for selling one's soul," Taylor said.

"You don't have to agree to this," Jonathan told her, ignoring Katrina, who was still talking.

He watched Taylor's internal battle. The only signs were a slight tightening of her too-wide mouth and a faint tension in her body. What was at stake for her? Why didn't she just tell him to go to hell?

And then he knew. Taylor thought she was right and she desperately wanted to beat him. But was her interest just about the book she wanted to sell or was it more personal?

"Interesting dilemma," he murmured. "Idealism battling plain, old-fashioned ambition."

"I'm sure I don't know what you're talking about," she said.

"I'm sure you do."

He stared at her until she looked away first. He'd come up with the idea of the bet on a whim. Now he was starting to see it was one of the best ideas he'd ever had.

Katrina glanced at them both. "Then we're in agreement? We're going to do this?"

Jonathan kept his gaze fixed firmly on Taylor. "Oh, yes. We're going to take this one all the way."

Chapter 2

"No, really. You were great," Marnie Boudine said two days later as she curled up in a chair in Taylor's living room. "You didn't let that Jonathan Kirby person distract you from your purpose for being on the show."

Taylor wanted to accept her friend's praise, but after ten years she knew that when given a choice between being honest and being kind, Marnie always chose kind. "I'm afraid I came off as too much of a bitch."

Marnie's green eyes widened. "Never. You were forceful," she said firmly. "There's a difference."

Taylor groaned and dropped her head to her hands. "I knew it. Men are allowed to be forceful. They're even encouraged to act that way. But never women." She rubbed her temples, then straightened. "I'll try not to think about the fact that all of America thinks I'm a bitch."

Marnie gave her a reassuring smile. "Honey, very little of America was watching your show. You're the only person I know who finds it entertaining."

"Publishers might have been watching," Taylor reminded her. "Do you think my performance on *Psychology in the News* is going to make them want to buy my thesis and publish it?"

"Absolutely."

Taylor couldn't help smiling. "Thanks. I'm sure I'll hear from my agent any second now with a book offer."

"If not now, then soon," Marnie told her. "Maybe after the contest."

Taylor held up her hand. "Please. Do not say the 'c' word in my presence. I can't believe I agreed to that. The whole experience of being on the show is like a bad dream. I keep having flashbacks."

Mostly of seeing Jonathan Kirby, she thought. She leaned back in her chair and wondered what she'd done to deserve having her carefully constructed world spun out of control by the one person she never, ever wanted to see again. The inevitability of disaster loomed like a force-five hurricane heading directly for land.

"At least the contest is going to take place in town," Marnie said helpfully. "You're going to have home field advantage."

Taylor tried to take comfort in the information, but she couldn't. "I don't think that's going to be enough," she said with a sigh. "This is my own fault. If I didn't want to sell my book so badly, I wouldn't have gone on that stupid show."

"I know." Marnie practically clucked her concern.

"It's just that I believe my theories make sense. They can help people."

"And the publicity won't hurt. Or the money if you got a book deal."

Taylor grinned. "Okay—that's true. I've been a

struggling single parent for sixteen years. I wouldn't say no to a career boost. But the contest."

Her humor faded. "Katrina Melon is like a terrier with a bone. The second she found out I lived in a place called Marriageville, she practically frothed at the mouth. 'Oh, we must have the contest in your little town,' " she said, mocking the host's cultured voice. " 'There's so much potential for publicity. And all those little people and their little businesses will be so grateful.' "

Marnie chuckled. "Maybe we could erect a statue to her honor. Something in plastic?"

Taylor's spirits brightened as she chuckled. "You noticed the face-lift?"

"Honey, you'd have to be on a different channel not to notice." Her smile faded. "Are you really upset about this?"

"I don't know. I'm confused. One second I was a guest on a show hoping to get a little media attention so I could sell my book. The next I'm in a contest with the Elvis of pop psychology."

She was having recurring nightmares about meeting Jonathan again. After all these years, how dare the man still get to her? She disagreed with everything he believed in, yet he still made her weak at the knees.

"I wish you'd been there," Taylor grumbled. "At least you would have distracted him."

Marnie laughed. "Dr. Kirby is a trained professional. I'm sure he'd be immune."

"He's a man and still breathing. He would have noticed."

Marnie twirled a lock of light brown hair around a finger. Taylor studied her friend, taking in the curls tumbling to the middle of her back and the cotton knit top clinging to her wildly impressive curves. Marnie had the body of a showgirl. She was five-feet-ten, with big hair and a beautiful face. To add insult to injury, she also had a head for numbers and her business sense rivaled an MBA's. Taylor supposed that if Marnie weren't such a sweet person, she would have been forced to kill her a long time ago.

"If only they'd warned me," she said, slumping back against the blue-and-white sofa as she looked out the big picture window. "I would have liked a chance to prepare before having to deal with him."

"He was impressed," Marnie said confidently. "I could tell."

"How? Did he hold up a sign?"

"No. It was how he acted. He kept looking at you."

"Marnie, you're imagining things. If he was looking at me it was because I was the other person on the show."

Marnie batted her long eyelashes. "Oh, but I *am* an expert. Haven't you been told?"

Taylor knew that if Marnie had been at the station, Jonathan wouldn't have been able to speak in complete sentences. Marnie left a trail of drooling men wherever she went. She also knew that her friend had only ever dated one man, whom she'd married and been faithful to all through the seven years of their marriage and in the three years since his passing.

Footsteps sounded on the hardwood floor of the hallway. Taylor smiled as her mother stepped into the living room. Linda McGuire held a tray in her hands. Taylor counted three large glasses of milk along with a plate of cookies.

"Don't you think I'm too old to have my problems solved by a snack?" she asked, even as she reached for a peanut butter cookie still warm from the oven.

"No one is that old," Linda said firmly after she'd set the tray on the coffee table in front of her daughter. She passed a glass of milk and several cookies to Marnie before settling on the far end of the sofa. "Are you all right?"

Taylor appreciated the softly spoken inquiry. She shrugged, then nibbled on the cookie. "I guess. I wish I didn't feel so stupid about the whole thing."

"You were interesting, dear. On television, isn't that all that matters?"

"I hope you're right."

"Did you talk to that Katrina woman about the contest?" Linda asked, reaching for her own glass of milk.

Taylor's mother sat with the graceful posture of a dancer. She'd trained for years before falling in love with Taylor's father and giving up her dreams of a stage career for the life of a wife and mother. Widowed at an early age, she'd opened a dress shop in town, raised her daughter and, for the past twenty years, served on the city council.

"We hashed it out this morning. That woman makes my skin crawl from a thousand miles away." She shuddered. "In approximately two weeks, our town of Marriageville, Texas, will be invaded by a gaggle of media types and an assortment of crazies. A contest will pit my well-researched theories on relationships against those of the pop-psychologist king himself, Dr. Jonathan Kirby."

As she spoke his name, she did her best not to picture him. Because imagining Jonathan made her want things—sexual things—she'd nearly forgotten about. One would think that seventeen years apart and any number of life experiences would have made her the slightest bit immune to his charms; however, one would be wrong.

"What do you mean, pitting the two of you against each other?" Marnie asked. "I thought there was going to be some kind of drawing."

"Nothing that simple," Taylor told her. "Forty couples will be involved. Twenty will be matched using the extensive questionnaire from my thesis, thus testing my theory of like people having a successful relationship. Twenty will be put together testing Dr. Kirby's ideas about opposites attracting."

"So he'll have a questionnaire, too?" Marnie asked.

"Right. There's going to have to be some kind of age restriction in Dr. Kirby's group or some seventy-year-old could end up with a twenty-something bride or groom."

Marnie grinned. "And that would be a problem how?"

Taylor ignored her friend. "The couples have to agree to live together for a month. If they survive the thirty days living in the same residence, they're entered into a drawing with the winning couple splitting the money."

Marnie pursed her full lips. "Those are one-in-forty odds for the million dollars. I like that."

"Then you're going to have to enter," Taylor told her. "You said you were thinking about starting to date."

Marnie shifted in her seat. "Taylor, starting to date and living with a man for a month are two very different propositions. How do you and Jonathan determine which of you wins?"

"Whichever of us has more couples wanting to stay together at the end of the contest time period is pronounced psychological guru of the year."

Her mother picked up a cookie. "Won't everyone tough it out for the money? After all, how hard could it be living in the same house? We're talking about a million dollars. People on TV eat bugs for less."

"I didn't make up the rules," Taylor said. "I guess the lawyers wanted people to have an out."

"Makes sense," her mother said.

"There's a press conference in a few days," Taylor said. "The details will all be worked out by then. If I don't have a heart attack first."

Marnie dismissed her concern with a flick of her slender wrist. Her coral nails, each decorated with a thin, diagonal line of silver, caught the light.

"You're going to do great. I think this is a fun idea. You're going to win and dozens of publishers will be begging to publish your book. Just as exciting, forty lucky couples are going to meet and fall madly in love."

Linda eyed her. "Don't you know being that upbeat gets on people's nerves?"

Marnie smiled as she rose and brushed off her slim skirt. It was the exact shade of deep coral as her knit top and nail polish. Strappy silver sandals emphasized her narrow feet and ankles. Nothing about the outfit should have been sexy, yet Marnie looked like a walking blow-up doll.

"I have to get back to work. You hang in there, Taylor. Everything is going to be great. You'll see." She headed for the front door. "Thank you for the cookies, Mrs. McGuire."

"Bye, Marnie," Taylor called after her. "I'll call you later."

"Okay. Bye."

Her mother picked up another cookie. "How many car accidents do you think she's going to cause as she sashays down Grand Avenue?"

"No more than usual."

Linda bit into her cookie, chewed, then swallowed. "Want to talk about it?"

Taylor shifted in her seat so that she faced her mother. Their eyes were the same color of gray-blue, thickly lashed, although the lashes were too pale to be visible without a liberal coat of mascara.

"You mean Jonathan," Taylor said.

"It's been a long time. I would imagine you had a shock seeing him again. I heard you pacing in your room last night, Taylor. Are you going to be all right through this?"

Taylor thought about all that could go wrong. "I hope so."

"I know how you like to plan your life," her mother said. "Jonathan is going to be something of a loose cannon."

"Then we're going to have to make sure he doesn't explode anywhere."

Her mother smiled. "I should have put him in jail when I had the chance."

Taylor laughed. "I should have let you. Jonathan's very handsome. He would have been quite the popular inmate."

Marnie paused at the corner of Grand and First. Her shop—Marnie's Palace of Beauty—was less than a block away. Across the street was Wilbur's Diner. A sensible woman would walk briskly toward her place of business, ignoring distractions along the way. A sensible woman would accept her limitations and the inevitable disappointments brought on by them.

Marnie drew in a deep breath. "Did I used to be sensible, George?" she asked softly as she checked traffic before crossing the street. "I can't remember."

Her late husband didn't answer her question. In fact he never answered or spoke back. She supposed that was a good sign. It was one thing to be friends with a psychologist; it was quite another to be forced into weekly sessions because she'd started hearing voices.

"It's just that you always knew me best," she said, continuing the one-way communication. "Taylor's a sweetie and I like her a lot, but it's not the same."

She paused outside of Wilbur's Diner, where a hand-painted and fading sign told all who were interested that the eatery had been established in 1941.

Marnie wasn't hungry. She'd had a big breakfast and Mrs. McGuire's yummy cookies. She was forever trying to lose ten pounds and buying a lunch she didn't need or want wasn't going to move her closer to her goal. However, if she went inside and ordered a salad to go, she would be standing right next to the counter. And from there it was only a few short steps to paradise.

"Spineless," she told herself as she pushed open the glass door and stepped inside.

It was nearly one in the afternoon, so the diner was only about two-thirds full. Marnie walked toward the counter, waving to those who called out greetings. All the booths by the front window were full, as were the tables in back. Up front there weren't as many people, although the small table in the corner contained one occupant.

Marnie told herself not to look. That looking was juvenile and obvious and . . .

He's gorgeous, she thought with a silent sigh as she caught sight of Will Ramsey sitting in his usual seat, his attention focused on the computer magazine in front of him. Soft, too-long sandy brown hair fell over his forehead and down to the bottom of his collar. Jeans and a short-sleeved white shirt hung loosely on his lean, runner's body. He wore wire-rimmed glasses and an expression of earnestness that made her bare toes curl ever so slightly in her silver sandals.

What was it about this man that made her simmer so? He was nothing like George, who had been open and easy to talk to. George who had seen past the big hair and bigger boobs. Will didn't seem to see past anything. He never looked at her, except by accident, and when that happened, he inevitably blushed and turned away. Obviously she wasn't his type.

She reached the counter and smiled at the red-headed waitress there. "Hey, Lorraine. A chicken Caesar salad to go," she said, trying not to glance at Will.

"Sure thing, Marnie." Lorraine jerked her head at the vacant stool by the cash register. "Take a load off while you wait."

Marnie did as the waitress suggested, settling onto the seat. She felt her skirt ride a little higher on her leg. Across the diner, Bobby Ray Tracer's eyes widened as he stared at her legs. He leered, not noticing the meat sliding out of his hamburger. After giving her a big ol' wink, he bit down, then frowned in confusion.

His buddies laughed and said something she didn't hear.

Marnie turned away from their amusement. She didn't want to watch grown men stumble when they caught sight of her or have endless conversations with the male population gazing at her chest rather than her face. She wanted what she'd had with George. A relationship with a nice man who loved her and recognized that there was a brain inside the shiny package.

Five minutes later Lorraine handed her the salad. "I'll put it on your tab," she said.

"Give yourself a nice tip, too," Marnie told her as she stood and headed out of the diner.

On her way to the door, she allowed herself one last peek at Will Ramsey, to see if he'd even noticed her. No such luck. He sat with his head still buried in his computer magazine.

"Do you think he's just not good with women?" she asked aloud as she crossed Grand and headed for Marnie's Palace of Beauty. "Or should I simply accept the fact that the man doesn't know I'm alive and has no interest in getting to know me?"

As usual, George remained silent on the subject. Marnie entered her shop, calling greetings to the four beauticians working at their stations. Marnie's Palace of Beauty stood in the center of town. It was a pink and gold homage to female pampering. Her sandals clicked on the shiny linoleum as she passed rows of dryers and sinks and her own nail station.

"Any calls?" she asked as she stepped into her office.

"Just some appointments," Mary Ann replied. "Mrs. Zucker is coming in tomorrow afternoon. She wants you to do those cute little moons on her nails again."

Marnie nodded, then closed her office door and leaned against the polished wood. She felt funny, like her life no longer fit as comfortably as it once had.

"What's wrong with me?" she asked, this time really wishing that George would answer. She straightened, then set her purse and her salad on the cherrywood desk she'd brought over from her house. Her office walls were creamy yellow with a border trim of cabbage roses. The carpet underfoot was thick enough and soft enough to double as a bed in a pinch, not that she'd ever tried. She had a business she loved, good friends, plenty of money, so what was her problem? Why did she ache so inside?

Marnie crossed to her desk. As she did so, she caught sight of herself in the full-length mirror next to the door. One would think that after living in her body for twenty-nine years she would be used to her reflection.

"I am too much," she said sadly. She fingered her long, full hair, then cupped her hands under her size 36DD breasts.

"You were man enough to handle me, George. You made me feel good about myself. All that's been lost since you've been gone and I don't know how to get it back."

She dropped her hands to her sides and sank into the chair in front of her desk. "I wish I could forget about Will. But I can't. There's something about him that appeals to me. He's a year or so younger, but I don't think that's gonna matter. He's smart and I like that. I don't think he cares about the money and I like that even more. And I've been so lonely since you've been gone. Why'd you have to go and die on me?"

She closed her eyes and could almost imagine George holding her close, making her feel safe. That had been his gift—making her feel as if she was right where she belonged.

"I miss you," she said quietly, knowing that if he could answer her, he would tell her to get over him and start living again.

"The men in my family don't make it much past seventy, darlin', so this is going to be a short marriage," George had warned her when he'd proposed. "But I would like to make it a happy one."

And it had been. Despite the age difference—he'd been sixty and she'd barely turned nineteen—she'd fallen in love with her husband and had truly mourned his passing. But it had been over three years and she was tired of being alone.

At one time the joyful shrieks from the front yard would have made Chris Harbaugh smile. She loved her kids and knowing they were happy brightened her day. Except not this morning. It was the first week of summer vacation and she was too tired to feel anything but sick to her stomach. She rinsed three more bowls and put them into the dishwasher, all the while wondering if a Disney video would keep them quiet until their father arrived to pick them up. Then she could sleep. *Just a couple of hours,* she thought longingly. *Is that too much to ask?*

The front door banged open. "Hey, babe."

Chris stiffened, then slowly wiped her hands on the tattered dish towel on the counter. Familiar footsteps thumped across the worn floor. She drew in a deep breath and braced herself before turning to face her ex-husband.

"Good morning, Rio."

As always, he was good-looking enough to take her breath away. Tall, blond, with Viking blue eyes and a body honed by physical labor. Even in faded jeans and a five-year-old T-shirt, he looked hot enough to melt ice in a snowstorm. Worse, he looked content and rested. Two things she couldn't remember feeling in oh, say the last five years.

He ambled up beside her and wrapped one strong arm around her waist, pulling her close. His tanned skin, the familiar heat and the awful wanting sensation in her midsection did nothing to improve her mood. Still, she forced herself to be pleasant. He was about to take the kids for the morning and Lord knew she needed the chance to sleep.

"What's that on your shirt?" he asked, releasing her and pointing to a stain on her sleeve.

She remembered the very long night she'd endured on her nursing shift in the ICU of Marriageville Hospital. "You don't want to know."

He grinned and her body went up in flames. Damn, but the man turned her on. She really hated that. She looked older by the minute and he still looked like a twenty-something poster boy. Worse, just being around him made her remember how long it had been since she'd had sex with someone other than herself.

"I got my overtime check," he said, giving her a last

squeeze before going to the coffeepot and pouring himself a cup. "That should get me just about caught up on child support."

"Great."

She tried to sound enthusiastic, but it was hard. Yes, Rio was caught up . . . for now. Until the next car race entry fee or new engine or transmission. Then he would do what he wanted and she would be the one left out in the cold. Or without the money to pay for car insurance or the phone or day care.

She turned toward the counter and reached for the dishcloth. "Rio, I appreciate that you try to stay current, but the fact is you fall behind a lot."

He swore. "Why do you always do this?" he demanded in an angry tone that made her spine stiffen. "I tell you I have extra money and instead of thanking me, you bring up something from the past or assume the worst."

Weariness made her hair hurt. "I work nights, Rio. A twelve-hour shift in the ICU. I'm on my feet constantly. I'm tired when I get home. It's not so bad when the kids are in school, but they're on summer break. Even the preschool is closed."

She shifted so she was leaning against the counter. Her gaze settled on his belligerent face. "I can't do this anymore," she told him. "I'm exhausted. I don't have any more to give."

"Yeah, well, I work all day. What do you want from me?"

"Nothing. We're divorced. I appreciate that you try to stay current with the child support, but the bottom line is I can't depend on you. Without knowing if the money is coming in, I have a tough time paying bills.

On my own I can only afford half the day care I need when they're out of school. When you short me child support, I have to keep them home, which means I don't get to sleep."

Guilt flashed across his face. Her first instinct was to go to him and hold him, telling him that everything would be okay. Except every time she did that, things only got worse.

"I can't keep doing this," she said quietly. "I want to make a fresh start."

He slammed the coffee cup onto the counter. "Dammit, Chris, you're not talking about moving to Dallas again, are you? You can't take my kids away from me. They need to grow up here."

"I know Marriageville is a good place to raise a family, but I don't have any support here. In Dallas I'd have my mom." She squared her shoulders. "You work in a garage. You could get a job there if you wanted to, but you're not interested in moving because it would mean being far away from your buddies and your car races."

He turned away from her. "Yeah, well…"

She studied him for a second, and then she knew. "You're not taking the kids today, are you?" she asked flatly.

He'd promised. He knew she was exhausted by the end of the week and he knew that she depended on him to at least keep them for the morning. She hadn't had more than two hours of sleep in three days.

Tears burned at the back of her eyes, but she blinked them away. "This is why I want to move," she told him. "My mom's willing to help and I can depend on her."

"You can depend on me," he said, spinning to face her.

"Just not this morning, right?"

"That's what I came to tell you. I meant to mention it before."

She reached for his coffee cup and dumped the contents down the sink. "I don't care, Rio. You're not a grown-up. You still want to run off and play with your friends rather than face your responsibilities. It's the reason I divorced you. You only think of yourself."

"You always say that, but it's not true. I've been here for you."

"Like when?" She put her hands on her hips, feeling the anger surge through her. "Were you here for me this time last year when you asked to borrow my car without telling me that you were going to race it? You crashed and because you were going a hundred and forty miles an hour in an illegal race, the insurance not only wouldn't cover the damage, they dropped me completely. I'm still making payments on a car I don't even have. Or were you there for me when Debbie was born? No. You were hunting. You missed her birth, but you got that deer, didn't you?"

She waited for him to say that Debbie was their second kid so what did it matter that he'd been gone? Instead he went on the attack.

"You want to take a look at your faults?" he asked. "What about all the things you've done wrong? Let's talk about the fact that you never wanted sex, you hate my friends, and you refuse to let my children spend time with their grandmother."

"Your mother is an alcoholic. She passes out every night."

"You're the one who got pregnant in the first place

so we had to get married," he yelled. "You were supposed to be on the goddamn pill. You're a nurse. You should have known taking antibiotics would screw things up."

Chris turned her head and saw the familiar battered table by the small kitchen window. She'd lived in this house nearly seven years. How many times had she and Rio had the exact same fights, using the same accusations, getting nowhere?

"I work hard," he said. "I don't think it's so wrong to take a little time off. I never asked for any of this, but I'm doing my best for my family."

She thought about telling him that his best wasn't good enough. But what was the point? Her anger faded, leaving only exhaustion. "I'm not going to fight with you anymore," she said quietly. "We divorced so we wouldn't have to fight. I appreciate that you're doing the best you can. You're a good father and the children love you. But the bottom line is that's not enough for me. I'm moving."

Chapter 3

"Taylor, darling!"

Taylor smiled as she tucked the phone receiver against her shoulder. "Alexi. You're calling me. Does this mean good news?"

"News? You want to talk of news? What of the joy of hearing my voice?"

Alexi Stratinoff, her literary agent, had arrived from the former Soviet Union back before the fall of the Berlin wall. With his charming accent and Slavic good looks, he was a popular figure, both in and out of publishing. She'd met him when she and Marnie had flown to New York for a long weekend. He'd been a friend of Marnie's late husband.

Taylor knew that he'd taken her on as a client out of respect and affection for Marnie, but she wasn't about to question her good fortune. Alexi had a reputation for being the best. After several months of hoping for her book to sell, she would settle for any crumb of good news.

"You are the light of my life," she said teasingly. "Especially if you're calling about an offer. I've been hoping that all the media attention about the upcoming contest would help."

"It has. You were very clever to come up with the idea. I have been in touch with several publishers."

No point in reminding Alexi that the idea had been Jonathan's. She'd been trying to forget him for days.

"And?" she prompted.

"There is an offer. But," he added hastily when she caught her breath, "not a big one. I said no."

She gasped. "Alexi! You turned it down?"

"Of course. If they are interested, they will come back with more. If they don't, they were not committed to the project. Trust me. Your contest hasn't even started. It will capture national attention, of that I am sure. Then, we will hear from others, you will get the contract of your dreams and we'll both make money, yes?"

She clutched the phone tighter. His words sounded so sensible, but had he really turned down a book offer? "Okay," she said through dry lips. "You're the expert."

"I am. You are the doctor, I know the publishing. Your job right now is to win your contest with Dr. Kirby. If you do that, I can promise you an advance in the range of the prize money."

If she hadn't already been sitting, she would have crumpled to the floor. "A million dollars?"

"You sound surprised."

"I . . . but . . ." She cleared her throat, not daring to imagine such an amount. "Okay. You do your thing and I'll win."

"That's my girl. Smile on camera. Show them how pretty you are. Give my love to Marnie."

He hung up. Taylor replaced the receiver and started to laugh. A million dollars? Her? Maybe this wasn't going to be quite the disaster she'd imagined.

Jonathan Kirby took the creaking elevator down to the lobby. The Royal Marriageville Hotel had once been as elegant and grand as its name, but that time had ended nearly a quarter of a century before. Now it was an aging matron of a structure, still beautiful but showing signs of wear around the edges. There were a few too many stains in the dark red, patterned carpet and scars on the gold and cream papered walls. Still, the hallways smelled of furniture polish and the stately four poster he'd slept in the previous night had been a genuine antique.

When the elevator groaned to a stop and slowly opened its doors, he walked out into a lobby built in a different era. There were stunning chandeliers hanging from the ceiling and gilded mirrors placed high on the walls. The bellmen (some of them young women) wore old-fashioned red uniforms, complete with pillbox hats.

"Oh, Jonathan. Over here!"

He turned toward the sound of a familiar, albeit unwelcome, voice. Katrina Melon waved as she hurried across the lobby. Today she wore a lavender suit accented by a string of pearls. Every hair was in place, every inch of her perfectly groomed.

"Jonathan, I've been waiting for you to come down. I thought we could walk to the press conference together."

"You read my mind," he said, lying through his

teeth. He hadn't known she was going to be in Marriageville this morning. "Will you be in town long?"

"A few days. I'm doing several follow-up pieces for the show. After all, I was there at the beginning. And I must say again, how brilliant your idea was for this contest. An innovative way to test two interesting theories by putting them to work in the real world."

He thought about telling Katrina the truth. That he'd challenged Taylor not because he'd wanted to make any kind of a statement or to test their respective theories on successful relationships, but because she'd looked so calm and in control sitting next to him. He couldn't resist tweaking her tail and making her spit. It appeared that there were still plenty of sparks between them.

He and Katrina walked out of the hotel. The late-May afternoon was hot and humid. He felt as if he'd stepped back in time, maybe to the 1950s. There was an old-fashioned movie theater across the street with a drugstore beside it advertising a soda fountain. Tall trees provided shade, while baskets of flowers hung from the fronts of the businesses. Cars drove slowly down the brick-edged street.

"The press conference is this way," Katrina said, slipping her hand around his arm.

So she hadn't given up trying to get him into her bed. Katrina was nothing if not persistent.

"Will you be in Marriageville for the entire month?" she asked.

"Is this an official interview or are you making conversation?"

She smiled. "A little of both."

"I have a weekend seminar scheduled in Milwaukee. After that, I'll be in town for the length of the contest."

"How will you stand a month in Hicksville? After all, you live in New York."

He thought about Taylor's long legs, and the way they'd once been unable to keep their hands off each other. "I'll manage."

"The couples will be chosen in about ten days?" she asked. "As soon as everyone gets entered into the computer?"

"Yes. Taylor's questions have already been programmed into the computer system. I e-mailed my questionnaire in yesterday so I'm sure they're working on it."

They walked past Wilbur's Diner, then crossed a street and entered the Ladies' Auxiliary meeting hall.

The large main room was filled with various members of the press. Men and women holding television cameras stood on either side, while several dozen chairs had been set up in rows, filling the center of the room.

"Dr. Kirby?"

Jonathan glanced down and saw an earnest young woman. "Yes?"

"You can join Dr. McGuire in there." She pointed to a closed door in the right front corner.

"Thanks."

The woman blushed slightly and slipped into the crowd. Katrina glanced around, at last disentangling herself from him. "I'd better find my crew and get set up. See you soon."

He nodded without replying and headed for the

closed door. Anticipation increased his stride. Then he pushed open the door and stepped into the small room.

There was no table, just a couple of chairs pushed against the side walls. Taylor sat in one of the chairs, reading a magazine. She barely glanced up as he entered.

"You're late," she said conversationally, setting the magazine on the floor. "I hope we're not keeping you from something more important."

"Nothing could be more important than this press conference."

She rose to her feet and stood in front of him. "Let me guess. No media opportunity is too small?"

"Exactly. There are no small opportunities, just small people."

"Do you memorize these little sayings or do they come to you on the spur of the moment?"

"You were always an inspiration."

Taylor surprised him by laughing. "Still as smooth as snake oil, Jonathan."

"Do snakes have oil? Personally, I think of them as dry creatures."

As she had for the television interview, she wore her blond hair back in a fancy braid. Her teal-colored suit made her eyes look more blue than gray and there was a flush of color on her cheeks. Her tiny pearl earrings were nearly the color of her skin. Except for her watch, she didn't wear any other jewelry. No wedding or engagement ring. Had she ever married?

She'd wanted to, he remembered. Once a husband and kids had meant everything to her. She'd wanted to belong and he'd wanted to be the best.

"Is your fan club here?" she asked.

He leaned against the wall. "I don't remember you being this mouthy when you were eighteen."

Taylor ignored his comment. "I'm only asking because I thought I saw Katrina's name on the list of television people attending the press conference. How long have you two been an item?"

"We don't have a personal relationship," he said easily. "She's not my type."

"Oh. Someone should tell her."

"Are you volunteering?"

"Not at all." She smiled. "She's very beautiful."

"So I've heard, but she would chew me up and spit me out before breakfast and that's not how I choose to start my day."

Taylor's gaze turned appraising. "Women always liked you, Jonathan. I guess that hasn't changed."

"It beats being liked by men."

She smiled, a faint curving of her lips that made the corner of her eyes crinkle. "Do you still get away with murder, too?"

"I haven't killed anyone recently, so I don't know."

She waved her hand, gesturing to the room. "I would say the answer is yes. You made one casual remark on a thirty-minute show and suddenly dozens of lives are going to be changed forever. What does it feel like to have that much power?"

"I make sure I only use it for good."

"I question your confidence on that subject, but then I don't agree with many of your theories." She stared at him. "I don't know why you suggested this contest. At first I thought it was to try to humiliate me, but then I reminded myself that would mean you were thinking of someone other than yourself."

"Ouch. Are you sure you want to draw blood on the first day?"

She ignored him. "I'm not the adoring teenager you remember. I'm all grown-up and I've learned a few things. I won't be charmed by you. I intend to win."

Taylor had been a pretty girl, but she'd matured into a beautiful woman. Just watching her move brought back dangerous memories of a long time ago. Back when passion had been easy . . . and frequent.

"Want to make a side bet?" he asked.

Her gaze narrowed, but she didn't speak.

He pushed off the wall and approached her. With a single finger, he drew a line from the curve of her cheek to the center of her bottom lip. He was rewarded by a slight dilation of her pupils.

"Want to bet that I *can* charm you? I would go so far as to say I could seduce you. What do you think, Taylor? It used to be damned good between us."

A knock on the door interrupted them. Taylor jerked away from his touch. If the fire shooting from her eyes had been real, he would have incinerated on the spot.

An older woman stepped into the room. She had short gray-blond hair like Katrina's but unlike the reporter, this woman had allowed herself to age gracefully. She pressed a clipboard against her red coatdress.

"It's time for the press conference to start. Are you two ready?"

Jonathan was surprised when instead of stiffening, Taylor actually relaxed. "Have you met?" she asked, looking at him and indicating the older woman.

"No." Jonathan turned and gave the visitor his best smile. He held out his hand. "I'm Jonathan Kirby."

The woman looked at his hand, then at his face. Her gaze narrowed. "I suppose you think you're God's gift to women. Well, let me tell you that you're not. I was just telling Taylor that I wish I'd thrown you in jail when I'd had the chance." With that, she turned and stalked out of the room.

Jonathan stared after her. He felt the blood rush from his head and for the first time in years, he couldn't think of a single thing to say.

Taylor laughed and patted him on the arm. "Mom's real happy to see you. Ready for the press conference?"

Twenty minutes later Jonathan was still glancing uneasily around the room, hoping to catch a glimpse of Taylor's mother. If he could keep his eye on her, he wouldn't be surprised with a .44 slug in the back. Not that he blamed her for being angry. If some jerk tried to run off with *his* sixteen-year-old daughter, he would have the boy's hide. The fact that he didn't have children didn't matter. Parental rage was a universal emotion.

Taylor read a prepared statement about the contest—explaining procedure and rules. He tried to tell if she was nervous. He thought he detected a slight tremor in her hands but wasn't sure. Based on the little he knew about her life, he doubted she spent much time speaking with the national media, yet she seemed calm and in control.

Impressive, he thought. She'd come a long way from the sobbing teenager who had protested she would die without him.

"Information packets are being handed out to each of you," she was saying. "Basically forty couples will be matched up using detailed questionnaires. Twenty couples will be matched using my theories on compatibility and twenty will be matched using Dr. Kirby's concepts of opposites attracting."

He leaned toward the microphone. "You left out sexual chemistry. That's very important."

Taylor rolled her eyes. "Right. Chemistry."

A woman in front raised her hand. "How do you measure sexual attraction?"

Jonathan grinned. "Very carefully."

A corner of Taylor's mouth twitched but she hid her smile. "There are some other basic restrictions. The couple will consist of one man and one woman, and they will be no more than seven years apart in age."

"Why?" a male reporter asked. "Don't you want May–December romances?"

"We have nothing against them," Taylor said. "However, anything more than ten years' difference would be considered statistically significant." She checked her notes. "Computer Tectronics, a local computer firm here in Marriageville, will write the program necessary to match the couples. They will also be inputting the questionnaire data. Once the forty couples are chosen, they will sign a fistful of documents, mostly holding me, Dr. Kirby and the town blameless for what they are about to do."

Several of the reporters chuckled.

Taylor laughed. "Hey, I'm not eligible for the million-dollar prize. I think a little protection against lawsuits isn't unreasonable."

"Good point," someone from the audience called out.

"The couples will agree to live together for one month," she continued. "They will have weekly appointments to check in with Dr. Kirby and myself. At the end of the month, the names of the couples who are still together will go into a hat. We will pull out the name of one couple and they will take home a million dollars."

Several hands shot up. Taylor nodded at an older man in the middle of the crowd.

"How do people enter the contest?"

"They go down to city hall and fill out a questionnaire," Taylor said. "While the applicants don't have to be residents, they must spend the month in town."

"How do you and Dr. Kirby determine who has the best theory on marriage?"

Jonathan stepped up to the second microphone and grinned. "We all know it's going to be me."

More laughter filled the room.

He glanced at Taylor who gave him an "in your dreams, buster" look. "Seriously," he said. "We will give each of the couples an exit interview to discover how many of them want to stay together in some kind of a relationship. Whoever of us has the most couples wanting to continue will be the victor. Whether or not the couples want to stay together, they'll be eligible for the prize money."

"Are you expecting a close race?"

"Absolutely," he said. "One thing I've learned through my years of studying marriages and teaching all over the country is that there isn't any one right way of doing things. I'm looking forward to learning from Dr. McGuire, watching her methods. I think she will equally benefit from close exposure to my way of doing things."

"What if the people hate each other?" a young woman in front asked. "Are you going to make them stay together?"

Taylor leaned toward the microphone. "Of course not. This isn't forced servitude. If a couple isn't getting along at all, they are welcome to withdraw from the contest and get back to their regular lives."

"Will they forfeit their chance at the money?"

"Yes."

Katrina raised her hand. "What do you two get out of this?" she asked.

Taylor hesitated, so he stepped in.

"Book sales for me," he said easily, making the crowd laugh. When the room quieted, he continued. "What we really get is a unique opportunity to test our theories in a real-world setting. This isn't a lab, there's no control group and it's not the least bit scientific, but that's what makes it exciting."

"But you don't believe Dr. McGuire's theories."

This comment came from Katrina. Jonathan deliberately winked at Taylor. "I'm open to being convinced by a strong argument."

She'd stiffened at Katrina's statement. Now she relaxed slightly. "I see Dr. Kirby is being as charming as we all know him to be. Despite that glib façade, he spoke the truth when he mentioned that there is no one right way of doing things. Marriage counseling is like dieting. Each individual is different and what works for one person won't work for another. I, too, am intrigued to watch our theories at work. What we are proposing here obviously has some entertainment value or you all wouldn't be here. But it's so much more than that. Forty lives are about to change. Forty-two if you count Dr. Kirby and myself. At the end of the month, there's no going back. Relationships—even temporary ones—should not be entered into lightly."

"It's interesting that both you and Dr. Kirby are considered excellent marriage counselors, yet neither of you are married," Katrina said.

Jonathan leaned toward his microphone. "You know what they say. Those who can, do, those who can't, teach. Or write about it."

The crowd laughed, with the exception of Taylor's mother, who bored holes into his head with her laser gaze.

"But don't you practice what you preach?" Katrina persisted.

Jonathan had the idea that he was being punished for all the dates he'd refused. He glanced at Taylor, who raised her hands in a gesture of mock surrender.

"You're the media expert, Dr. Kirby. I'll let you answer the question."

He smiled. "Thanks. Okay, yes, it would seem that two very qualified counselors would have wonderful marriages. I, for one, was married many years ago and it was an unqualified disaster. I'm sure my ex-wife would be pleased to explain why the failure was all my fault."

Several of the men chuckled. Jonathan shrugged. "We're not perfect. We're people trying to make a difference. No better and no worse than anyone else."

"What about you, Dr. McGuire?" Katrina asked, turning her attention to Taylor. "You've never married?"

"No. Staying single wasn't a difficult choice for me. I've led a full and active life."

"Why didn't you marry?" Katrina persisted.

Taylor shifted slightly. "There wasn't any one particular reason."

"I would think that as a psychologist you'd want your child to have two parents."

Taylor clutched the edge of her podium. She should have realized Piranha Woman would check on her. Not that she'd kept her daughter a secret. Not exactly. But she hadn't expected the information to come out like this. A burst of panic flared to life in her stomach.

Jonathan glanced at her quizzically, then faced the reporters. "From the perspective of the average male, I would answer that Dr. McGuire's decision to not marry wasn't from lack of offers. Any other questions?"

Taylor released the breath she'd been holding. Score one for Jonathan. She hadn't expected the save, but she sure appreciated it. She wondered what questions he was going to have when they were alone. She didn't doubt that there would be dozens. She didn't know if he'd thought about her or not in the past few years, but she doubted he'd pictured her with a child.

"Once we get our partners hooked up, we'll be providing weekly updates, letting you know how our couples are progressing," Jonathan was saying. "A week from Friday the fun begins. It's going to be a Texas-size party, so you'll all want to be here."

Two or three people yelled out questions, but Jonathan only waved. He took Taylor's arm and led her back into the small, private room at the rear of the hall. She ignored the way the light pressure of his fingers against her suit jacket made her go all tingly inside. She was a mental health professional. She did *not* go tingly under any circumstances.

"I'm glad that's over," she said, stepping away from him as soon as they were alone. "Now we can get down to actually working on this project."

"You were great with them," he said as he shoved his hands into his trouser pockets. He wore an expensively tailored suit that emphasized the strong build of his body. "No one is going to suspect that was your first press conference."

She didn't ask how he knew. With her lifestyle, the information was fairly apparent. "Thank you," she said grudgingly, wishing he hadn't complimented her. Did Jonathan really think he could make her *like* him? She refused to think about his preposterous advances earlier. Him seduce her? Not while the earth continued to rotate around the sun. She'd already been burned by that particular experience and she wasn't stupid enough to do it again.

"So, you have a child."

The quick change in subject made the room tilt slightly. Taylor sucked in a deep breath and thought about a calm, quiet lake scene, just like she'd learned in yoga. *Relax,* she told herself. *Act normal.*

"I have a daughter. Her name is Linnie." She pressed her lips together, not wanting to say too much.

Nothing flickered in his dark eyes. No hint of suspicion, no questions.

"I'd like to meet her sometime," he said.

"Sure." She pretended a casualness she didn't feel. "She's away at summer camp right now, but she'll be home on break soon." Not that Taylor had any intention of letting Linnie meet this man.

"How old is she?"

Taylor forced a laugh. "She's a teenager. So far it hasn't been too awful, but we're still in the early stages." Okay, that was a slight exaggeration. Taylor knew she was deliberately making Linnie sound thirteen rather than sixteen. However, desperate times and all that. "Mom says that the teen years get worse before they get better."

"I don't want to talk about your mother," he muttered. "I think she wants to hang me."

"Not by the neck," Taylor offered sweetly.

"Gee, thanks." He swallowed. "Summer camp?"

"Yes. It's for deaf children. Linnie learned sign language last year."

He looked as if he was about to ask another question, so she beat him to the punch.

"Tell me about your ex-wife. Was it the grad student? What was her name? Rita?"

He looked so blank, she wanted to hit him. "Rita," she repeated, speaking slowly. "You know, the one you moved in with after we broke up?"

He frowned. "Yeah, I remember. No. She and I didn't go out for very long."

The urge to hit him got stronger. Taylor sighed. Great. Jonathan didn't even remember the woman he'd left her for. She'd been crushed, thinking her life was over and he barely remembered the situation. How typical. Life was all about perspective.

"I guess we've really changed," she said at last.

"For the better?"

She couldn't help smiling. "I have."

He pulled his hands out of his pockets. "I'm going to ignore that. We need to talk about the logistics of the next month. How we're going to handle the follow-up appointments. We should probably set some ground rules."

She thought about the forty couples who were about to have their lives changed. "I agree. When are you free?"

"I'm leaving town in a couple of hours. I have a seminar this weekend in Milwaukee. How about the first part of next week. The contest begins Friday, so, say Monday or Tuesday?"

"Monday's fine." She thought of her mother's less than enthusiastic greeting and grinned. "You could come to my place."

"Why do I know you and your mom share a house?"

"I don't know, but we do. It's been in the family for over a hundred years. It's beautiful. You'll love it."

"I don't think so." He rubbed his neck. "I'd like to stay in one piece for the next few weeks and I don't think that's her goal. How about you coming to my hotel? I have a suite with a large dining room table. We'd have plenty of room to work."

She thought about his threat to seduce her, then acknowledged her slightly fluttering heart. Okay, so there was still some minor attraction between them. So what? She would handle herself professionally and if Jonathan tried anything, she would tell him off. After all, she had the weekend to practice pithy comebacks.

"Your hotel is fine," she said.

He smiled—a male now-I-have-you smile that

made her skin break out in goose bumps. "Close quarters with a beautiful woman. There's nothing I like more."

"Do you make more as a gigolo or a psychologist?" she asked.

He didn't even have the decency to look embarrassed. "Both lines of work can be seasonal, so it depends."

She found herself wanting to ask which season it was now. *Trouble,* she thought. When she got home she was going to have to give herself a stern talking-to. No way was she going to fall for Jonathan Kirby again. Not even for a million-dollar book deal.

Chapter
4

*M*arnie Boudine fingered the visitor's badge she wore on a chain around her neck and followed the receptionist to the end of the corridor. The young woman pointed to the left, toward a windowless office along a wall.

"He's in there."

Marnie smiled her thanks, squared her shoulders and crossed her fingers for luck. Here went nothing.

She walked to the open door and lightly knocked. Instantly the occupant, a thirty-something computer engineer with glasses and a receding hairline, glanced up. "Yes?"

He was adorable. Big eyes, an easy smile. Kind of froggy looking. Kathy Ennis was so lucky, Marnie thought mournfully. If only she could get lucky, too.

"Mark Ennis?" she asked.

He nodded. Amazingly his gaze only slid to her breasts twice before he shook his head and motioned to the chair beside his desk.

"I'm Mark," he said. "And you are?"

"Marnie Boudine." She held out her hand as she settled into the seat. "You don't know me. I do your wife's nails. I saw Kathy earlier this morning and she said I should come to see you right away."

Mark frowned. "I don't understand. Kathy sent you?"

Marnie glanced over her shoulder to make sure no one lurked in the walkway outside. The open end of several cubicles faced Mark's open door, but they were empty at the moment. Even so, she lowered her voice.

"I have something of a delicate nature to discuss with you."

Mark swallowed. "Okay."

He wore a short-sleeved blue plaid shirt with a gray and pink bargain-basement tie. Marnie wanted to lean over and pinch his cheek, he was so cute. Not as cute as Will, but plenty attractive.

"I understand that you're in charge of the computer program for the marriage contest," she said.

Behind his glasses, his eyes widened. "Look, I have nothing to do with the money."

Marnie dismissed him with a wave, then smoothed the hem of her skirt. She'd deliberately dressed conservatively today, pairing a sleeveless pink T-shirt with a denim skirt. Her cream nail polish was decorated with matching pink and blue hearts.

"I'm not interested in the money. Believe me, I have plenty. What I want instead is a chance to be matched with someone who interests me."

Mark drew his eyebrows together. "I don't understand."

"He doesn't know I'm alive. I don't know how else to meet him. So I was hoping that you could sort of make things happen."

"Look, ah, Marnie, you're gorgeous. Who wouldn't want you?"

She sighed. "You are so sweet. No wonder Kathy's crazy about you."

Mark blushed and ducked his head. "Yeah. Well, thanks." He cleared his throat. "My point is you could get any guy you wanted."

"Not really. I can't get Will Ramsey to give me the time of day."

Mark stared at her. "Will? The guy even the other techs think is nerdy? The guy who wouldn't know what a social event is even if it bit him on the ass? Pardon my French."

Marnie sighed and crossed her legs. "That's him. I can't work up the courage to talk to him and he's sure not approaching me. I thought for a while that maybe he was gay, but Kathy says he's not."

Mark nodded. "We had him over to a Christmas party last year. Kathy's cousin is gay and spent the evening with the guy. He said Will's just clueless."

"I could change that."

Mark laughed. "I'll bet you could. Okay. I could probably fix things so that you got matched up with Will. Using the opposites attract matching would be easiest. But how do you know he's going to enter?"

She glanced down at her nails. "That would be my other problem."

"I could get him entered," Mark said, slowly leaning back in his chair. "I could fill out the forms and tell him after the fact. You know he's backward as hell. Are you sure?"

"Yes. I want to spend time with him. Get to know him." *Fall in love with him,* but she didn't say that.

"You'd probably kill him," Mark muttered, "but it would be a great way to go."

Hope made her straighten in her chair. "You'll do it?"

"If I don't agree now, Kathy's going to bug me until I cave, so I might as well make it easy on myself. Sure. I'll do it. Who knows? Will might even thank me."

"Hey, Dad, you're not late," eight-year-old Justin Harbaugh said as he opened the front door.

Rio grinned at his son, even though the comment stung. "I'm always here on time."

Justin, dark like his mother, with her curly hair, pulled the door open wider and stepped back. "That's not what Mom says."

Rio walked into the small house he'd once called home. He and Chris had been divorced for a year, but it still felt funny to have to knock when he came over to look after his kids.

He gave his son a quick hug. "Where are the girls?"

"Watching TV." Justin rolled his eyes. "It's their turn to pick the video and they picked some stupid girl thing."

"Tough break."

Justin was the oldest of their three, with six-year-old Debbie in the middle and four-year-old Molly as the baby.

Rio glanced around at the tidy living room. The tract house they'd bought seven years ago had taken every penny of their savings, but Chris had insisted.

She'd been tired of living in an apartment, so she'd found this place. It wasn't huge, but it had a formal living room—God knows why she'd wanted it, they never entertained—four bedrooms and a decent-size family room in back.

He inhaled the smell of meatloaf and his stomach growled. "Did Mom leave any leftovers for me?" he asked.

"I dunno."

"Okay. I'll go say hi to Mom, then check on the girls."

Justin headed upstairs while Rio walked toward the master suite back behind the living room. He knocked once, then opened the door without waiting for a response.

Chris stood beside the bed. She wore a plain white bra and panties, and was in the process of stepping into her blue scrubs. Long curly hair tumbled down her bare back. Three kids had changed her body but he still found her appealing, especially with his sex life currently being in the toilet.

"Hey," he said.

Chris jumped when she heard his voice and reached for her scrubs shirt to cover herself. "Dammit, Rio, you can't just barge in here."

"Why not? I've seen it all before."

She glared, her brown eyes shooting angry sparks. "We're not married. You have no right to be in my bedroom."

"This used to be my house, too."

"It isn't anymore. You're a guest when you come here and I would appreciate it if you would respect my privacy."

She dropped the shirt and pulled on her pants, then

drew the top over her head. As she dressed, he focused his attention on her breasts. A flicker of desire sparked to life inside of him.

"You seeing anyone?" he asked.

"I'm not answering that," she said, turning away from him to face the mirror. She separated her thick, curly hair into three sections and braided it. She looked at him in the mirror. "You can't fix the issue of child support or privacy with sex," she told him. "It solved your problems when we were married, but it only made mine worse. Your needs were taken care of while mine got ignored."

"If you'd ever bothered to want sex, I might have paid attention to what you said you needed."

She didn't say anything as she finished with her braid, then fastened the end with a blue stretchy band that matched her scrubs.

Finally she turned to face him directly. "Just once I would like to argue about something different," she said quietly. "Or not argue at all."

He reached into his back pocket and pulled out several papers. "I have something here we can agree on. Have you heard about that marriage contest?"

"Yes," she said flatly. "You're entering?"

"No. *We're* entering."

"I already divorced you once. I don't want to marry you again."

He ignored the jab. "I don't want to marry you, either, but that's not the point. The contest isn't about getting married, it's about living together for money. We did it for nearly eight years, so what's another month? At the end of that time, we'd go into a drawing for a million dollars. Do you know what the money could do for us?"

Chris pulled on her watch, then opened a drawer and removed a pair of white socks. She sat on the edge of the bed to pull them on.

"What makes you think we'd get picked at all, let alone picked as a couple?"

"Because half the couples fill out a questionnaire to see how much they have in common. We could do that together, saying we liked the same stuff. In fact, I can fill the form out tonight and you can check my answers."

She reached for her Nikes. "I don't doubt you'll get all my answers wrong."

He ignored her ill temper. He was used to ignoring Chris, so it wasn't hard. "It's a million dollars. That should be worth a little effort."

"Like I said, I already divorced you once."

"And if we do this and win, you'll never have to sweat me showing up on time, or day care or any of that."

She reached for the papers he held out, studied them, then set them on the bed. "I'll think about it."

He grinned. "You won't be sorry, babe."

"Like I haven't heard that line before."

"Hi, Mom."

Taylor smiled as she adjusted the phone. She checked the clock and saw that it was nearly nine in the evening back east. "Hi, Linnie. This is a nice surprise."

Her sixteen-year-old daughter laughed. "I saw you on CNN, Mom. I had to call. You're famous."

Taylor was torn between delight at hearing her only child's voice and horror at the thought of being on the national news. She sank into a kitchen chair. "Was it awful?"

"No. You were great. You looked fabulous. That teal suit is my favorite. And Dr. Kirby is a hunk. At least you don't have to work with a troll."

"Isn't that a plus," Taylor murmured. "How's camp?"

"Don't change the subject," Linnie scolded. "He's hot, Mom."

"He's a little old for you, dear."

"I meant for you. I'm gone. You should take advantage of that. Be wild. Go on a date or something."

"I don't do wild and Dr. Kirby isn't my type." *Not anymore,* Taylor thought.

"Did he take your quiz?"

Taylor frowned. "I don't think so. Why?"

Linnie chuckled. "If he didn't take your quiz, you can't know that he's not your type. I say give him a chance."

"And I say, no thanks." Just what she needed—romantic advice from a sixteen-year-old. *Of course, it was unlikely a sixteen-year-old would have made more mistakes,* she thought wryly. "So, how's camp?"

"Great. I'm getting better at ASL every day. Maybe next year I can study Japanese."

Linnie had taken a year of American sign language at school, then had found a summer job working at a camp for deaf kids. Her daughter never failed to amaze her. And always in a good way. "Yes, I can see how speaking French, German, Italian and ASL isn't enough for anyone. Of course you'd want to add another language to your list."

"Mo-om, you're teasing me."

"A little. But only because you're terrific. All this drive, not to mention intelligence *and* beauty."

"I get it from you and Grandma."

Maybe the brains, Taylor thought, *but not the drive.* That came from Linnie's father.

"Have you met any interesting boys?" Taylor asked, changing the subject.

"It's a girl's camp. There aren't boys here."

"There are boys at nearby camps. I know you have shared events. And don't tell me the boys are all ten. There are male camp counselors."

"Okay. No, I haven't met any interesting boys. I've met some uninteresting ones, if that counts."

"I know the feeling," Taylor told her.

Linnie drew in a deep breath. "Mom, during your interview, one of the reporters asked why you'd never married. Is it because of me?"

Taylor leaned back in the kitchen chair. "Honey, no. We've had this conversation before. The reason I never married is because I never met a man who made me want that kind of relationship. I love you very much. You're incredibly important to me, but you're not my whole world. I wasn't holding back, I was waiting for the right feelings. I guess it's a McGuire woman thing. Grandma never remarried after Grandpa died. We're darned picky. We want a spark."

Like the one I'd felt when Jonathan had touched my face, she thought, then pushed the idea away. No. She absolutely was *not* going to feel attracted to him. Not when they had to spend the next month practically living in each other's pockets.

"I just want you to be happy," Linnie told her.

"I appreciate that. I want the same thing for myself and for you."

They talked more about Linnie's life at camp before her daughter reminded her that she was due home in three weeks. Taylor had known of the week-long visit, but still the mention of it made her clutch the phone tightly.

"I'm looking forward to seeing you," she said. "I miss you."

"I miss you, too."

"Do you want to speak to your grandmother?" she asked.

"Sure."

They said good-bye, then Taylor called for her mother to pick up the phone. When she heard her mother's voice, she replaced the receiver and sighed.

Linnie was the most wonderful daughter on the planet. Taylor couldn't wait to see her. But if she could think of an excuse to keep her from coming home, should she do it?

Fifteen minutes later her mother walked into the kitchen. She headed for the stove and collected the kettle, then moved to the sink where she ran water.

"Linnie's coming home soon," Linda said as she finished filling the kettle.

"I know. In three weeks."

"She's interested in what's going on in town. She'll want to meet Jonathan."

"It's inevitable." Taylor wondered if there was a way to turn back time and avoid going on *Psychology in the News*.

"Neither of them are stupid."

Taylor nodded.

"I've brought this on myself," she admitted. "When we were on that show and he was shooting down my theories, I just lost it. Worse, I let a lot of old feelings distract me. I agreed to the contest, and Katrina insisted it be held here and now Linnie's coming home. They're going to meet and I don't know what to do."

She rested her elbows on the kitchen table and covered her face with her hands. "Alexi told me if I win the contest, he might be able to get me a million-dollar advance, which is nearly too incredible to believe. A part of me desperately wants the money. I want to repay you for all you've done for Linnie and me. I want to be able to pay for my daughter's college education myself and not have her sweat getting a scholarship. Yet this is all such a mess. I feel like I'm selling my soul to the devil."

"As bad as all that," her mother said lightly.

Taylor looked at her. "I detect a distinct lack of sympathy on your part."

"I'm sympathetic—to a point." Linda joined her at the table. "You knew they were going to meet eventually. You always said you would tell Linnie about her father when she turned eighteen. So it will happen sooner than you imagined. Is that so horrible?"

"I don't know," Taylor admitted. "Who is Jonathan Kirby and how is he going to react to the news that he has a sixteen-year-old daughter? What kind of father will he be, assuming he even wants the job? Being good at making babies has nothing to do with being good at raising children."

"Are you upset because of your concerns about Linnie or because you're not in control of the situation?"

Taylor winced. "I hate it when you cut to the heart of the matter like that. Can't you at least pretend to walk around the point for a while?"

Her mom rose and kissed Taylor's forehead. "Like mother, like daughter. I suggest you start practicing what you're going to say when Linnie and Jonathan find out the truth."

Chapter 5

Taylor squared her shoulders and gave herself a last-minute pep talk. She was smart, she was prepared, she was immune. Okay, maybe that last affirmation needed a little work, because she was afraid she *wasn't* immune to Jonathan Kirby—at least not physically. But she was in control and she would stay that way. There was no reason for him to know that ever since their recent meeting on the talk show, she'd been having recurring sex dreams about him.

That decided, she knocked sharply on the door to his suite and braced herself to face temptation incarnate.

He opened the door. "Good morning," he said with a smile.

It was exactly eleven and Jonathan looked better than he had last night in her dreams. Taylor forced herself to smile in return and hold out her hand, pretending to be the consummate professional when all she really wanted was forty-five minutes of hot, sinus-clearing sex.

"Come on in," said the spider to the oh, so willing fly.

Knowing the smartest course of action would be to run, Taylor crossed the spacious living room of the suite. The room had been decorated in blues and greens, with a print sofa facing an entertainment unit. There were two wing chairs on the left, a dining room table with six chairs on the right and double windows overlooking downtown Marriageville in the far wall.

"How was your seminar?" she asked, taking a seat on one end of the sofa and setting her briefcase on the beige carpet. She forced herself to think calm, professional thoughts that had nothing to do with sex . . . or even naked bodies.

"Good. It was more of a refresher course for couples who have attended other groups I've held."

"Sounds interesting."

"I don't believe you," he said as he settled into the wing chair closest to her and leaned back. "You hate my theories and think my seminars are just smoke and mirrors."

She was grateful she'd worn her dark purple pantsuit. The flattering color always made her feel confident. Now she followed his lead and relaxed in her seat. Casually, she crossed her legs, careful to keep her upper-body posture open. No way was she going to give anything away through her body language.

"Saying that I hate your theories implies a level of energy and caring I simply don't have. We're both professionals who disagree. That's all."

He didn't look the least bit impressed by her speech. "Sell it somewhere else, Taylor. You can be as cool as you want when we're together, but I know you despise my ideas about opposites attracting. The only thing you find more annoying is my insistence that sexual attraction is essential in any successful marriage."

Damn the man—he was right. But she would face torture rather than admit the fact. She leaned toward him. "Amazingly enough, I don't think about you or your theories at all. My life is full and successful, even when you're not a part of it. However, I'll happily support your need to be the center of the universe in whatever small way I can. I understand that you've built a fragile, egocentric world view and I would so hate to be the cause of that world cracking."

He grinned. "You always were smart. Now you're not afraid to let people know."

"I've come a long way from the young girl you remember." She studied his face. "You've changed as well. You always told me you were going to make it to the top, and you did. Is it everything you thought it would be?"

"It's better. I heard you had a book offer."

The change of topic caught her flat-footed. *Score one for the devil,* she thought, unable to keep her mouth from dropping open. She closed it quickly. "Word travels fast."

"I hear things. You've got a good agent. I'm sure Alexi told you to hold out for the big bucks. I hope you listen. This is a great opportunity for you."

"Imagine how great it will be when I win our contest."

"I don't remember you being this competitive," he said. "Is it something new?"

No. It was something specifically about him. "I have faith in my abilities. I don't see that as a weakness."

"Fair enough. Want something to drink? Coffee?" He nodded toward a small table at the side of the room. On top was a carafe and several cups.

"Sure. With a little milk, please."

He rose and walked toward the table. She glanced around the room and noticed the open door leading to his bedroom. The bed was unmade and several suitcases stood open. She quickly averted her eyes and found herself staring at a partially set up computer on the dining room table. Several file folders lay next to the keyboard.

"Another book?" she asked, pointing to the pile.

"Always."

"Books and seminars. Any patients?"

He handed her a cup of coffee, then carried a second mug to the wing chair and resumed his seat. "No. I haven't worked in a private practice in years."

The information surprised her. "Isn't that what psychology is all about? Dealing with real people?"

"I did it for a while. I prefer writing."

"What about the case studies for your books? I can't believe even you would make them up."

He sipped his coffee. "Your confidence in me is flattering. I use couples from my seminars, or establish a group for research purposes." He eyed her over his mug. "Tell me, Dr. McGuire, is it a coincidence that you ended up in the same field I was studying when we met?"

"It's not a coincidence at all." She hesitated, then figured there wasn't any point in avoiding the truth. "It took me a while to get over you, but once I did, I knew I wanted to go to college. I didn't actually have a major in mind. One of my general education classes was psychology and I really enjoyed it. I'm sure some of that was because you were always talking about it while we were together."

His dark eyes turned knowing. "Interesting. You didn't once think 'if he can do it, I can do it better'?"

She laughed. "Well, duh. Of course I thought that. You dumped me so I had something to prove. Besides, besting you turned out to be a great help. Whenever I felt I couldn't possibly get through my classes, I thought of you and told myself that if you could do well, so could I."

"Am I allowed to say I'm proud of you?"

"Not if you want to escape unbloodied."

His dark eyes flickered with something that might have been respect. Or was it desire? Taylor hated that she really wanted it to be the latter. Just sitting in the same room with him was a major turn-on. Like she needed the complication.

She made a show of checking her watch, mostly because looking at him made her forget to breathe. "Are you ready to get to work? I have the new press releases," she said. "They were delivered to my office this morning. Also, we have to talk about how we're going to handle meeting with the couples."

"You've got it all figured out."

"Not really, but I'm determined to get a handle on this circus we've created."

"I might write about this experience," he said. "Or we could talk about collaborating."

"You don't work well with others."

"How do you know?"

"You never did before."

"Maybe I've changed."

She studied his face—the shape of his mouth and the way his gaze never left hers. She remembered when he'd still been idealistic about his career, more interested in helping people than in writing books. "You're right. You have changed. But I'm not interested in playing."

"It could be fun."

She didn't doubt that. "No thanks."

"Too bad. Because I thought of you quite a bit this weekend. You were a distraction."

He spoke the last word slowly, drawing it out sensuously, making her shiver.

"Do you really think seducing me is going to help you win this contest?" she asked pleasantly, striving for a "how's the weather" kind of tone.

"No, but it will make the time in Marriageville more pleasant. Besides, we're going to be working together. You know that I strongly believe sexual attraction makes relationships more successful."

"Sexual attraction in romantic relationships," she clarified, ignoring the way her mouth had gone dry. "We're collaborators in a somewhat twisted scientific experiment. While the thought of being your diversion for the next month is just too exciting for words, I'm going to have to pass. I have a life in progress and I don't need you mucking it up."

"I don't muck." He leaned toward her. "I offered you a side bet, Taylor. You interested?"

More than words could say. "Why are you coming on to me?"

He straightened, obviously surprised by the question. "It was good between us. Maybe it would be again."

She sensed he was telling the truth, but also holding

back. Not a combination to make her sleep better at night.

"It wasn't all that good," she reminded him. "We were both really young. We fought a lot."

"The making up was damn sweet."

Suddenly her pantsuit seemed a little too tight. She wanted to tug at her collar, but she wouldn't give him the satisfaction. "Yes, the sex was great, we have those memories, yada, yada. I've enjoyed our trip down memory lane. Can we get back to the subject at hand, namely the contest?"

Jonathan didn't look the least bit insulted by her feigned indifference. "Fire away."

She set her cup on the coffee table, then pulled several papers out of her briefcase. For a second her brain refused to function, then rational thought returned. Contest. She was here to talk to him about the contest.

"Do you want to see the new press releases?" she asked.

"Sure." One corner of his mouth quirked up. "I'm intrigued by what you said about me."

She handed him the papers. "I didn't write these, although I did make a few suggestions."

He read for several minutes. "These look fine. Getting support from the local clergy was smart. Your idea?"

"Yes." She tried not to be pleased by his praise. "I consider what we're doing more entertainment than serious study. Still, people *will* be living together without the benefit of marriage. I don't doubt we'll be criticized by an assortment of folks, so I would like to head off as much as possible."

"Those who choose to participate do so freely.

They're going to learn something about themselves, possibly meet the love of their life and have a shot at a million dollars. That's hardly a problem."

"I want to make sure everyone sees it that way."

He waved the papers he held. "We're going to be meeting with the participants every week. You're not going to have much free time for your regular patients."

"I know. I'm working out a temporary schedule, seeing them bi-weekly when possible."

He crossed his legs, resting his ankle on his opposite knee. "We can't give every couple in this contest personal attention. Counseling for forty couples would mean at least forty hours a week."

"I agree. However, I think we should be available for anyone who needs help."

"Pro bono work?"

She smiled. "Let me guess. Along with avoiding private practice, you don't do charity work, either?"

He shrugged. "I've been known to be persuaded from time to time." He glanced toward the window. "Marriageville doesn't strike me as the kind of place with a lot of problems."

"We have our share of troubles. Kids get involved with drugs, or drink too much. There's crime."

"I don't believe that. Any murders?"

"Not in the past couple of years." She looked at him. "We consider that a *good* thing."

"So you live a bucolic existence."

"We have a low crime rate when compared with the rest of the nation, but we're not all functioning with dull-normal IQs."

"Sorry. I didn't mean to tread on your toes."

"You didn't." She reached for her coffee. "I'm a little sensitive on the subject because I've been fielding the press since word got out about our contest. Most of them have made assumptions about Marriageville and they're amazingly similar to what you just said. Why is it people from big cities have to put down small towns? Do you really think you're that much better or are you overcompensating?"

Jonathan grinned. "Both."

"You're still insufferable," she said.

"Charming," he corrected. "The word you're looking for is *charming.*"

"You were always that." She sipped her coffee. "So, Dr. Kirby, what have you been doing with your life in the past sixteen or seventeen years?"

"Working. Writing. And you?"

"About the same."

He studied her. "What happened when you came back here? Was your mother angry?"

Taylor thought about that time. She'd been eighteen, heartbroken and, as she'd discovered a month after she'd crawled home, pregnant. "I think she'd been saving up her lectures for the two years I'd been gone, but I was in pretty bad shape when I arrived, so she gave me a break."

Linda had taken one look at her, then held out her arms. Even now Taylor could remember the feeling of being so empty inside that she thought she was going to simply fade away.

"I'm sorry," he told her. "For what happened and how it ended. I shouldn't have taken you away from your family. You were way too young."

His apology should have come too late to matter—

at least that's what she told herself. Yet a part of her was comforted by the words. "Agreed, but I wanted to be with you." She smiled slightly. "And don't you dare say it was just teenage hormones and sex."

He nodded. "There was plenty of that. But we had more going on."

"I was so in love with you," she said with a sigh.

He uncrossed his legs and leaned toward her. "I loved you, too. I just wasn't ready to settle down and get married."

"I know." She'd wanted to love him forever, and he'd wanted to move on.

"Taylor, I—"

He stopped talking. At the same moment she realized this was an incredibly intimate conversation to be having with a man who was a virtual stranger, she also found herself remembering all those teenage hormones and sex. Her heart might have recovered just fine, but her body seemed to be stuck in the past. Worse, she could remember what it had been like when being physically intimate with him had been the best part of her day.

Something dark flickered in Jonathan's gaze. At the same time she noticed the air seemed to crackle with tension. She could swear that she could hear his heartbeat.

They stared at each other, then both glanced away. An awkward silence filled the room. Taylor broke it first. She set her coffee mug on the table and reached back into her briefcase.

"Here are the papers the couples are going to sign. They hold us blameless for anything we might say in the course of the contest."

"What about holding each other blameless?"

"You and I or each of them?"

"Both."

"Are you planning to sue me, Jonathan? Should I be worried?"

"Not about that."

He'd used that sexy voice again. The one that made her turn as pliable as bread dough. She needed a man. Or a very powerful vibrator.

He stood and crossed to the sofa. Taylor nearly fainted as he sat next to her and took the papers from her hands.

"This is all legal stuff," he said, dismissing it. "Where are the ground rules for the relationships?"

"Each couple should establish their own. What works for one couple won't work for another."

"You're the one who promotes questionnaires and getting to know people," he said, sitting way too close. "We should come up with suggestions for ways to communicate. It's very important for a couple to communicate."

"Yes. Of course."

She could feel the heat of him. Hating herself for being so weak, she imagined him gathering her so close that she could feel his hard, muscled body pressing against hers. He'd always had the power to make her feel safe.

"And sex," he said.

She blinked at him. "Excuse me?"

"We need to have some rules about sex. For the couples."

"They're not going to do it!"

He gave her another of his sexy smiles. "*Do it?* Taylor, I would think that you of all people would want to use more professional terminology. 'Doing it' sounds like kids getting it on in the backseat of a car."

She and Jonathan had made love in a car, she thought, unable to keep herself from flashing back to how amazing it had been when the two of them had been going at it like rabbits. They'd made love in every location possible, in every position and with a frequency that bordered on pathological. It had been wonderful.

She cleared her throat and sat a little straighter, trying to put some distance between them. "Perhaps a few well-chosen comments on the potential hazards of physical intimacy would be a good idea."

"We have to talk about touching, too."

Then she got it.

"Nice work," she said, patting him on the cheek. "Moving closer, switching the conversation to something personal and sexual. Lowering the tone of your voice. I'm impressed. You've used nearly every known technique to indicate physical interest and illicit a response from me."

She practically quivered with pleasure and pride from figuring it out before she did something stupid like throw herself at him.

His gaze narrowed. "So this is the downside of seducing a psychologist."

"I can't speak for the profession in general, but it would be the downside of trying to seduce me." She raised her eyebrows. "Did you really think I'd be that easy?"

"Hey, I'm using my best material and you just shot me down. My sense of self-worth has been shattered and it's all your fault. This is many things, Taylor, but easy isn't one of them."

"I suspect no permanent damage has been done. You'll recover nicely and without my help."

"You think?"

And then he kissed her.

There was no warning, no chance for her to prepare. Taylor sat immobilized by shock as his mouth settled on hers. Worse, she felt herself spontaneously combust as his lips pressed against hers with a sensually exciting, familiar pressure. His scent and heat surrounded her and before she knew what she was doing, she found herself wrapping her arms around his shoulders and pulling him close. A voice in her head screamed for control and sanity. A rush of liquid passion drowned out the words.

Even as his tongue stroked against her bottom lip, she wanted to press against him. She wanted to touch all of him, relearning hollows and planes that had so entranced her all those years ago.

He teased the seam of her lips, and she parted for him. He entered slowly, as if savoring the moment. She focused all of her attention on the sensations generated by his tongue gently rubbing the inside of her bottom lip. Rational thought fled. Need flared until all she could think about was being with this man. Her breasts ached, her thighs trembled. His taste intoxicated her.

They danced, tongues circling, sweeping, rubbing until she knew she no longer had the will to deny him anything. No one else had ever made her feel that her body had been created solely to provide pleasure. But she'd felt it with him before, and she felt it now. She felt it more.

It was the realization that the passion was hotter, stronger and more tempting that made her jerk back.

She scrambled to her feet, grabbing the back of the sofa for support when her weak legs didn't want to straighten.

"Taylor—"

"Don't," she told him hotly as she reached for her briefcase, then headed for the door. There was no one word to describe how she felt at the moment. Humiliated, flustered, shocked, embarrassed, but mostly aroused. She needed a new word to explain the conflicting emotions swirling through her.

"We'll pick this up later," she said, then shook her head. "The discussion, not the rest of it."

Not if she was going to survive the next few weeks. She absolutely, positively could *not* have a sexual relationship with Jonathan Kirby. Once she'd told him her little secret, all bets would be off.

Chapter 6

The series of math equations scrolled down Will Ramsey's computer screen at Computer Tectronics. The error lay buried in the code somewhere. He just had to find it. Easier said than done. In the latest run-through he'd found that—

Something slapped against his desk, followed by the command to, "Sign this, Will."

Without taking his attention off the computer screen, he fumbled to his right for a pen and hastily scrawled his name. "What did I just sign?"

"You don't want to know," Mark Ennis, his boss, told him.

Something about the sequence maybe, he thought, staring back at the screen. He could start there.

Sometime later he smelled coffee and looked up. Mark handed him a steaming mug, then settled on the corner of his desk. "You don't even blink," Mark said. "It's amazing. Pure concentration. But the not blinking . . . weird. I thought everyone had to do that."

Will pushed his wire-rimmed glasses a little higher on his nose. "I blink."

"No way. I've been thinking about it and my guess is that it's like that old movie, *Tron.* You know the one— the computer programmers get sucked in by the CPU. I'm not saying that's what's happening, but you connect with the computer like you're part of it. Kinda eerie."

"Thanks," Will muttered.

He knew he was in trouble when the other computer nerds thought he was too involved with his work. When he got home he should pull out one of those books he'd bought. The ones on getting along in the workplace.

He glanced at the calendar and realized it was Wednesday. *Ask something personal,* the books always encouraged. Okay, he could either ask Mark about his previous weekend, or the one coming up. He weighed the possibilities and decided the future was safer.

"Do you have any plans for the weekend?"

Mark grinned knowingly. Will fought against a familiar sinking sensation. Had Mark told him about something significant, like his wife having a baby?

"There's that contest in town. You know the one that matches up couples and they have to live together for a month to get a chance at a million dollars. Kathy and I thought we'd go watch what was going on."

Will blinked. Ah, so he *did* do that from time to time, he thought, pleased. "Contest?" he repeated.

Mark's smile broadened. "You should know all about it. It's been in the local paper and you recently entered."

Will's normally lightning-speed brain faltered. Fact—he did remember reading about the bizarre experiment pitting two psychologists against each other.

Was that starting this weekend? Fact—he didn't remember entering the contest and he was sure he would have remembered something that important.

Then a thought teased at the edge of his consciousness. Mark shoving a paper in front of him and ordering him to sign.

"You entered me," he said, his voice more stunned than accusing.

"Guilty as charged," Mark said cheerfully and without remorse. "I'm your boss, and from what I can tell, you have no life. You know the old saying, All work and no play. It's time you got out there and played." Mark paused and winked. "With a woman. You like women, don't you?"

"Sure," Will said automatically.

Like didn't come close. He longed to be with a woman, to talk with her and touch her and maybe even have her like him. He wasn't stupid enough to expect an actual long-term relationship, although he did have occasional fantasies about marriage and kids.

Mark patted his shoulder. "Then you'll be fine. With a little luck, you'll get matched up with the lady of your dreams. You get to play married for a whole month. Even *you* should manage to get lucky in that time."

Intense longing filled Will. A month of living with a woman? "I might not get chosen," he said.

"You will." Mark sounded confident.

"But what if she doesn't like me?"

"You worry too much. Will, you're what, twenty-six?"

"Twenty-eight."

Mark pointed to the screen. "There's more to life than working all the time. Be wild for once. Take a chance. Besides, you don't have a choice. I turned in the paperwork this morning. Face it. You're going to have to spend a month in the real world. The good news is you might just like it."

Will opened his mouth to protest but before he could form words, his computer started beeping. As he glanced at the screen, he saw the carefully constructed program had crashed.

"That still has design flaws," Mark said unnecessarily.

He might have said something else, but Will wasn't listening. He tapped keys and in less than a second, everything around him faded to black.

Rio tried to keep his temper in check. He'd filled out the damned contest entries himself, he'd come over early so that he and Chris could talk about them before she left for work, and was she the least bit grateful? Of course not. All she did was complain, as usual.

"I shouldn't have let you talk me into this," Chris said as she slapped their two plates of spaghetti on the table and put her hands on her hips. "I don't want to spend my evenings going out dancing," she said.

"Mommy, you dance pretty," Molly, their youngest, offered, as she finished the last of her dinner.

Chris spared the curly headed four-year-old a smile. "Thank you, sweetie."

Molly beamed back, then carefully wiped her mouth on a napkin. She missed most of the spaghetti sauce. Chris finished the job, then pulled back her daughter's chair. Molly scampered off to join her siblings in front of the TV.

Usually Chris insisted they all eat together, but

tonight she'd had the kids eat first so they wouldn't hear their parents argue. She'd said "argue" while glaring at him. Like this was all *his* fault. Rio was only trying to help them win a million dollars, but in her mind, he was still the bad guy.

He threw up his hands. "Since when don't you like to go dancing? We always went dancing before."

"Exactly. Before. Before I had three kids and no time to sleep. Before I spent my twelve-hour shift on my feet. When I get home after work, I'm exhausted. When I have a night off, I want to relax, not head out to a nightclub and wear high heels. That's not fun, it's torture."

He had a brief thought about putting his fist through a wall, but he knew from personal experience that it would hurt way more than it would help. Instead, he waved the contest forms in front of her. "So what do you want me to put down?"

"Gardening and reading."

Rio couldn't believe it. "That's crazy. I've never seen you with a book in your hands and our garden looks like sh—" He glanced toward the living room, then lowered his voice. "Crap. It looks like crap."

She sat across from him. "You never noticed," she said quietly.

"What?"

"You never looked closely enough to see a book in my hands. Every week I locked myself in the bathroom for a couple of hours and took a bath. What did you think I was doing all that time?"

"I dunno."

He didn't know. He'd never much thought about

her weekly time alone as anything but an inconvenience to himself.

"I was reading," she said. "I've always enjoyed reading. I didn't do it much around you because you made it clear early in our relationship that you thought it was a waste of time. So I read when you weren't around. Or weren't paying attention."

Her tone indicated he'd done the latter as much as the former. Rio wanted to protest, but he didn't think he had the right. Now that he and Chris had been divorced for a year, he was willing to admit that he might have been a little selfish while they were together. He'd gone racing whenever he'd wanted, feeling free to take money from their savings to pay for parts or entry fees. He'd missed birthday parties and been late when he'd promised to look after the kids. Still, how could he not have known his wife liked to read?

"What about the garden?" he asked. "It's just a bunch of dirt and weeds."

Chris rested her elbows on the table and cupped her chin in her hands. "I know. It makes me feel bad to see it like that, but there's no sprinkler system. We don't even have a hose hookup outside. I used to carry buckets of water to my plants, but eventually I gave up."

"Gardening," he muttered, and scribbled the change in their contest applications.

"You might as well add car racing and picnics," she said. "Just to be fair."

He stared at her. Chris was dressed for work. Today she wore reddish scrubs she referred to as cranberry. She'd pulled her long hair back but as always, a few corkscrew curls escaped. She didn't wear much makeup, but she was still one of the prettiest women he'd ever met. He'd been shocked as hell when she'd agreed to marry him. Even though she'd been pregnant, he'd half expected her to laugh in his face.

"How'd you know I like picnics?" he asked.

She rolled her eyes. "You only took me on at least forty-seven when we were dating. How could I not remember?"

Yet he hadn't figured out she liked to read. He didn't even recall having a conversation during which he'd told her reading was a waste of time, although he didn't doubt it had happened. He tended to say things without thinking, assuming they would quickly be forgotten. But not with Chris. She remembered everything, and usually made sure it came back and bit him on the ass.

"I'm sorry I didn't know about the reading," he said.

"Whatever. You were too busy being trapped to notice anything but your suffering." She stirred her fork through the pasta, but didn't eat.

He sensed her frustration and sadness. Unfortunately, he didn't know what to do about it, which made him angry.

"How come if you knew I liked picnics so much, we stopped taking them?"

She raised her gaze to his. "Because I was mad at you and I wanted to punish you by not doing things you liked. I was trying to get your attention so you'd pay attention to things I liked, too. It didn't work."

"I'm sorry," he said lamely, wishing for a better answer.

She nodded, her expression softening. "I know, Rio. I'm sorry, too. I just wish being sorry made a difference."

He stared at the application in front of him and wondered if this crazy idea was going to work. And if it did, would he and Chris survive living together for a month?

"Last but not least," the broadcaster said as he grinned at the camera. "Preparations are under way in Marriageville, Texas, for the first-ever relationship contest. Feuding psychologists Jonathan Kirby and Taylor McGuire have set very interesting events in motion. Forty couples will be matched up, half based on opposites attracting and potential sexual chemistry and half using an extensive compatibility questionnaire developed by Dr. McGuire. All forty couples are expected to live together for a month, after which they're eligible for a million-dollar drawing."

The perfectly coiffed man kept talking, but Grace Anderson hit the mute button on her television remote, then glanced at her large marmalade cat dozing next to her.

"What do you think, Alexander?" she asked, then paused as if expecting the large cat to do more than twitch his ears. He didn't. He opened one eyelid, then closed it slowly.

"My thoughts exactly," Grace told him. She was used to Alexander not saying much, so she filled in the quiet bits for him. He didn't seem to mind and she had the illusion of someone to talk to.

She rose and headed for the kitchen to get more tea. As she crossed the dining room, she caught sight of herself in the mirror over the buffet.

Normally Grace didn't pay any attention to her appearance, but now she stopped to stare at her reflection. Her once-blond hair had turned completely white. It surrounded her forehead and cheeks in soft waves, thanks to her grandma Jean, who had always had perfectly waved hair. Lines framed her eyes and her mouth, pulling down her skin and scoring her neck. She still had most of her slender figure. For thirty years she'd hated her small breasts, but now she was grateful. Tiny though they were, they'd stayed where they belonged instead of heading for her knees.

With her knit pants and loose shirt hiding the other wrinkles and signs of aging, she told herself that if one didn't look too closely, she wasn't unattractive. Not for a woman closer to seventy than sixty. She almost believed herself, too.

"I'm a fool," she whispered to her reflection. A lonely fool who had grown tired of her own company. She turned her attention to the papers on the lace-covered dining room table and touched the top sheet. She'd nearly finished filling everything in.

According to the contest rules, she wouldn't be matched with anyone more than seven years in age difference. How many old men would bother to enter? So the odds of her getting matched with anyone seemed small. Still, she thought she might have to try. That or she would die from being so very alone.

When she was out in town she observed other women her age. They always traveled in groups, talking and laughing. She envied them and wished she could join, but she didn't know how. She'd always been painfully shy. She'd married Alan when she'd been eighteen, because he'd asked and she'd never thought anyone would. Between the constant moving as Alan forever chased his elusive dreams of success and fortune and her own awkwardness at making friends, she'd been alone. Over the years her family had passed on. Then ten years ago, Alan had started drinking.

She pushed those ugly memories away and pulled out a dining room chair, then settled onto the seat. Her reading glasses were there. She put them on and quickly finished filling out the application. When she was done, she closed her eyes.

"Dear God, please send me someone kind," she prayed aloud. "A gentle man who will talk with me and tell me he likes my cooking. I'm sorry for such a selfish prayer and I hope you'll see fit to forgive me for it and grant me this one request."

Taylor sat at her office desk, sorting through files. At least that's what she was supposed to be doing this afternoon. She had paperwork to finish that night after dinner, clients to meet with in a couple of hours and the ridiculous contest beginning at the end of the week. A contest she wanted to win—for the sake of her potential publishing career *and* her pride. She couldn't afford to waste any time.

She also couldn't concentrate. It had been all of twenty-seven hours since her encounter with Jonathan—twenty-seven hours of doing everything in her power to forget how the man had kissed her.

And how she'd let herself kiss him back.

What on earth had she been thinking? Or better yet, why *hadn't* she been thinking? She had to work with him. They were going to have to be in very close quarters for the next month. She had withheld incredibly significant information from him that she may have to share relatively soon. Starting a physical relationship, or even just sharing a kiss, was not going to make any of that easier.

She tried telling herself that it was *just* a kiss. Not important, not to be repeated, nothing more than a sensual stroll down memory lane. Yes, it had been very nice. Perhaps even a little better than what she remembered. But it didn't have to *mean* anything. She had always been cautious about her sexual encounters. In fact, they'd been extremely rare events. She could change that by accepting the next invitation that came her way. Easy enough.

As long as Jonathan wasn't the one doing the inviting. She didn't need that kind of trouble.

She straightened in her chair. She would gird herself against his appeal and charm, remind herself that she was forged of strong moral steel. If that didn't work, she would remember what had happened the last time she'd fallen for Jonathan.

She would simply make sure they were never alone again. Or if that wasn't possible, she would—

She slammed her hands down on the table and swore aloud. What was it about him that got to her? She was a sensible, intelligent, articulate woman. Not some sex-starved groupie desperate for love in whatever its form. She knew better.

Unfortunately this seemed to be one of those situations in which knowing better and doing better had very little in common.

* * *

Marnie hovered over the large wooden box in the foyer of city hall. She glanced from the folded paper she held to Linda McGuire, Taylor's mother.

"This looks like one of the town's ballot boxes," Marnie said, still not sure she could go through with it.

"It is. There was no point in wasting the money to buy a special box when we could simply reuse these."

Linda pointed to the two boxes set up on separate tables. Each was clearly marked with a sign indicating the criteria for matching. Both boxes were carefully guarded.

Linda touched the paper in Marnie's hand. "Are you going to do it?"

"I don't know," she admitted. "It's been three years since George died. I still miss him, but…"

Linda patted her hand. "You're young and very beautiful, Marnie. Go ahead. Have a little fun."

Easy for Linda to say. She hadn't arranged to cheat, nor was she the one who would be punished by the Almighty. "Do you think whoever I get will like me?"

"Of course." Linda patted her arm. "Honey, you're beautiful, you're smart, and you're rich. What would be the problem?"

"I guess." Marnie briefly squeezed her eyes shut, then dropped her application into the box. If Mark didn't come through, Lord knew who she would be matched with. She didn't want to think about that.

Instead she turned her attention to Taylor's mother. "Are you going to enter?"

"No. I thought about it, but I've already had the love of my life. I don't want anyone else." Linda smiled. "Don't take that wrong. I'm not judging you. It's just that the women in my family seem to only love one man. If I ever meet anyone who makes me feel half as good as Taylor's father, I'll marry him in a heartbeat. But it's been nearly thirty years and that hasn't happened. I've stopped expecting it."

Marnie wondered if she should stop expecting it, too. She glanced at the box.

"Can I get my paper back?"

"Not in this lifetime. You, young lady, are about to have an adventure. Enjoy every minute of it."

"I've seen a lot of talk shows fail," Jonathan said calmly, refusing to be sucked in by the syndication suits sitting across from him. The deal was everything he'd ever wanted but they didn't have to know that. "Major stars have tried to make the format work and they've fallen on their famous asses. What makes you think I'd do any better?"

The programming executives gushed about his wit, his charm, his people skills, and how the camera loved him. He didn't doubt that if Taylor were here, she would be pleased to tell them forty-seven reasons why they were wrong.

Taylor. He tried to push her from his mind. The last thing he needed right now was to remember how she spit fire at him every time she opened her mouth . . . and the way she felt in his arms.

He'd called her a distraction and he'd been right. He'd spent the past seventeen years doing whatever was necessary to claw his way to the top and now all he'd ever wanted was within his grasp. So why the hell was he thinking about Taylor?

Focus, he told himself. And returned his attention to the meeting.

Fifteen minutes later, Irene Grant, Jonathan's long-time agent, closed her folder. "Gentlemen, you've given us a lot to think about. My client and I will discuss the show and get back to you."

The men shook hands with him. "Don't forget to win," the head of the syndication company said as he walked to the door. "That's all we need to get you on right after Oprah."

"I always liked Oprah," Jonathan said when the men had left.

Irene turned in her chair and grinned at him. "Her show or her money? You said you were looking for something different, Jonathan. Here it is. Win the contest and you write your own ticket. I spoke to your esteemed editor earlier this morning. Jack says the new book is debuting at number one. You've never been hotter."

"Due to you, in no small part."

Irene shrugged. "I look for opportunities. You write the books. We're a good team."

Jonathan crossed to the window of his agent's office and stared down at the busy New York streets below. All the publicity about the contest had sent book orders through the roof and had caused the syndication people to come calling. Adrenaline coursed through him.

"A talk show," he said. "What do you think they'll offer?"

"We'll hold out for a percentage," Irene said. "We're talking millions."

Someone knocked on the door to the conference

room. A young woman stuck her head into the room. "Irene, it's that call from Paris."

Irene excused herself. "I'll just be a couple of minutes. Think about it," she advised. "You want to be on at four in the morning or do you want to go on after Oprah?"

If he got the show, he'd have it all, he thought when he was alone. More money, more success. Irene said the contest was pure genius. While he didn't disagree, he hadn't been thinking of his career when he'd issued the challenge. He'd been thinking of Taylor.

The successful, acerbic Taylor McGuire he knew now was very different from the young woman who had once adored him. She should annoy him, yet he found himself unable to stop thinking about her. Or the kiss they'd shared.

He couldn't remember the last time he'd wanted someone the way he wanted her. He was reasonably confident he could seduce her into his bed. The question was what did he do with her once he got her there?

Will Ramsey hunched over his desk. His program still had bugs but that wasn't what captured his attention. Instead he pored over chapter five of Jonathan Kirby's *What on Earth Was I Thinking?*, a guide to help men understand women.

Will had already read the book twice to grasp the content. Now he was going back and reading more slowly, taking notes, trying to figure out what it was he always did wrong where the fairer sex was concerned. Dr. Kirby had a lot of suggestions but they all took place in a context Will didn't understand.

Listen while they talked, Dr. Kirby said. Don't interrupt, don't offer opinions, don't try to fix. Just listen. Make small noises to show that you're listening.

"Like what?" Will muttered under his breath. "A grunt? An uh-huh?" Couldn't the man be specific? Besides, he nearly always listened attentively when a woman spoke to him, mostly because it happened so seldom. Yet no matter how intently he paid attention, he inevitably said something wrong and the female in question looked at him as if he was an idiot.

He turned to the chapter on being more sensitive. Dr. Kirby lectured on the value of frequent small gifts instead of one or two big gifts a year. Okay, that made sense. Except Will usually struck out there, too. He still remembered his excitement when he'd finally asked a girl out on a date. He'd been eighteen and already in his Ph.D. program at M.I.T. She'd been a sixteen-year-old junior from a local high school. They'd met during a campus tour. Hailey had been considering attending the university.

Will had carefully chosen a small but beautiful plant to take to her house. By the time they'd returned from their date, and just before he could gather the courage to kiss Hailey, her mother had come running out of the house in tears. Little Fluffy, the family cat, had snacked on the plant gift, had a fit and promptly died. Hailey had never returned Will's calls after that.

A few years later he'd served shrimp dip to a woman deathly allergic to seafood and they'd spent the majority of their first date in a hospital emergency room. He'd broken an antique platter at another woman's house and had worn a leather jacket on a date with a confirmed vegetarian and animal lover who worked for PETA. She'd spent the entire evening lecturing him on the brutal conditions under which cattle were raised and slaughtered.

Will supposed that if he was like other men, the entire male-female situation wouldn't be so complicated. But he wasn't like other men. He'd been in college before his voice changed and in a graduate program before he could drive. When he was sixteen, his peers were in their twenties. He'd never had a normal relationship with a woman.

He closed the book and removed his glasses so that he could rub his eyes. Maybe he was going about this all wrong. Statistically there wasn't much reason for him to worry. There were probably going to be hundreds of entries and only forty couples would be matched. The odds of him getting picked were slim. If he did, well, he'd worry then.

He turned to his computer, but before he touched the keyboard he found himself thinking about how it might be, if his luck ever changed. He wouldn't mind meeting a nice woman. Someone quiet and shy. A bookworm. She didn't have to be pretty. He'd never cared about looks. He was fairly nerdy, so he was in no position to make demands in the appearance department. But he'd like someone nice who could talk about things. He didn't care if they didn't have much in common—he could like what she liked. Even cats. He'd always felt bad about Fluffy.

A librarian, he thought happily. A mathematician would be even better, but he wasn't getting his hopes up. Then, without warning, he suddenly pictured the bombshell brunette who sashayed through Wilbur's Diner every day. She was tall, curvy and possibly the most beautiful creature he'd ever seen. She scared the life out of him.

Not her, he thought firmly, telling himself it was unlikely she would even enter. He switched on his monitor to study his program. Anyone else, but not her.

Chapter 7

"This is something out of a sixties sitcom," Jonathan said as he paused by a street vendor and bought two ice cream cones.

Taylor took the one he handed her and gave him a smile. The hot afternoon made her appreciate the cool, sweet ice cream.

"What do you know about the sixties?" she asked. "You weren't around for very much of them, and as an infant, I doubt you were watching TV."

"I've seen reruns." He motioned to the open area around them. "What was everyone thinking?" he asked. "Honeymoon Avenue? Engagement Way? I thought you had normal street names."

"We do. Just not here around Marriageville Square."

It was nearly three on Friday and the contest would begin in less than an hour. Through a series of unexpected circumstances—Jonathan being called to New York for the day, her having a sudden rush of appointments—they hadn't seen each other since Monday. Or, as she thought of it in the privacy of her mind, since "The Kiss."

When Jonathan had called and suggested she meet him before the event began, she'd hesitated, not sure if she was ready to face him again. But he'd acted as if nothing had happened between them. She refused to be the first person to bring it up, so she'd agreed.

Now she was stuck spending time with him, trying to pretend every inch of her skin wasn't hypersensitive and quivering at the thought of his touch.

"Tell me about Marriageville Square," he said, pointing to a bench, then taking a seat when she nodded.

Taylor sat down as well, making sure they weren't too close.

"Your hotel is on Grand," she said, then licked the cone. "There's Main Street and First Avenue, like most small towns. But here, by the square, it's all marriage, all the time."

She pointed to the white gazebos set close to each corner and the lush gardens, currently displaying the beginning of the rose-blooming season.

"The square was designed for outdoor weddings. We also have the churches if people prefer."

Jonathan glanced toward the corner in front of them. A white church stood there.

"Turn around," she said, fighting back a grin.

He did as she suggested, noticing another church. He turned again. "Four churches?"

"Absolutely. We aim to please as many people as possible. There are also several nondenominational facilities, along with a very lovely botanical garden. Most of the restaurants will cater, there are halls to rent, a couple of old mansions. Getting married is big business here. It has been for nearly eighty years."

"Hence the name."

"Exactly. My mother owns a bridal shop that carries bridesmaids' dresses along with other formal gowns. Before I started my private practice, I used to work there."

He glanced at her. "When you weren't running off with teenage boys."

"There was only one boy."

She licked her cone, then leaned back on the bench and refused to get nostalgic. Above them, the wide-open Texas sky was a stunning shade of blue. There weren't any clouds and the temperature would climb close to ninety.

Taylor adjusted her napkin so she wouldn't drip on her light gray silk suit. She'd made a special trip up to Dallas to buy it. After all, today's event practically guaranteed national media attention. She might be shaking in her pumps, but they were designer expensive. As a major player in the month-long circus she'd brought to town, she wanted to look her best. Jonathan's appreciative stare was an added bonus.

"I remember you saying you liked growing up here," he said.

"It's great for a kid. We have a minor league baseball team in the spring and summer. High school football is practically a religion. There's the lake for swimming and fishing, plenty of open space to play. Plus the people are special."

"How?"

She sighed. "My dad died when I was five. When my mom showed no signs of remarrying, the town stepped in and helped us out. One of the local contractors always made sure the house was in good shape. Pastor Greene taught me to ride a bike, then later, to drive. Someone was always willing to take me to any of the father-daughter functions. A couple of the guys even screened my dates."

"They never met me. I doubt I would have passed inspection."

She grinned. "You were a little old for me. All of nineteen to my very naïve sixteen."

"I have tremendous ambivalence about that time," he admitted. "You *were* much too young, but I wasn't that much older. We were playing house. I can't believe your mother didn't throw me in jail. She mentioned wanting to."

"I remember. She followed me to Boston and demanded I come home with her. I threatened to disappear if she did and never come home again, so she backed off."

He winced. "You really went to bat for me."

"Yes, I did. And look at what a sorry creature you turned out to be."

He laughed. The sound seemed to vibrate inside of her, making her slightly nervous stomach even more jumpy.

Taylor took a last bite of her ice cream and tossed the rest of the cone into a nearby trash can. After wiping her fingers, she let her gaze settle on Jonathan.

He wore a suit, which wasn't a surprise. She hadn't seen him in anything else. Did the man even own jeans? Not that his clothes did anything but emphasize his muscled body and masculine good looks.

"Are you sorry?" he asked.

It took her a second to figure out he was talking about the past. "I was hurt when it ended. I'll admit running away with you wasn't the smartest thing I ever did, but sorry? No."

"Do you worry about history repeating itself with your daughter?"

She'd already told him about Linnie, so his comment shouldn't have surprised her. Still, she found herself fighting butterflies in her stomach. Linnie wasn't just *her* daughter. When was she going to tell Jonathan about their child? Seventeen years ago she'd made the decision not to trap him by confessing she was pregnant, but this was a different situation. *Timing*, she thought. She needed good timing.

"My daughter has a sensible head on her shoulders." Something else Linnie inherited from her father. "Plus I've been pretty honest about my past, so she knows my concerns."

"You can't protect her forever."

"Agreed, but I can try. You asked me if I had any regrets about our relationship. I do have one. That I hurt my mom. I didn't realize how much until I had a daughter of my own. When I think about all the times my mom dragged me back and how I kept running away."

"You were determined."

"I was in love."

Jonathan tossed the rest of his cone into the trash. "Life was more intense then."

"I thought I'd die if we weren't together. Probably not a healthy manifestation, but I was too young to be mature about it."

He looked at her. "And now?"

At first she thought he was talking about her feelings for him, but then she realized he meant other men in her life. She hesitated. Honestly, no one had ever gotten to her the way he had, but did she want to admit that?

"And now I know better. I'm the queen of mental health."

"A single queen."

"The queen bee."

"So you have boy toys just waiting to have their way with you?"

She couldn't help laughing. "I wish, but no." She angled toward him. "Does everything have to be about sex?"

"Pretty much. It's important. Or don't you cover that in your therapy sessions?"

"We discuss many things. I have couples longing to stay together but not knowing how. I give them skills, direction. They do the work and by participating and making an effort, they have a sense of coming together. Bonding over the process. The love is still there, it just gets a little misplaced."

"What they need is more sex."

"You're obsessed."

"I'm right."

"You're not even close. I've read your books." He raised his eyebrows and she dismissed him with a wave. "I read everyone. Don't get all excited thinking I've spent the past seventeen years pining for you. I haven't. My point is, you talk about a whole lot more than the wild thing."

"Maybe you bring out the animal in me."

Wouldn't that be nice, she thought, before she could stop herself. *Don't go there,* she reminded herself. As a way to switch gears, she thought about Linnie. What would Jonathan say if she told him about his daughter?

When. Not if.

"You're looking serious about something," Jonathan said. "Want to talk about it?"

"I thought you didn't do private therapy," she teased.

"I might make an exception."

"I couldn't afford your rates."

"We could work out a deal."

"I think there might be a conflict of interest. Besides," she pointed to the crowd collecting in the square, "it's time."

They rose. "Coward," he murmured as they headed for the stage.

"I prefer to think of this as a strategic retreat."

"You're not getting off that easy."

She didn't doubt his words. Once she told him about his daughter, they would be sharing a lot more than sexual attraction.

Marnie knew she was going to be punished. Life had very specific rules and she'd broken a big one. God was going to get her.

"Welcome, everyone."

Linda McGuire spoke into a microphone from the podium. Marnie thought about running away but knew it was too late for second thoughts and remorse. She'd created the situation—now she was going to have to live with it. That or she was going to have a heart attack and die right here in the middle of Marriageville Square.

All around her crowds of people pressed closer to hear what Linda was saying. Taylor's mother explained about the contest. Marnie strained to hear her words. Everything sounded faint and garbled. She didn't dare glance around. What if she saw Will? What if he knew what she'd done and thought she was a horrible person? What if something went wrong and she was matched up with an icky guy?

That was it, she thought glumly. That was how God was going to punish her. He would make the computer put her with someone awful. A smelly, toothless, tattooed man with bad breath and wandering hands. She was going to throw up.

Instead she shook her head and stared fixedly at Linda. Eventually she was able to make out the older woman's words.

". . . two groups. Everyone participating will sign a whole truckload of legal documents so you can't sue the city or anyone else."

The crowd chuckled. For the first time Marnie noticed all the media in attendance. They circled the square, video cameras recording the event.

"Once your name is called, come on up and meet your prospective significant other. You'll have a few minutes to talk, then if you both agree, you'll sign the papers and make your arrangements to live together. While most of you are here for the chance at a million dollars, there's also two interesting theories on the line. You'll be meeting with the good doctors every week and filling out a bunch of questionnaires.

Not to be biased, but I do want to mention that my daughter, Taylor, is one of the psychologists involved."

More laughter drifted from the crowd.

Linda grinned. "Just so you get my point."

Marnie fastened and unfastened the top button of her white shirt. She'd tucked the blouse into black jeans and had pulled on her favorite red cowboy boots. The heels made her a hair under six feet, but Will was taller, so she didn't think her height would be a problem. Maybe she should have worn a dress. Or a dressier pants outfit. Or maybe her hair was too big, or he'd hate the little state of Texas decals she'd glued onto her nails. Maybe—

"Let's get this started," Linda said as a young man handed her a folder. She slipped on her reading glasses.

Marnie took a step back, trodding on the man behind her. She apologized quickly, then started to make her way out of the crowd. She was crazy. She couldn't do this. She had to get away before lightning came out of the clear sky and struck her where she stood.

"Cameron Waverly and Sara Potter."

Marnie froze. This was really going to happen, she thought stunned by the sudden realization of reality. What had she done?

Three more couples were called.

Linda turned to the next page, hesitated, then looked out into the crowd. In that second, Marnie knew.

"William Ramsey and Marnie Boudine."

"All right. Will's got a woman."

Mark pounded Will on the back while Mark's wife, Kathy, offered a quick hug of congratulations.

"Are you excited?" she asked, an odd expression in her brown eyes.

Excited? Try stunned. Thrilled. Horrified. He'd been given a chance and there wasn't a doubt in his mind that he was going to screw it up.

"Yeah," he managed, speaking carefully so he wouldn't choke on his words. "It's great." He paused. "Marnie Boudine. Why does that name sound familiar?"

Mark and Kathy exchanged a glance. "Gee, I don't know," she said, but it was obvious she was lying.

A knot formed in Will's stomach. Was she really boring and not very bright? Ugly? How could he explain to these people that he wasn't interested in looks so much as personality and brains?

"I don't mind if she's not real pretty," he said.

Kathy gave him a sympathetic smile. "Honey, that's not going to be a problem."

Rio reached over and took Chris's hand. They were in the middle of a gathering crowd, listening to Councilwoman McGuire read the names of the couples. Chris tried not to notice the familiar feel of her ex-husband's fingers lacing with hers, or the unexpected urge to lean her head against his broad shoulder.

It was the circumstances, she told herself. The fact that it was just the two of them, away from the house. They'd left the kids with a sitter, rather than explain what they were doing.

Rio grinned at her. "I have a good feeling about this."

"I hope you're right."

Chris felt unsettled by the whole situation. It was almost as if she and Rio were being given a second chance, which was crazy. She didn't want a second chance. She glanced at her ex and realized that what she wanted didn't matter. Rio had been a lousy husband, but he was a great father and he adored their kids. She owed Justin, Debbie, and Molly.

"I mean it, Rio. If we're picked I want the kids to stay with my mom. Getting back together for a month would be too confusing for them. We'll visit when we can, but I don't want them knowing we're living together."

He looked like he was going to argue, then he nodded. "It'll be worth it," he told her.

"Now we'll move onto the second group," Ms. McGuire was saying. She took another folder and opened it. "I'm most interested in this group," she said, smiling out at the crowd. "Let's see who's compatible."

She read off a half-dozen names, then said, "Christine Harbaugh and Rio Harbaugh." Ms. McGuire paused. "Uh-oh. This could be interesting."

Rio turned to Chris and pulled her into his arms. "This is it, babe. That million dollars is practically in our pockets."

She let him spin her around the crowd. She laughed and tried not to notice how good it felt to be close to him. She was a complete idiot. She didn't for one minute think they were going to win the money, so why was she doing this?

There was no time for introspection. They walked to the tables beside the stage and were given fistfuls of paperwork to read and fill out.

"You know we're going to have to tell them the truth," she reminded Rio as they wrote and signed their names. "That we were married before. They're going to know something is up from the last names."

"I know, I know."

They'd already fought about coming clean, but she'd managed to convince him it was the right thing to do. The rules hadn't said anything about divorced couples entering.

Chris noticed several people talking around the tables. Other couples who had just met weren't so quick to begin the process of filling out the paperwork. She knew that she would have been a tad reluctant if Rio was a stranger.

"What if they throw us out?" Rio complained when they'd finished signing everything and were escorted across the street to an office in the rear of the Baptist church. There they waited to speak with the two psychologists.

"They're going to be challenged," Chris said. "Think of how much they're going to want to get us back together. Just be willing to work with them and everything will be fine."

Thirty minutes later they were shown into a small office. Two people sat behind adjoining desks. The man was in his mid-thirties, with dark hair and eyes, and a smile that instantly put her at ease. The woman, Taylor McGuire, Chris recognized from the news reports.

Taylor's elegant, Southern, blond beauty made Chris feel frumpy by comparison. Because of the heat, Chris wore shorts and a T-shirt. Taylor's light gray suit looked as if she'd stepped into it moments before. She was open, friendly and it was hard not to like her, although Chris thought she might give it a try.

Taylor glanced at their paperwork. "Chris Harbaugh and Rio . . ." Her voice trailed off.

Rio shifted in his seat, but Chris leaned forward, intending to take charge. "Can you believe it? We divorced a year ago," she said with a little laugh. "I knew we'd both entered, but wow, look what happened."

Taylor picked up on her cues, as Chris had thought she might.

"I can't even imagine what you two feel," the female psychologist said, placing her well-manicured hands on the desk. "Is this going to be too uncomfortable?"

Chris glanced at her ex. "I think we can manage to keep from killing each other." She returned her attention to Taylor. "I'm not looking forward to having the same old arguments again, though."

Dr. Kirby leaned toward them. "Interesting that Dr. McGuire's questionnaire matched a divorced couple. You two must have had more in common than you realized."

"I guess." Chris didn't sound convinced because she knew it wasn't true.

Taylor smiled. "We're supposed to have weekly sessions with the couples. I think you and Rio might benefit from a little more than just a check-in. What if we scheduled an actual counseling hour? We could discuss some of the problems you had before in your marriage and see if we can get them solved."

Chris glanced at Rio. "I don't know. You never wanted to talk to anyone about what was wrong."

She saw the corner of his mouth twitch. He was enjoying their game. "Gee, honey, I always thought you were the problem, but I guess if these two nice people want to share their expertise, I can listen."

"Good." Taylor scribbled into an appointment book. "What about next Tuesday. What time is good for you both?"

Chapter 8

Jonathan stared after the departing couple, then turned his attention to Taylor.

"I can see I'm going to have to call my editor and tell him that my book is going to be late. I'd thought I might be able to work on it while I'm here, but you're going to make sure that every second is taken up with pro bono counseling."

"You can afford it," she said sweetly. "What with your millions."

He grinned. "Agreed, but some compensation seems only fair."

Humor filled her gray-blue eyes. "Whatever you're thinking—stop!"

Teasing her made him feel good. He tried to remember the last time he'd done something for pleasure and not because it would help his career.

He leaned close so that he could speak directly in her ear. "Perhaps some kind of exchange of services? I'll give you what you want and you'll do the same."

He was close enough to hear her soft intake of air and watch the color spread across her cheek.

"Stop doing that," she said, but the words were more of an invitation than an order.

"Doing what?" he asked innocently even as he rested his hand on hers. He curled his fingers around her wrist and felt the fluttering beat of her heart.

"Why are you so fired up to have sex with me?"

"For the same reason you can't stop thinking about being in *my* bed. We were spectacular together. We could be again."

She stiffened and pulled her hand away. "We are professionals and competitors. Need I remind you that I'm determined to win this contest? I will *not* be seduced into forgetting my purpose."

He adored her when she sounded righteous. "Tell you what, Taylor. We won't let the sex interfere with the contest. May the best theory win and all that."

She tried to hide her grin. "I don't think so."

"I guess you're right. If you win, the best theory has lost."

"I can't believe this," she told him. "You are nothing more than a sexual predator."

"I'm flattered."

"Don't be. I don't mean it in a nice way."

"Sure you do."

She sighed. "Will you please be serious?"

She angled her chair away from him and concentrated on shuffling the papers in front of her. "Chris and Rio have three kids. They used to be a family. Isn't that worth saving?"

It took him a second to change gears. "I don't doubt

the worthiness of the cause, just the practicality of dealing with all these people." He turned and caught her looking at him. He winked. "All right. I'll concede. We can give Chris and Rio as much therapy as they can stand. How's that?"

"Don't do this for me. Do it for the betterment of humanity."

"That's a bit of a stretch."

She cleared her throat. "Yes, well, they didn't take very long to make up their minds," she said, counting the stack of cards they'd received from the contestants who had already been to see them. "Barely half the people have signed the necessary paperwork so far."

He raised his eyebrows. "You sound surprised. How easy would it be for you to meet a perfect stranger and agree to live together for a month?"

She gave him a smile. "If he was perfect, I might not have any trouble at all."

"Thank you for clarifying that."

He relaxed in his chair. They were using a room in the Baptist church because it was close to the staging area for the contest. Jonathan tried to remember the last time he'd been in church . . . or believed in God.

"Do you really think we can help them?" he asked, tapping the file of the couple who had just left.

"I don't know. We'll need to talk to them, see what the problems were. Most married couples seem to fall into bad communication patterns. The woman—Chris—made the comment about not wanting to have the same arguments over and over again. I think we could help them break that cycle. If there was a bigger problem such as an addiction or abuse then I would be less optimistic."

He watched her as she spoke, seeing the light of conviction in her blue-gray eyes. She uttered each word with an intensity that made him feel old.

"What?" she asked. "Why are you looking at me like that?"

"Because you believe everything you're saying."

"Of course I do. There are certain skills and insights a therapist brings to the table that often make the difference."

"In the end, it's the couple who makes the decision to change or not. Most of them don't bother. It's too much work and they'd rather be right than be together."

Taylor touched his arm. "You can't believe that. It's so sad."

He liked the light brush of her fingers. He would like her to keep touching him. Unfortunately his wayward thoughts were already creating trouble and they were about to be interrupted. So there was no point in getting worked up . . . not yet. Maybe the next time they were alone.

"It's not sad, it's realistic. How many couples have you seriously helped?"

"Dozens," she said, her eyes wide with concern. "Between your seminars and your books, I would say you've helped thousands. You must get letters and have people tell you what a difference you've made in their lives."

He shrugged. "There are people who can't be helped," he said. "Couples who should make it and be completely happy together. Yet their relationships fall apart. Why?"

"I don't have all the answers. No one does. But we have to try."

"You're still idealistic."

"When did you get so cynical?"

"I'm a realist."

"Not in my world."

He believed that. She lived in a town called Marriageville where people probably didn't lock their doors at night. She had a private practice and her idea of the big deal was an article in a psychology journal. He lived in New York, gave seminars to thousands and was willing to do just about anything to end up on top.

They had nothing in common but great sexual tension. Apparently twenty-*one* couples were going to be testing his theory.

Will found himself standing alone in front of the stage. It was his worst nightmare coming to life. He'd been stood up in front of an entire crowd.

A middle-aged woman holding a clipboard approached. "What's your name?"

"Will Ramsey."

She scanned a list. "That's right. You're here. Where's Marnie?"

"She's *not* here," he said glumly.

"Maybe having second thoughts," the woman said brightly. "It happens under the best of circumstances. My Celia ran out on her own wedding. I told her if she ever did it again, I would break both her legs." The woman smiled cheerfully. "I'm sure Marnie will show up. When she does, come find me and we'll get started on the paperwork."

He nodded, knowing there wasn't any hope. Probably she'd seen him walking toward the stage and had been so disgusted that she'd—

"Will?"

He turned slowly toward the voice. Hope flared, then crashed and burned when his gaze settled on the tall, busty, gorgeous woman standing next to him.

It was the bombshell from the coffee shop. The walking, breathing, sexpot who made every man in a fifty-mile radius salivate and indulge in marginally illegal sexual fantasies.

He opened his mouth, then closed it. No. This wasn't really happening. She couldn't possibly be—

"I'm Marnie," she said, holding out her hand to him.

He blinked. Her thick hair tumbled around her shoulders. A white blouse, which should have been conservative, even boring, clung to breasts large enough to have their own zip code. She had a tiny waist, curvy hips and great legs, all outlined by black jeans and red cowboy boots.

"We're in real trouble if we can't even shake hands," she said.

"What? Oh."

He took the hand she offered, noticing that she had tiny decals in the shape of Texas on her nails. He forced himself to look at her face. If only she were ugly, he might be able to forget the showgirl body. But she wasn't. Wide green cat eyes gazed at him. Her features were perfectly even. He remembered reading an interesting study about symmetrical features and how most humans found them appealing. She had high cheekbones, a full mouth, and truly amazing breasts.

He dropped her hand when he realized he was staring at her chest. Worse, he was painfully aroused and if she happened to glance down she would see that he was as sophisticated as a sixteen-year-old.

"I'm real happy we were matched together," she said, in her soft voice. He couldn't place the accent. Oklahoma, maybe?

"Why?" he asked. "I mean, I'm not your type."

She was tall but he was taller. She had to tilt her head slightly to gaze into his eyes. A slow smile tugged at her lips. "Don't believe everything you hear about me. I know I look like a bimbo, but I'm actually pretty smart and I enjoy the company of intelligent men."

He didn't feel very intelligent right now. Instead he felt as if he were on the verge of babbling. "Ah, yeah, I, ah, work at Tectronics." As soon as the words were out he wanted to groan. Could he have sounded more geeky?

"I own Marnie's Palace of Beauty." She waved her hands in front of her. "I do nails. It's not that interesting, but it gets me out of the house."

Several pieces of information clicked into place. She'd been married to that old guy. He'd died, leaving her a fortune. He could only imagine what she'd been doing when she'd met her late husband.

Marnie cleared her throat. "So, is this something you want to do?"

"What?"

"The contest. Did you want to enter it with me?"

He thought about his fantasies for a nice quiet librarian or a scientist. Someone he could talk to. Someone he would have something in common with. Someone not Marnie.

But there wasn't anyone else, and he couldn't imagine telling the people running the contest that he wanted to be matched with a more suitable woman. They would think he was crazy.

"I, ah, guess it would be fine."

She smiled. A bright, happy smile that made his erection pulse painfully and his mouth go dry.

"Great. So where do you want to live? My house is plenty big, but if you wouldn't be comfortable there, I wouldn't mind your place."

They were going to have to live together. He clenched his hands into fists and vowed that he would make Mark pay for this, one way or the other.

"I have a one-bedroom apartment," he muttered. "Your place would probably be better."

"Okay." She touched his arm. "Ready to sign our lives away?"

If she touched him again, he was going to explode. He couldn't believe the heat that jumped between them or the way his hands started to shake. This was going to be a disaster, he realized. He wasn't just bad at relationships, he was toxic. And the thought of Marnie Boudine laughing at him was more than he could stand.

"Marnie? What on earth?"

Marnie shrugged at Taylor and held out the paperwork. "I thought I'd told you I'd entered the contest," she said with a calmness belying the thundering of her heart. She didn't remember ever being this nervous before.

She was half afraid that Will was either going to pass out or bolt. He'd had a terrified look in his eyes ever since she'd introduced herself. She'd known she was going to be too much for him, but there wasn't any way for her to change that.

Taylor continued to study her, then she turned her attention to Will. At once recognition and understanding crossed her face. She glanced at the man sitting next to her.

"Jonathan, this is Marnie Boudine, a close friend of mine. And the gentleman with her is . . ." she glanced at the papers Marnie had given her ". . . William Ramsey."

"Will," he corrected.

Jonathan gave Marnie a wink. "So you know all of Taylor's deep dark secrets. I'm going to have to pump you for information later."

Taylor laughed. "Not in my lifetime. Ignore him," she said, speaking to Will who sat stiffly in his chair. "Hi. I'm Taylor McGuire and the comedian over here is Jonathan Kirby."

"Nice to meet you," Will said awkwardly.

Taylor looked at Marnie. "Okay, here's what we've been saying to everyone. You do realize what you're getting into, don't you? You've agreed to live together for one month. There will be weekly follow-up visits with Jonathan and myself. At the end of that time, we'll discuss whether or not you considered the relationship a success."

Marnie doubted Will would ever think the relationship was a success. The poor man looked as if he were about to be executed. She wished there was a way to tell him that it wasn't going to be that bad. She'd just been looking for a way for them to get to know each other. As much as she wanted him to get past her body to learn about her personality, she wanted to do the same with him. She adored that he was smart and a bit of a nerd, but she didn't know that much about him. She hoped he was sweet-natured and funny, but he could be a real jerk for all she knew.

"What if we can't stand each other?" Marnie asked, more for Will than herself.

"No one is going to force you to stay together," Taylor said. "You can end things whenever you'd like. Of course, that means you're not eligible for the drawing."

Marnie thought about pointing out that she didn't need the money, but she held back. A million dollars would certainly matter to Will.

Jonathan glanced from one to the other. "Any questions?"

Will shook his head.

"Have you talked about your living arrangements?" Jonathan asked.

Will cleared his throat. "I'm, ah, going to be moving in with Marnie. For the month. In her house."

Taylor smiled sympathetically. "You'll be fine, Will. I've known Marnie for years and she's very easy to get along with."

He cast Marnie a quick glance that didn't seem to rise above her breasts. She sighed softly. God was already punishing her.

"Did you know your mother has invited me to Sunday supper?" Jonathan asked.

"No." Taylor stared at him. "I wonder if she's planning to poison you."

"My thoughts exactly." He actually looked worried. "Does she keep rat poison around?"

Taylor laughed. "Jonathan, I was kidding. She doesn't hate you." She hesitated. "At least not that much. It's been a long time."

While Taylor was surprised by the invitation, she thought she understood it. No doubt her mother wanted to get to know the man who had fathered her grandchild, and start forming tentative familial bonds in case he found out about Linnie.

Taylor nibbled on the inside of her mouth. Actually there wasn't any "in case." She'd decided to tell Jonathan the truth as soon as she figured out what to say.

She'd always told Linnie that she would tell her about her father when Linnie turned eighteen. Then it would be her decision to find him or not. But this contest had ruined all her carefully constructed plans.

"You'll adore my mother," Taylor reassured him. "She's a lovely hostess. Very gracious and a fabulous cook. Come hungry."

"We'll all be eating the same food, right? There won't be any *special* dishes just for me?"

"Not a one. I'll be your official taster if you'd like."

"Why? I would have thought you'd want me dead. I'm the competition."

She collected the papers on the table and placed them in her briefcase. "No way, mister. I'm not winning by default. I intend to take first prize because I've earned it, not because you're dead."

Chapter
9

$\mathcal{G}$race Anderson dusted her front room for the fourth time that morning. She was so nervous, she thought she might have a heart attack. The flutterings in her chest made it difficult to move her dustrag across the already polished surface of her coffee table.

"I'm giddy," she confessed, pausing to pat Alexander. "That saying is true—'There's no fool like an old fool.'"

She finished dusting and walked into the kitchen to tuck the rag into the bucket under the sink. Once she'd washed her hands, she checked the plate of homemade cookies. There was also brewed coffee, heated water for tea, regular cookies, sugar-free brownies (in case Mr. Reed had a blood-sugar problem), and cream and sugar in the crystal containers. Now if only her heart would stop pounding so.

Of course it was difficult not to be nervous when she'd invited a stranger into her home. She and Mr. Reed had met the previous afternoon in Marriageville Square. He'd seemed nice enough. Actually, she'd been pleasantly surprised to find out that the mysterious computer had seen fit to match her with anyone. Alan had always told her that she was lucky he put up with her—that no one else would ever want her.

"No," she said firmly. "I will not ruin this pleasant afternoon with thoughts of him."

A knock on the front door made her jump. Her heart rate increased even more, making it difficult for her to catch her breath. She walked quickly into the living room and saw Mr. Reed standing on her porch. With a last silent prayer, she opened the door.

"Hello, Grace," Nelson Reed said with a smile.

Grace found herself smiling back as she motioned for him to come into her house.

"Hello, ah, Nelson." Her lips felt awkward speaking his Christian name. After all, she'd been thinking of him as "Mr. Reed" ever since they'd met the previous day.

He stepped into the living room and glanced around. Grace followed his gaze, taking in the comfortable but worn sofa, the shelves of her beloved books, Alexander sprawled out on a cushion in a patch of sunshine.

What did he see? That she'd worked hard to make a pleasant home? Or did he see the shabby furnishings and air of loneliness that lingered in the room?

"You have a lovely home," he said, then took the seat she offered.

"I have coffee and tea ready," she said quickly, desperate to do something. "Cookies, sugar-free brownies. Whatever you'd like."

He smiled at her again, a gentle smile that made his eyes twinkle. "What I would like is a chance to talk with you for a bit. We've gotten ourselves into an awkward situation. Why don't we discuss things until we're both more comfortable."

Grace nodded, then settled onto the sofa, sitting next to Alexander and patting him as an excuse not to look at Nelson. Yet despite her resolve, she kept glancing at the man across from her out of the corner of her eye. He was handsome. Tall and lean, with white hair and kindly blue eyes. He reminded her a little of Charlton Heston, whom she'd always admired. *The Naked Jungle* had been one of her favorite movies.

He sat comfortably, his large hands resting on his thighs. Silence stretched between them for nearly a minute. Finally Nelson smiled. "I can go first, if you'd like."

Grace nodded. She didn't know what was expected of her. She didn't want to put a foot wrong, or make him angry.

"I was born here in Marriageville, went to seminary back east and settled with a ministry in Ohio. I lived there forty years before retiring. When I retired, I came home, to Marriageville."

She remembered now that yesterday Nelson had said he'd been a pastor. While she prayed several times a day, she'd never been a churchgoer. Alan hadn't allowed it.

"You're a widower?" she asked at last, when it became apparent he expected a reply.

"Yes. My wife passed away nearly five years ago. I've been lonely and asking God to send me a little companionship. One day I saw an article about the contest in the newspaper. I realized the good Lord couldn't have made His point more clear without tattooing it on my forehead."

Despite her nervousness, Grace smiled. Nelson didn't seem to be a frightening man at all.

"Do you have children?" she asked.

His good humor faded slightly at her question, but he spoke before she could call it back.

"Two sons. They're both missionaries in the Far East." He paused. "I'm proud, of course. But I miss them. Sometimes I think I did too good a job with them. They're both dedicated to their service. I'd like them to come home more but they have too much work. When I tell them I get lonely, they tell me to talk to God."

Nelson looked at her. The sadness faded from his eyes as he winked. "The good Lord is a tad less chatty than some might think."

Grace found herself relaxing as she laughed. Alexander stood, stretched, then curled back up, this time on her lap.

"That's a fine-looking cat," Nelson said. "Have you had him long?"

"Four years."

She'd always wanted a cat, but Alan hadn't let her have pets. She'd been alone for nearly two years before she worked up the courage to adopt the small kitten that would grow up to be her most constant companion.

"And your husband?" Nelson asked.

Grace pressed her lips together. "I'm a widow. Alan died nearly seven years ago."

Understanding softened Nelson's expression. "I'm sorry to hear that."

His practiced graciousness made her realize she hadn't made the same kind of polite comment when he'd mentioned the death of his wife. She flushed at her own rudeness.

"Yes, well, I'm sorry for your loss, too. I mean, I should have said something before. I'm sorry."

She hated the tremor in her voice. Worse, she hated the shaking in her body. Fear filled her. Fear that had been gone for so long that she'd nearly forgotten how it felt to be so very cold inside.

"I am sorry," she repeated. Why had she done this? Why had she allowed a man into her home? Being lonely was a small price to pay for being safe.

Nelson studied her for a long time and when he spoke, his voice was soft and persuasive.

"You have no need to apologize, although I thank you for your sympathy. I can see that you're a compassionate woman. If you don't mind, I'd very much like to hear about Alan. What did he do?"

"He worked for the county, running a road crew."

"How did he die?"

Shame filled her. Shame and regret that she'd stayed in her marriage so long.

"He'd visited a local sports bar. It was spring, raining. They think he had a heart attack on the way to his truck. He fell by the side of the road and drowned in the gutter."

She knew it was wrong, but the horrible way Alan had died had restored her faith in God. Perhaps it had been chance and not retribution at all, but she liked to think an angel somewhere had set her free.

"You have no children?"

His softly voiced question caught her unaware. She should have expected it—she'd asked him the same thing. And yet the pain sliced through her, nearly suffocating her with its intensity.

"No," she whispered. "No children."

She'd been pregnant so many times. Each child had arrived too early—only little Becky had survived more than a day, but even she hadn't made it past a week.

Nelson didn't say anything for a long time.

"I see sadness in your eyes," he told her. "My words are too small and empty to be much comfort."

She stared at him. His compassion was a tangible presence in the room. "Thank you."

He studied her. "Grace, do I frighten you?"

She swallowed. Against her will, she whispered the truth. "Yes."

"Why did you enter the contest?"

She pressed her lips together, tears so very near the surface. "I'm so tired of being alone."

"It was an act of great courage." He smiled. "Grace Anderson, you have my word of honor that I've done my best to be a good man. I've never raised a hand to a woman in my life. I'll admit to spanking the boys a time or two when they were growing up, but there's a difference between a spanking and a beating."

"I know."

"I'll never hurt you, either, or do anything to frighten you, but as my sons would say, you don't know me from a rock. So if you're not comfortable taking my word on that, I'll walk out of this house and you'll never have to see me again."

He was right—she had no reason to believe him. And yet she did. Deep in her heart she sensed that he would never hurt her. But the years with Alan were not easily forgotten.

"I'll try not to be afraid," she said.

"I appreciate that. Now, while we're baring our

souls, I should probably confess that I have my share of faults. I'm not always as attentive as I should be. My late wife used to complain about that all the time. I read four newspapers a day and I hate it when someone reads them before me. I have an even temper, but I'm occasionally impatient." He grinned. "There are other flaws, but that should be enough for us to make a start. That is, if you still want me here."

Did she? Grace considered the matter. While she was afraid, she was also lonely.

"I'd like to try," she said.

"Good. I've always been in favor of a best effort. That's what we'll do. And if I act in a way that bothers you, just wave a heavy fry pan in my direction and I'll get the message."

She nodded, suddenly feeling awkward. Nelson rescued her.

"How about that coffee now?" he asked. "Then you can show me to my room."

"I made the quilt myself," she blurted before she could stop herself.

He rewarded her with a smile. "I'll bet it's beautiful. I want you to tell me all about it. And show me everything else you've made around here. I've always admired women who know how to make a house a home."

Silly words, she told herself as she rose and walked into the kitchen. Meaningless phrases designed to put her at her ease. And darn the man—they worked.

Marnie paced the length of the black-and-white tiled foyer, keeping watch for Will's arrival. She felt nervous—so nervous that she'd been unable to eat breakfast. For someone who carried cookies and chocolate in her purse just to make sure she never was hungry, this was a huge deal.

"George, am I crazy?" she asked aloud, turning at the base of the stairs and walking back toward the front door. "I nearly couldn't go through with it yesterday. I almost left when they called out our names."

She paused, wishing that she could have just ten minutes with her late husband. She would give up every penny of his estate and whatever else was necessary, just to see George one more time—to hear the sound of his voice and feel his arms wrapping around her. Instead, she was simply alone.

Marnie crossed her arms over her chest. As she waited for Will's arrival, she raised her head slightly and glanced at the imported French chandelier hanging from the second-story ceiling. The foyer was bigger than most houses in Marriageville, certainly three or four times the size of the double-wide she'd lived in as a child. There were eight bedrooms, a formal living room, a parlor, family room, great room, media room, small and large dining room. The six-car garage had once held George's toys, as he'd called the sports cars he collected but never drove. Instead his day-to-day transportation had been a truck.

Most of the vast art collection was on loan to various museums, as was some of the antique furniture. A decorator came through once a year and redid sections of the house. The kitchen had the capacity to prepare meals for thirty.

She'd thought about selling the place. She didn't need the space. George hadn't needed it either, but he'd grown up in a sharecropper's shack and he'd been determined to live like a king once he'd made his fortune. Now, with him gone, Marnie felt lost in the house. But she couldn't seem to make herself part with it. Not as long as she could slip into George's study and still feel close to him.

"About Will," she said, but before she could finish her thought, she heard a faint sound.

She crossed to the window by the double door. A silver Ford pickup drove slowly along the half-mile drive from the main road. Her heart line-danced across her chest and her mouth went dry. Wishing she could be comfortable in difficult situations, she smoothed her hands against the legs of her jeans. She'd dressed casually—jeans, T-shirt and Nikes. She'd pulled her hair back in a simple ponytail and had put on very little makeup. Even her nails were plain, tinted with barely-there pink.

She waited until Will pulled up in front of the house before stepping out onto the wide porch. She forced a smile when all she wanted to do was bolt.

He turned off the engine and slowly opened the door. She started to shove her hands into her back pockets, then thought better of the idea. The last thing she needed was to thrust her chest forward.

As he climbed out of the truck, she had a chance to study him. He was tall and rangy, with a lean runner's body. The morning sunlight caught the edge of his gold-rimmed glasses and made his brown hair gleam. He looked more nervous than she felt, which was pretty bad. *Could this be more awkward?* she wondered, then wished she hadn't tempted fate by asking the question.

"Hi," she said with a brief wave in his general direction. "You found the place okay?"

"Yes. Your directions were very precise. Although it's

seven-tenths of a mile from the road to the house, not half a mile."

His comment made her smile and eased some of her tension. "Gee, thanks for putting a finer point on it."

She shoved her hands into her front pockets and rounded her shoulders. Will seemed to be avoiding looking at her directly. Instead he darted glances at her out of the corner of his eye.

He finally closed the driver's door and turned his attention to the house. Apparently he hadn't really noticed it before because his expression shifted to stunned.

"This place is huge."

"I know." She sighed. "My late husband wanted a mansion so that's what he built. There are tons of rooms I never use."

She turned toward the three-story structure. The wood-trimmed, brick house rose toward the Texas sky. Part plantation manor, part traditional colonial, it should have looked uncomfortable, but instead it sprawled gracefully in the middle of George's private paradise. Sunlight glittered on sparkling windows. The garden was lush and blooming, the porch wide and welcoming.

Will pushed up his glasses. "You don't have children?"

"No."

Marnie forced a lightness she didn't feel. She'd wanted children, but George had felt he was too old to be a father. He'd known he wouldn't live to see them graduate high school. So he'd had himself fixed. He'd been mighty proud to be getting a vasectomy at the ripe old age of sixty. Marnie had been heartbroken.

She headed toward the front door, waving at Will to

follow her. "There's a day staff, but no one spends the night. I know you work long hours at your job, so I'll make sure there's plenty of food in the fridge. Just help yourself to whatever you want."

She didn't want to be talking about the cleaning service or what they were going to eat. She wanted to ask if he was as scared as she was, and did he regret that they were going to spend the next month together. She wanted to know about his past. Why wasn't he married and who had been his first love? She wanted them to be friends.

Marnie showed him the kitchen, living room and parlor, then they headed upstairs. The landing opened into the great room. Will grinned at the large pool table, the wide-screen television and sophisticated electronics sitting on shelves. Excitement chased away some of his trepidation.

"Great setup," he said.

"I know how to turn on the television and tape a show," she said with a laugh. "The rest of it is way too complicated for me."

He bent down and examined several dials on a piece of equipment she'd never figured out. Like her he wore jeans, but instead of a T-shirt, he'd tucked a short-sleeved polo shirt into his waistband. He looked strong, in a wiry kind of way, and she shivered as she wondered what it would be like to be held by him.

Vague guilt accompanied the speculation. After all, she'd never been with anyone but George. Did she have the right to want another man?

"You can use this," she said, waving at the system. "I don't bother very much. I have a TV in my room. If I want to catch the news or check out what's new on

QVC, I use that one." She paused. "Would you like to see your room?"

"Ah, sure."

He followed her down the hall, past her room. The door was closed and she didn't mention it was hers. She wasn't sure she wanted him to know.

She'd put him into a suite at the end of the hall; this guest room had the best view. She'd converted the living room of the suite into an office, providing him with a computer desk, modem, extra phone line, a fax machine and several bright floor lamps.

He poked his head into the adjoining bedroom and nodded. "It's very nice."

"I'm glad you like it."

Then they both stood there like lumps. Marnie sighed. Things had been a whole lot easier with George. He'd taken charge until she was comfortable participating. Looks like that was going to have to be her role here.

"I thought we'd have dinner or something," she said. "So we could get to know each other."

He nodded.

"Okay," she said, backing out of the room. "Around seven?"

He nodded again. She gave a vague smile, then turned on her heel and practically ran to her room. *Disaster,* she thought, stepping into the sanctuary of her bedroom. *This was just plain going to be a disaster.*

Chapter 10

"So you're the man who stole my little girl," Linda McGuire said as she opened her front door Sunday night.

This time Jonathan wasn't thrown by her attitude. Prepared to smooth troubled waters, he handed over the spray of flowers he'd brought with him and gave her his best smile.

"You have every right to be furious with me," he said sincerely. "What I did was irresponsible and wrong. My only excuses are youth and the fact that your daughter was irresistible."

Linda and Taylor had the same color eyes and were of similar height. An expression of "tell me another one" crossed Linda's face, but instead of tormenting him, she merely smiled and held open the door.

"You can come in. You weren't my favorite person when my daughter came home with her heart broken, but I guess it's too late to punish you now." She sniffed the flowers.

Jonathan stepped into the large house. "You have a

lovely home," he said, moving toward the formally furnished room with tufted sofas and Queen Anne tables. He knew all about Queen Anne furniture—his ex-wife had tortured him endlessly by discussing, buying, and rearranging it the entire time they were married.

Linda followed him as he walked to the fireplace and studied a picture showing a much younger Linda, a grinning toddler and a man who had died many years before. There was so much love in the adults' eyes. Affection for each other, and the happy child they held between them. He turned back to his hostess.

"I'm sorry," he said sincerely, not sure if he was talking about what he'd done to Taylor or the loss of her husband nearly thirty years before.

"I suspect you just might be." Linda sighed heavily. "I guess I'll go put the flowers in water and tell my daughter that I've decided to let you live through dinner."

"Jonathan will be pleased to know that," Taylor said as she entered the room. She paused to touch one of the roses, then turned her attention to him. "Was she threatening you?"

"Not at all. Your mother possesses that graciousness Southern women are famous for. I feel like an honored guest."

Linda glanced at her daughter. "I see what you mean. He's charming, and not too flashy. Maybe *I'll* run off with him this time."

Jonathan laughed. "I'd be thrilled."

"No, you'd be terrified."

Taylor stepped back to allow her mother to leave, then headed for the sofa where she sank onto the seat and motioned for him to do the same. She wore a sleeveless, blue tunic top over matching slacks. Strappy gold sandals covered her feet, exposing her bare toes. Her hairstyle was different. Soft curls tumbled to her shoulders. She looked tousled and sexy—a combination designed to tempt any breathing man.

"The flowers were nice," she said as he settled across from her. "But don't be surprised if that's not enough to win her over."

"You don't have to tell me. I've already figured out that neither McGuire woman is easy."

"Oh, but we're so worth the effort."

"Agreed."

Linda returned to the living room. She set down a tray on the table in front of him. There was a bottle of wine and three glasses. "I'd appreciate it if you'd do the honors."

"My pleasure," he murmured, determined to win her to his side. If only he could find something they had in common—something other than Taylor.

"I'm enjoying learning about the history of the region," he said as he unwrapped the foil around the bottle of Chardonnay. "Taylor's been filling me in on all the particulars."

"I'm sure it's a change from the big city."

"Yes, but a nice one."

Linda sat in the chair next to his. "Tell me, Jonathan, what do you get out of the contest?"

"A chance to test my theories in a real-world situation." He poured a glass of wine and handed it to her. She murmured a thank you that was barely audible.

"Yes, I know all that. But what do you *really* get out of it. So what is it? Another book contract?"

Jonathan knew where Taylor had inherited her tenacity.

"A talk show. I've spoken with some people in syndication and they're interested in having me host a show."

Her eyes, so much like Taylor's, narrowed. "And if you win?"

"I follow Oprah on the schedule."

Linda took a sip of her wine. "This does make for an interesting horse race."

He turned his attention to Taylor who was watching, obviously fascinated. "What are your offers up to with the book?" he asked.

"I'd rather not say."

"I have a lot of experience in publishing, Taylor. My knowing what's going on isn't going to affect the deal. I'm happy to offer advice."

She hesitated. He could read her indecision. When she glanced at her mother, he half expected to see Linda shake her head. Instead the older Ms. McGuire shrugged.

"He's sold dozens of books, dear," Linda said. "It might do you good to speak with him."

He couldn't help gaping in surprise.

Linda sipped her wine, then gazed at him over the glass. "I might not approve of you running off with my daughter all those years ago, Jonathan, and I might think I've earned a pound or two of flesh from you, but I'm not a fool. You have information Taylor needs. As you said yourself, you knowing the details of the deal isn't going to change anything and it might help her."

"I'm impressed," he said easily.

Linda smiled. "I hear that all the time."

He returned his attention to Taylor. "Want to talk about it?"

"Maybe." She drew in a deep breath. "Alexi, my agent, called yesterday. The last offer was for two hundred thousand dollars." She shook her head. "I can't even believe I'm saying that out loud. It's so much money."

"Hold out for more," he told her.

"That's what Alexi said."

"Then listen to him. The contest is just beginning. Over the next few weeks there's going to be a media frenzy. That will only help your position."

"Thanks for the advice."

Linda raised her eyebrows. "Jonathan, you're going to make it very difficult for me to continue disliking you."

"Is that what you want?"

"I suppose it had been my plan, but I'll have to re-think it." She cupped her glass in her hand. "I remember hearing at the first news conference that you weren't married. Any children?"

"No. My ex-wife and I weren't together that long."

"How long does it take?"

He grinned. "Good point. Okay, we waited and then the marriage ended."

"I'm sorry to hear that. Children can be a blessing."

He didn't know what to say. He'd never thought about having kids. His lifestyle—with work always being number one—didn't leave much room for a personal life, let alone children.

"If things had been different, I suppose I would have liked a couple of kids," he said when it was obvious Linda was waiting for more.

Linda exchanged a glance with her daughter. "I'll

leave you two to chat while I get dinner on the table." She rose and left the room.

Taylor set her wine on the coffee table. "Still hungry?"

"She wasn't so bad."

"I appreciate the advice about the book contract."

"I mean it, Taylor. Hold out for more."

"I will."

"Good." He stared at her. "So you want a big money book contract and I want a talk show. It seems that more than just our professional ideas are on the line."

"A battle to the death?" she teased.

"Nothing so dramatic."

He glanced around the high-ceilinged living room and found, despite the Queen Anne furniture and the fact that Linda McGuire had once wanted him dead, he felt pretty much at home here. What on earth was wrong with this picture?

Two hours later Taylor crossed her legs and inhaled the sweet evening air.

"I feel like I'm an extra in a movie," Jonathan said from his place next to her on the old-fashioned porch swing. "The real world isn't like this."

"Big porches and hot summer nights also exist in Texas," she said. "Haven't you figured out we have the best of everything here?"

He patted his stomach. "Certainly the best pecan pie. Did your mom really bake that? I couldn't taste the rat poison at all."

"I'm ignoring that last remark. Yes, she made the pie and we fried the chicken ourselves. Welcome to a world where not everything comes wrapped in plastic."

"I'm too full to listen to you lecture me." He pushed a foot against the worn floorboards and set the swing in motion. "Tell me how Marriageville got its name."

Taylor paused to collect her thoughts, all the while trying not to notice the man sitting next to her. Maybe it was the sugar coursing through her veins or the heat of the evening. Either way she found herself hungry for something other than food.

"My great-great-uncle Andrew founded the town. It was originally called Henderson, for reasons no one can figure out. He was a preacher and marrying people was his passion. He thought it was far more interesting than preaching or baptizing. So he performed as many weddings as he could. From what I can gather, the ceremonies were fairly spectacular and people began traveling from all over to be married by him. The weddings were good for business. Eventually the townspeople voted to change the name and around you, you see the final result."

"Was Uncle Andrew the first mayor?"

"Of course. I come from a long line of public servants. Eventually I'll be called to serve in some capacity. It's required of the McGuire family."

She wondered if her daughter would stay in town and make a life here after college. If she did, Linnie would find herself running for city council or taking her turn at being mayor. But young people liked to explore the world. There was a time when she, Taylor, had thought she wanted to live just about anywhere else. Yet here she was—making her life in Marriageville.

"My grandfather was involved in both city and state

government," she said, gazing up at the clear starlit sky. "He was—"

Jonathan turned to her in mid-sentence. He leaned toward her, wrapped his arms around her and kissed her before she'd even taken a breath.

As his mouth settled on hers, she reminded herself that she'd sworn she wasn't going to do this again. Not now, not with him. They had a lot of unfinished business between them and getting physically involved was only going to make it messy. Then he moved against her, softening the kiss, pulling her closer and she found she couldn't think of anything at all. Not when all she wanted was to spend the rest of her life in this perfect embrace.

The heat was instant, as was the passion. It danced around her like fire, warming, consuming, making her ache until all she could do was cling to him. It was as good as it had been the last time he kissed her and better than it had been before—when she'd been young and foolish and so much in love.

Her body remembered as she moved her head slightly to allow him to deepen the kiss. Familiar needs pulsed in time with her heartbeat. Every part of her trembled in anticipation. When his tongue brushed against hers, she softly moaned, trying to swallow the sound, yet unable to control herself.

His strong hands moved up and down her back, then slid to her arms. The feel of his palms on her bare skin made her breasts ache and swell. She clutched at his shoulders, pulling him closer, wanting more. Always more.

Sitting next to each other made the embrace awkward. Taylor had a sudden vision of them stretching out on her bed, removing clothes. Images of them making love fueled her growing passion, making her close her lips around his tongue and suck gently. He gasped.

Then as quickly as it had begun, the kiss was over. Jonathan straightened, released her and leaned forward, resting his forearms on his thighs.

"I shouldn't have done that," he said quietly.

His admission shocked her. "What happened to trying to seduce me?"

"Oh, I still want that," he said, turning to look at her.

So why was he sorry about the kiss? She swallowed uncomfortably.

"I envy your life here," he said.

She hesitated, then accepted the change in subject. "What happened to New York City being Nirvana?"

He smiled. "I meant growing up here."

She glanced around at the grounds. "I liked it. My mom was a terrific parent. She still is." Taylor knew any claim to fame in the mothering department with her own daughter was due to Linda's influence. "You grew up back east, right?"

"That was me—a product of the suburbs."

"Don't you think it's strange that we both lost our dads? Although you were older than I."

"I was fourteen."

Her father had died when she was five. "What happened?"

"He was drunk and got into an accident. Fortunately he only killed himself."

There was something in his voice. Something that if he'd been a patient, would have caused her to push harder. Instead she let it go.

She drew her knees to her chest and wrapped her arms around her legs. Nothing made sense. Her lips still tingled from Jonathan's kiss, she was determined to whip his butt in their contest, and she couldn't help wanting him in bed. Oh, and there was the matter of the child he didn't know about. She was definitely a finalist for Strangest Life of the Year.

Silence stretched between them. Jonathan straightened, then angled toward her, resting his arm along the back of the swing.

"I'm sorry your marriage didn't work out," she said and was pleased to find out she *almost* meant it. Not that she wished Jonathan unhappiness—it was just that his being married right now would complicate things.

"Thanks."

"Want to talk about what went wrong?"

He looked at her. "As a professional? No, thanks."

"Actually, I was thinking more as a friend."

"Are we friends?"

"I hope so."

He rocked the swing. "The bigger question is why I married her in the first place. I guess I thought it was time. It didn't take me long to be grateful for her endless business trips. I don't know. We could talk about anything, we had similar values. It should have worked and it didn't." He shrugged. "What's your excuse for being single, Dr. McGuire? No wealthy ranchers in the neighborhood to tempt you?"

"Not that I've met," she said easily. "Being a single mom in a small town cuts down on one's opportunities."

"Good line and I don't buy it for a second."

"Buy what you want." She raised her eyebrows. "At any one time there are approximately six single men in Marriageville, not counting the priest. You, however, live in a city of what, six or seven million, where more than half of them are women. People with unsuccessful personal lives shouldn't throw stones."

He laughed. "So did any of the six eligible bachelors take the infamous McGuire quiz?"

"A couple."

"Linnie's father?"

She chuckled. "No. He wasn't the quiz type."

"Want to talk about him?"

She didn't doubt he was curious. "Not really."

"Did any of the prospective husbands pass the test?"

"It's not a pass–fail situation. In the end, it didn't matter how well we got along. I never felt the spark."

He winked. "Not like with us?"

"You keep bringing that up. If I give you a plaque or something, will you stop mentioning it?"

"Yeah. I want a really big plaque, though. At least three feet across."

They laughed together. Something stirred in her chest. Not passion, which she could accept. Instead it was something far more dangerous. Liking.

She pushed him out of the swing. "It's late. You need to head back to the hotel."

"Want to come with me?"

In that heartbeat, she did. "No, but thanks for asking."

His humor faded as he stared at her face. "Thanks for tonight, Taylor."

"You're welcome."

She watched him walk away, all the while listening to warning sirens going off all around her.

Marnie's alarm went off at 5:50 in the morning on Monday, a time she normally never tried to experience in real life, except through the glory of sleep. Determinedly, she climbed out of bed before she could give in to weakness, then staggered to the bathroom where she completed an abbreviated form of her ablutions and pulled a green jersey robe over her matching nightshirt.

"Coffee," she murmured softly as she headed toward the stairs. "Life will be better after coffee."

Fortunately she'd prepared everything the night before so all she had to do was push the button and wait for water and grounds to create magic. Stifling a yawn, she wandered over to the refrigerator and pulled out fixings for breakfast. She didn't know what Will liked to eat in the morning, but she was determined to tempt him into staying in her presence for more than thirty-five seconds, which was about all she'd seen him for over the weekend.

After he'd arrived on Saturday, he'd disappeared into his room, coming out long enough to tell her he couldn't make dinner. She'd spent Saturday night alone and missing George. Sunday morning Will had left on a run before she'd been up. By the time he'd returned, she'd been leaving for church. When she'd returned home after service, she'd found a note saying he would be spending the day at work, and she hadn't seen him since.

This was not what she'd had in mind when she'd arranged for them to be linked up together.

When there was enough coffee to pour into a mug, she sipped gratefully at the steaming liquid. Feeling returned to her body and she was able to function. Then it was just a matter of starting the pancakes, frying up sausages and bacon, whipping eggs and waiting for Mr. Wonderful to make his appearance.

At six-twenty she heard footsteps on the stairs. Determined not to let him slip through her fingers, she strolled into the foyer, an extra mug of coffee in her hands. Will saw her and froze, not quite halfway down the stairs, his eyes wide, his mouth open.

She'd spent the last couple of nights having second thoughts about all this, but the look on his face eased some of her bruised feelings. The whole starving-man-staring-at-a-woman-like-a-last-meal analogy had always seemed a bit over the top for her. Women weren't meals and men didn't starve for them. At least most men didn't. Based on the hunger in Will's eyes, he'd been dieting for way too long.

His hazel gaze traveled all over her body, from her bare toes with her bright pink painted nails, up her legs, to the hem of her robe several inches above her knee. She thought he lingered there for a second before traveling to her breasts, unbound and barely contained, then to her face. She hadn't put on any makeup and her hair was a little tousled, but she hadn't thought she'd looked all that bad. Will swallowed.

"Ah, good morning."

"Morning," she said, giving him a little smile and holding out the coffee mug. "I made breakfast."

He took two steps, stumbled, caught himself and made it the rest of the way down the stairs without mishap. When he reached her, his face was flame red and he kept compulsively pushing up his glasses.

"I'm, ah, not much of a morning eater."

Marnie couldn't help it. She knew she scared Will and she should probably make it easy on him, but she just didn't have the self-control required.

"When *do* you like to eat?"

She asked the question slowly, lowering her voice slightly and leaning toward him. It was fun to flirt. She'd never been good at it through her teens. George had been the one to teach her the pleasure in a double entendre.

He gaped like a fish.

Marnie took pity on him and handed him the coffee. "If you won't have anything, you have to at least come and admire what I've made so far."

Acting more brazen than she felt, she put her arm through his and led the way.

Will allowed her to take him into the kitchen. Once there she released him and he put his briefcase on the counter and studied the cooked sausage and bacon, then nodded at the blueberry pancake mix.

"I'm surprised you cook," he said at last.

"I'm not an idiot. Of course I cook."

He flushed again. "I didn't mean to imply you weren't capable. I thought you would have a staff."

She picked up her mug and took a sip. "I have people who clean and decorate. I take care of my own cooking because I like it and cooking for one isn't much of a challenge." She looked at him over the rim of her cup. "Are you sure I can't fix you something?"

He wore khakis and a white shirt, both with painfully perfect creases. Yesterday he'd looked fabulous while sweating. The thing was while she thought he was kind of sexy in a charmingly inept way and knew he was smart, five-sentence conversations weren't going to help them get to know each other. If they didn't sit down and talk, how was she supposed to figure out if her crush on him was just a waste of time?

"I'm really running late, ah, Marnie," he said, putting down his coffee. "I have a seven o'clock meeting."

"Could we have dinner?"

"I work very late and usually order in."

She pressed her lips together. "Will, are you going to spend the entire month avoiding me? If that's your plan, why did you enter?"

A nanosecond too late she remembered *she'd* been the one who had made sure his name was slipped into the computer. *Oops.*

He stared at something just over her left shoulder. "A friend entered me in the contest."

"Oh." She leaned against the counter. "So why did you go this far?"

"I thought I might meet someone suitable."

Now it was her turn to blush. Marnie knew she had many terrific qualities, but suitability wasn't one of them. She wrapped her fingers around the opening of her robe and pulled the two ends together.

"Okay," she said quietly. "I'll go see the folks in charge and let them know this has been a mistake. I'm sorry to have taken up your time."

She didn't look at him as she turned to leave the room.

"Marnie, wait."

She paused without turning around. Behind her, Will sighed.

"I'm doing this all wrong. I always do it wrong. I'm not saying you're not perfectly fine. I'm a little nervous being around you because you're not a librarian or a math teacher."

She spun to face him. "You're saying I'm not smart enough for you?"

"No. Not that. You're just so pretty and—" He gestured helplessly. "You're pretty and I'm really bad with women. I don't want to bore you or anything."

He was worse at the whole male–female thing than she was. Once again, she felt comforted.

"I won't assume you're a boring computer nerd if you won't assume I'm a bimbo," she said. "How's that?"

"I, ah, okay."

"We should probably actually get to know each other. I mean we *are* living together for a whole month. How about a home-cooked meal?"

"Sure."

"What night?"

He hesitated, then pushed up his glasses. "Friday?"

That was way too far away, but she decided not to complain. She gave him her best smile and spoke the truth. "I can't wait."

Chapter 11

"So, how are things going?" Marnie asked.

Taylor slid into the booth opposite her friend and shook her head. "To be honest, I don't have a clue."

"What do you mean?"

Taylor thought about the recent twists and turns in her life. "Instead of running a small but successful private practice, I'm suddenly involved in a media event that puts both my reputation and my financial future on the line."

"You're doing great," Marnie said loyally. "You're going to win the contest and get a really great book deal."

"I hope so. I'm shallow enough to admit that the money would mean a lot to me. I never thought I'd be in my thirties and still living at home."

Marnie frowned. "It's more complicated than that. You needed Linda's help with Linnie. Plus it's not like you're sharing a one-bedroom apartment. That house has been in your family for nearly a hundred years. It's huge. You have your own wing."

"I know." She shook her head. "It's not just that." Taylor glanced around to see if they were alone—at least as alone as one could be at Wilbur's during the lunch crush. "Jonathan is also a problem."

Marnie grinned. "Now *this* is getting interesting. Tell me everything. I want details."

Before Taylor could figure out how to spill them, Lorraine, their waitress, appeared at the side of the table. "Okay, girls. What's it gonna be?"

She stood snapping her gum, pencil poised, her posture warning them that she didn't have much time.

"A burger and fries," Marnie said. "Small salad on the side, blue cheese dressing, and a Diet Coke."

Taylor rolled her eyes. "Because the Diet Coke is going to help with all those other calories?"

Marnie grinned.

"I'll take the grilled chicken salad," Taylor said. "Low-fat ranch dressing on the side, no bread. I'll drink water."

When Lorraine had left, Taylor leaned back in the booth. "I keep thinking you're going to start putting on weight as you get older, but it doesn't happen. It's not fair. You don't even exercise."

"I do. I walked here from the shop."

"Wow. Nearly half a block. Did you have to stop and rest on the way?"

Marnie lowered her voice. "Taylor, you need a man. You're getting a little short-tempered these days. Why do I know that this *problem* with Jonathan is contributing to your crankiness?"

"Because it is. But there's a whole lot more going on."

Lorraine reappeared with their drinks, giving her

time to compose herself and try to forget about their encounter the previous Sunday. Why did the man keep kissing her and why did she not stop him?

"I don't talk much about Linnie's father," she began slowly as she peeled the paper from her straw.

"Actually you've never said a word about him." Marnie held up her hands. "I'm clarifying, not judging."

"I know. Thanks for understanding. I haven't said anything to anyone for a lot of reasons. We'd already broken up when I found out I was pregnant. He'd made it really clear he wasn't interested in staying together. I wanted to get married and have kids and he wanted a successful career."

"Some people do both."

"He didn't. I think he was already sort of involved with someone else when we broke up. It doesn't matter."

Marnie nodded sympathetically. "So Jonathan reminds you of him?"

"Actually, Jonathan *is* him. Jonathan is Linnie's father."

Marnie gasped. Unfortunately she was drinking at the time and started choking. Three men from different ends of the restaurant rushed to pound her on the back. One offered mouth-to-mouth resuscitation. Marnie shooed them all away.

"What? Linnie's father?" She kept her voice low but still sounded stunned. "He's the one you ran off with when you were sixteen? He's the one you lived with while he was going to college? Him? Dr. Kirby?"

"What's so surprising about that?"

"I don't know. It's just . . . I never expected him to be a real person."

Despite her confusion and the fact that her life was

spinning out of control, Taylor started to laugh. "Immaculate conception?"

"No, just he was always 'this guy.' Not someone I've actually met."

"I've actually kissed him," Taylor said before she could stop herself.

Marnie's eyes widened. "So the spark is still there?"

"Oh, yeah. Which complicates things." She swallowed. "I'm going to tell him about Linnie. I'd always planned to wait until she was eighteen before outing him, but fate or circumstances or whatever has brought him here."

"Geez, what are you going to say?"

"I have no idea. I've been trying to figure that out for days. I need the right words and the right time. And I need to get through the conversation without throwing up or passing out. The thing is, I'm running out of time. Linnie will be home Friday for a week. Between now and then I have to figure out what I want to say."

Marnie shook her head. "Wow. Jonathan Kirby." She frowned slightly. "You know, now that you mention it, I can see the resemblance a little. What do you think is going to happen when you tell them?"

"I have no idea. Linnie will be thrilled to find out who her father is. I'm not sure what Jonathan's reaction is going to be. I'm confident they'll both want to kill me for keeping this information from them for so long. I don't look forward to that."

"I don't blame you. But they'll get over it and then the three of you . . ." She paused. "What will the three of you be?"

"Uneasy relatives."

Lorraine returned with their order. Marnie spread mustard on her burger.

"I thought I had problems," her friend said, "but you've put my life in perspective."

"I live to serve." Taylor picked at her salad, then looked up. "What problems?"

Marnie was one of the most honest people Taylor knew so she was surprised when an expression of guilt crossed her face.

"Nothing," Marnie said innocently.

"Don't give me that. What's going on?"

She sighed. "It's no big deal. I mean it's not like I wanted the money or anything."

Taylor put down her fork. "What are you talking about?"

Marnie stared at her burger. "I really wanted to get to know Will. I've had a crush on him forever, but he would never look at me, so I spoke with one of the guys programming the computer. He fixed things so that Will and I were put together. That's all."

Taylor's stomach turned over a couple of times. She felt the blood rush from her head. "You fixed the contest?"

The concept horrified her. What if Jonathan found out? Or the publishers? It could ruin everything.

"Just one little part." Marnie leaned toward her. "Don't be mad, Taylor. I just wanted to see if he was anything like I thought. How else was I going to meet him?"

"You could have introduced yourself for a start. 'Hi, I'm Marnie, want to have coffee?' "

Her friend glared at her. "Yeah, right. And then I

could watch him trip and fall in his rush to get away from me. Taylor, you know I don't attract normal men. George was the only one who bothered to figure out there was an actual person behind this body. Do you think I enjoy being thought of as a cross between a hooker and a blow-up doll?"

Taylor forced herself to take a couple of deep breaths. Maybe the situation wasn't so bad. Then she looked at Marnie and gazed at what the rest of the world saw.

Her friend wore a dark purple sleeveless shirt, a black skirt and black sandals. Onyx and amethyst earrings dangled from her ears. Her long hair tumbled in its usual disarray of curls; makeup highlighted her features. She shouldn't have been anything but ordinary. Except this was Marnie.

Her large breasts seemed to strain against the material of the blouse. Technically the fabric wasn't tight across her chest at all, but there was something about her size or shape that made one wait for flesh to spill out. Her dark skirt emphasized long legs and slender hips. Her walk was purely sexual in a way Taylor had long given up hope of ever imitating. When they were together, she felt like a platypus following a gazelle.

Then there was Marnie's face. Big green eyes, a full mouth, perfect skin and porn-star hair. Full and big and sexy as hell.

"I forget how gorgeous you are," Taylor admitted. "You're right. I don't want to admit it but you'd scare off any regular guy. He'd either be completely intimidated and decide you weren't in his league, or he'd overcompensate. Worse, he'd probably assume you were stupid. But, geez, Marnie, couldn't you have picked a different way to meet Will?"

"I'm sorry. I didn't mean to make trouble. I just didn't know what else to do. I miss George. It's been three years and I know I have to get on with my life. I need to love somebody, Taylor. That's what I do best. I'm a nurturer, like you. I take care of the world."

Taylor thought about protesting that she didn't take care of the world, but she supposed with her chosen profession, it wouldn't be much of an argument.

"So how are things going?" she asked. "Is Will falling under your spell?"

"So far he's just avoiding me. I had to get up before six on Monday just to catch sight of him. But we're supposed to have dinner on Friday. I'm hoping that will help." Marnie leaned an elbow on the table. "The irony is I don't even know if I'm going to like him. That's what I wanted this month to be about. Exploring possibilities."

"Go slow," Taylor advised.

Marnie laughed. "Honey, I've been with exactly one man in my life. I don't know any other way to go."

The couple in front of them reminded Jonathan of Jack Sprat and his wife. He and Taylor sat in two club chairs with an end table between them. Across the coffee table was a sofa on which sat two of the most mismatched people he'd ever seen.

The man was tall and thin with precisely combed hair, a perfect knot in his tie and trouser creases sharp enough to draw blood. The woman was much shorter and very round. She had dimpled cheeks, fussy hair and dangling earrings of painted cats. They sat as far from each other as possible.

"We're not really getting along," Velma was saying, dabbing at her moist eyes with a white handkerchief trimmed in paw prints.

She wore a cat print shirt over jeans and her voluminous bag sitting on the carpet next to her featured the face of a calico.

Taylor nodded sympathetically. "You and Walter were matched according to Dr. Kirby's questionnaire?" she asked.

Jonathan shot her a look, but she simply smiled innocently. He knew what she was thinking—that the first couple to drop out of the contest came from his side. Score one for her.

He leaned toward the couple. "I've pulled your responses. It seems that you're pretty much opposites, which should make things exciting. Is there any chemistry at all?" He avoided defining the chemistry as sexual. No matter how he tried, he couldn't imagine these two in bed together.

Velma shook her head. "We've tried. I know it's only been a few days, but it seems so much longer."

"We have different lifestyles," Walter said, studiously avoiding looking at Velma. "She has cats and I'm allergic. I like a nice dinner with steak and a fine wine, she's a nondrinking vegetarian."

"I feed the cats meat," Velma said quickly. "I'm very careful about their diets. Natural food with none of those chemicals in commercial brands. Only the best for my babies."

"Of course," Jonathan murmured, trying to keep

from laughing. He probably should be annoyed that a couple on his team was dropping out, but the situation was too comical.

Rather than give in to humor, he glanced around the room. They were in Taylor's suite of offices. Light peach walls gave the space a warm glow. Several Impressionist prints added color without being too distracting. Her furniture was comfortable, and there were plenty of boxes of tissue within reach. Everything a therapist could want. Except for these two.

"He's been divorced," Velma said, speaking the words in the same tone one would use to discuss a pedophile. "Three times."

"And she has never been married."

Taylor made some notes. Jonathan glanced at her pad and saw she'd written "HELP" in oversize letters. They exchanged a sympathetic glance.

"Why did you enter the contest?" Taylor asked.

Velma shifted uncomfortably. Walter stared at the ceiling.

"I'm going to guess it was for the money," Jonathan said.

They both nodded.

"Then you have that in common," Taylor offered. "There's a place to start. What about movies you both have liked? Or books? Hobbies?"

Velma leaned forward. Jonathan noticed that she had small three-dimensional cats covering the buttons down the front of her shirt. "We just don't like each other very much."

Walter offered a pained smile. "We have that in common. Do we have to stay together?"

"Not at all." Jonathan looked at them. "You do realize that if you split up now, you won't be eligible for the money. You could simply tough it out and avoid each other as much as possible for the next couple of weeks."

Velma and Walter both shook their heads. "There isn't enough money in the world to keep us together," Walter said.

"Exactly." Velma touched her hankie to the corner of her eye.

"Then consider yourselves out of the contest," Taylor said. "All you have to do is sign papers saying you'll no longer be a part of things. You'll have to go to city hall to do that." She wrote on a fresh page from her pad and handed it to Velma. "Linda McGuire can help you. Here's her office and phone numbers." She glanced at her watch. "You should be able to catch her right now."

Velma and Walter barely paused to say good-bye. In their haste to leave and dissolve their union, they practically pushed each other out the door. When Jonathan and Taylor were alone, they burst into laughter.

"Talk about a mistake," Taylor said, tossing her pad on the table. "They were so uncomfortable together."

"No wonder. He was prissy and she had all that cat stuff. Did you see her buttons?"

Taylor nodded, still chuckling. "I actually liked them."

"You're lying."

"No, but don't worry. I won't be getting you any for a present."

"I suspect you'll have to get them through the mail. No self-respecting retailer is going to sell items like that."

"Want to bet?" She stopped laughing. "Okay, Dr. Kirby, we've lost one couple from your column. That should make you nervous."

"It doesn't matter that they pulled out. Our competition is based on couples who want to stay together when the month is over. I didn't have a chance with them. However, I'm still going to win."

"Not in this lifetime." She raised her arms in a gesture of victory. "I bet the town will have a parade in my honor when I win."

"I wouldn't start planning the route. We have a long way to go and I have every confidence in my people."

"Not counting Mr. Prissy and the Cat Lady."

"Not counting them," he agreed.

She lowered her arms and shifted in her seat. "Jonathan, I have to tell you something. Actually I have two things to tell you. The first relates to the contest. I'm hesitating because you have every right to use it against me, but I'm hoping you won't."

She sounded serious, but not upset. He leaned back in his chair and assumed his most serious, most concerned psychologist voice.

"With hard work and commitment on both our parts I know we can work through whatever personal problems you may have."

She shot him a mock glare. "Don't even begin to think you can psychoanalyze me, Dr. Kirby. This is about a friend of mine."

"Oh—a *friend*. Of course. What is your *friend's* problem?"

She shook her head. "I'm being serious. Someone I know rigged the computer so that she would be matched with the man of her dreams. Or so she hopes."

He straightened. "How'd she do that?"

"I didn't ask, but Marnie has her ways. She confessed today at lunch and I'm passing the information along. She's not interested in winning the money. Marnie has plenty in her own right. It's really just about the guy—but it does break the rules. Do you want to report the irregularity?"

She was so damned earnest. "I think we can keep this to ourselves. However, we'll have to come to some kind of arrangement to keep the situation equitable. If I don't tell on you, what are you going to do for me?"

She rolled her eyes. "Is this about sex again? Do you ever *not* think about it?"

"I believe four to six times an hour is average for my age group. You should be pleased that at least three of those times I'm imagining you in the fantasy."

"Who else do you fantasize about?"

"No one you know."

He kept his tone light so she wouldn't guess he was lying. Since seeing Taylor again, he'd been unable to think of anyone but her. It had been that way while they'd been together, as well as for months after. He might not have been willing to commit to her all those years ago, but he hadn't been able to stop wanting her.

She wore a navy pantsuit with a white silky blouse. Very professional and far too sexy for his taste. Of course he'd find Taylor sexy in anything . . . or nothing at all.

Regretfully he glanced at his watch. "I hate to cut this short, but I have to go. I have a plane to catch."

Her eyes widened. "What?"

"Duty calls. I'm a last-minute guest on a couple of talk shows. The syndication folks are testing me in various markets. I'm flying to New York today, then to Los Angeles. Don't worry. It's only for a couple of days. I'll be back in town in time for our Saturday morning press conference."

Taylor stood. "Fate has an interesting sense of humor."

"In what way?" he asked as he rose as well.

"Oh, it's difficult to explain. I'd hoped we would have some time to talk."

"I have a few minutes."

"This will take longer." She touched his arm. "It's about our past. Just some things I wanted to clear up. When do you get back?"

"Late Friday." He frowned. "Should I be worried?"

"Not at all. I swear." She made an X over her heart. "What about meeting Friday when you get back?"

"I'll be counting the hours."

Chapter
12

*W*ill stared at the computer screen and wished the world would end. It was Friday. Friday at four, to be exact. Friday when he was expected to have dinner with Marnie Boudine—Marriageville's answer to Mae West, Anna Nicole Smith, the Mayflower Madam and Julia Roberts all rolled into one.

"Tonight's the big night, eh?" Mark asked as he walked into Will's cubicle. "Dinner with the old lady."

Despite the hard drive–sized knot in his stomach, Will smiled. Marnie could be described as many things, but "old lady" wasn't one of them.

He had to clear his throat before he could talk. "Yes. She's cooking dinner tonight."

Mark settled on the corner of his desk and winked. "So, you seen her naked yet?"

Will nervously pushed up his glasses, all the while keeping his attention firmly fixed on his computer screen. "No. Just in a short robe."

He tried to speak casually, hoping to ignore the instant

arousal that throbbed to life the nanosecond he'd mentally pictured Marnie in her A.M. wardrobe. While she hadn't fixed him breakfast since Monday, she always had coffee waiting for him before he left. She didn't say much, just sort of smiled as she handed him a steaming mug.

"How short?" Mark asked gleefully.

The image of Marnie's long legs filled Will's brain. Long, perfect legs that seemed to stretch on forever. Legs he would have sold his soul to touch. "You don't want to know."

Two hours later Will stepped out of the shower. The cold water had temporarily alleviated his aroused condition. Despite telling himself that this wasn't a date, he felt awkward and nervous. He hadn't had an evening with a woman go well more than once or twice in his life and he couldn't remember the last time it had happened. What were they going to talk about? What if she figured out he didn't know the first thing about being a normal person? What if he couldn't get past her breasts to stare into her eyes?

A thousand disastrous scenarios ran through his head. It was like watching a hideous movie of relationship bloopers with him starring in every scene. Despite the entertainment, he managed to get dressed and shave without drawing blood. Then he picked up the box of long-stemmed white roses he'd bought and took them downstairs.

He heard country music drifting out from the direction of the kitchen. An off-key voice sang along, making him smile. He clutched the gold florist's box tightly against his chest and walked toward the singing.

She stood in the center of the kitchen, leaning against the island. A sleeveless peach-colored dress skimmed over her curves before falling to mid-calf. Her hair had been pulled back into a thick braid and her feet were bare. She looked casual and incredibly sexy.

"You're right on time," she said, moving toward him. "I like that quality in a man." She glanced at the box. "Are those for me?"

"What? Oh. Yes." He thrust the flowers toward her, careful to keep from touching her.

She set them on the counter, then lifted the cover. Instantly the scent of roses filled the room. "They're beautiful."

"You're not allergic, are you?" he asked anxiously.

"Not at all."

She walked to the far side of the kitchen and opened a cupboard. Despite being about five-foot-eight, she had to stand on tiptoes to reach the top shelf. Her dress rose with her, tightening slightly around her high, full rear. Will's mouth went dry as he stared at the enticing curves. Every part of her was perfect.

Don't think about that, he ordered himself, as she returned with a vase. *Make conversation.* He searched his brain frantically before finally remembering something he'd read in one of Dr. Kirby's books. That women like to be appreciated with compliments.

"You look very nice," he said, hoping he sounded sincere, because he really meant it. She looked incredible.

Marnie's smile deepened. "Thank you. I hope you don't mind us going casual tonight. I thought it would be easier. I've got salad in the refrigerator, potatoes baking in the oven and two big steaks ready to grill."

He thought about the rabid vegetarian he'd dated and breathed a sigh of relief. "That sounds really nice."

She arranged the flowers in the vase, then set them on the island. "What about something to drink?" she asked. "I have beer in the fridge, or wine. There's liquor in the butler's pantry."

"Beer's fine."

She crossed to the refrigerator. As she did so, she walked close enough to him that he could inhale the scent of her. Not perfume, exactly. At least he didn't think it was. More like soap or shampoo, or maybe just Marnie herself.

What would it be like to know someone so intimately that it would be possible to recognize her by scent alone? He wanted that. He wanted a woman's scent to linger on his sheets. He wanted to be like those guys at work who complained when their wives stole their sweatshirts for an afternoon and left a fragrance of perfume in the fabric. He wanted—

"Here you go."

Marnie handed him a beer and a bottle opener. She moved over to the grill and turned on the burner. "So how was your day? I heard that your team has nearly completed their networking project, which means you're ahead of schedule."

Will had brought the bottle to his mouth, but he put it down, untouched. "How do you know that?"

"It was in the paper yesterday," she told him. "I always read the business section first thing in the morning."

"Why?"

She dropped her hands to her hips. "Will Ramsey, if you insist on treating me like a bimbo with the intelligence of a dress-up doll, we're not going to get along at all. I can read. I can even do math."

She smiled as she spoke, but he thought he saw something else lurking in her green eyes. Pain, maybe. And disappointment. He let his gaze travel down the length of her body, pausing at her breasts, before moving to a narrow waist, rounded hips and those incredible legs. Was she trying to tell him she was all this and smart, too?

"I'm sorry," he said, knowing he was doing it all wrong. "I know you can read."

"Good. Try to remember that. George always told me that I could be more than a pretty face. With his help, that happened."

He blinked. "George?"

"My late husband." She walked to the refrigerator and pulled out a package of meat.

"Ah, right."

She closed the door with her hip. It was one of those easy moves women make all the time. To Will, it was as lovely as a ballet.

"You want the long version or the short version of my life?" she asked, returning to the grill.

Better her talking than him, he thought. "The long version."

She chuckled. "I know you're lying. No one wants that. But thanks for pretending. Let's see. I was born in a tiny west Texas town. My parents didn't have much money, so the understanding was the kids would leave when we turned eighteen. I'd never enjoyed school so I didn't want to go to college. Instead I packed my bag and took a bus to the big city." She put the steaks on the grill. "That would be Houston. How do you like your steak?"

"Medium rare."

"Me, too." She winked, then continued. "I worked at fast-food places while earning enough to put myself through beauty school. When I graduated, I got a job at a fancy hotel and about six months later, I met George."

Her expression softened as she spoke the other man's name. Will pulled out a stool by the island and sat down.

"He was older," Marnie said, glancing at him over her shoulder. "Sixty to my nineteen. He said he wanted a young, pretty wife at his side during the twilight of his life. He didn't have any family, he was rich and kind and he was willing to leave it all to me. After my childhood I wasn't about to turn down the security."

She leaned against the counter. "I liked him. I wouldn't have married him if I hadn't. But I didn't love him. That came later. He'd told me that the men in his family didn't make it to seventy, so it wasn't going to be a long commitment for me. We were married and moved here. George had grown up in Marriageville."

She turned the steaks over. "During that first year, we got to know each other. He learned that he still had a lot of life in him and I learned I was smarter than I thought. George wanted me to be sensible about the money, so I took a few financial courses, found out I had an interest in politics and a head for business. One day I realized I'd fallen in love with my husband."

The corners of her mouth trembled. Will thought he should probably say something, or ask a question. He couldn't think of anything. Fortunately, Marnie continued without prompting.

"We never had children. George didn't want me to be a single mother. I tried to press him, but he was firm on the matter. Then one day he up and died. It was nearly four years ago and here I am."

She opened the oven and pulled out two potatoes, setting them on a plate by the grill. "I probably shouldn't have said all that," she murmured so softly he could barely hear her. "It was silly."

"No. I don't mind hearing about George." He didn't even care that she was still in love with the man. It wasn't as if Will expected her to fall for him.

"Thanks. You're a real gentleman and I appreciate that." She took a sip of her wine. "What about you, Will? Tell me your life story."

He'd been in the process of taking a drink of his beer when she spoke. The bubbly liquid went down the wrong way, making him cough. Marnie hurried to his side where she began patting him on the back. Her left breast brushed against his upper arm, making him even more painfully hard.

"I'm fine," he gasped, needing her to stop before he did something stupid like lose control right there. "Really."

She eyed him doubtfully. "Don't die on me, Will. I'm real sensitive to that sort of thing."

He held up a hand to show he was fine, and she returned to the grill.

"You know we have our first interview with the psychologists next week," she said. "I haven't ever been in therapy, have you?"

"Ah, no."

"Think they'll ask anything embarrassing?"

"I hope not."

She turned the meat again. "These are about ready.

Why don't you pour some wine for dinner. I left it in the dining room."

He walked in the direction she'd pointed and found himself in a large formal room. The cherrywood table could easily seat twenty. Two place settings sat on the polished table, one at the far end and one next to it.

Will saw the bottle of red wine on a small tray next to two glasses. He removed the cork without mishap, then poured the ruby-colored liquid. By the time he finished, Marnie carried in a tray with their dinner. She served them, then motioned for him to take his seat.

The previous evening Will had stayed awake long into the night rereading Dr. Kirby's book on understanding women. He'd made up a list of several topics to discuss during their meal.

"Your house is very beautiful," he said awkwardly.

"It's big," Marnie admitted. "I don't know. I keep thinking about selling it, but I don't have anywhere else I'd rather be. It does take a lot of work to keep up everything, though."

When she finished speaking, there was only silence. Will swallowed. Why did other people know how to make conversation? They did it all the time, with what appeared to be great ease. He searched his mental list again.

"Thank you for cooking dinner. It's very good. Do you like to cook?"

She stared at him. "I'm glad you like the meal, but grilling a steak and throwing a couple of potatoes into the oven hardly counts as cooking."

"Oh."

"Do I make you nervous?"

He pushed at the bridge of his glasses and studied his wine. "Why do you ask?"

"You seem . . ." She sighed. "Maybe it's me. I haven't been on a date since George died. I probably shouldn't have talked about him. I didn't mean to make you uncomfortable."

He risked glancing at her and saw she'd ducked her head. "You didn't make me uncomfortable," he blurted. "Really. I liked hearing about you and George."

He instantly regretted admitting that. Could he have sounded more like an idiot? But instead of rolling her eyes in disgust, Marnie raised her gaze to his. Something like relief filled her eyes.

"You did?"

"Yes. You had a happy marriage. That doesn't happen often enough these days."

"Oh." She smiled. "Well, good." She planted her elbows on the table and leaned toward him. "I just realized that I asked you to tell me about your past, but we never actually talked about it. How did a brilliant computer guy like you end up in little ol' Marriageville?"

Brilliant? She thought he was brilliant? "I, ah, was offered a job."

Marnie laughed and lightly touched his hand. "I figured that, Will. Start at the beginning."

Her fingers seared his skin. So much blood rushed to his groin that he felt light-headed. "I'd always had an aptitude for math and science," he said, barely able to string the sentence together. "School was very easy for me. I started college when I was thirteen and graduated at sixteen."

She pulled back her hand and his ability to think returned.

"Sixteen? You got your bachelor's degree at sixteen?"

He nodded. "I entered a Ph.D. program immediately, finishing my advanced work before I was twenty. I accepted a position with a small firm in California. Four years ago I came to work for Tectronics."

She studied him. "I'm guessing you were too young to date much during college."

She didn't know the half of it, he thought grimly. "Yes. Way too young."

"It must be hard to be so gifted," she said, then sipped her wine. "On the one hand, you're incredibly intelligent, but on the other hand, you missed out on so much of a regular life. Do you have regrets?"

Too many, he thought. But he wasn't about to bare his soul to a virtual stranger.

"I'm very comfortable with the course I've chosen," he said, hoping he didn't sound too stupid. "So tell me about your business. It's here in town, right? Marnie's Palace of Beauty?"

She laughed and began explaining about owning a beauty shop in the heart of Texas. By agreeing and nodding, he kept her talking all through the meal. When they'd finished, she sent him out on the porch while she prepared their dessert.

Will stepped out into the hot summer evening. There were a thousand stars in the sky. When he gazed up, he wished he'd taken more time to study other sciences. His knowledge of astronomy and astrophysics was minimal at best. Perhaps he could take up quantum theory as a hobby, or—

He sank onto the bench by the back door and dropped his head into his hands. Quantum theory as a hobby? He didn't need to read a chapter in Dr. Kirby's book on women to know that wasn't normal. The average guy had sports hobbies, or collected stamps.

Noises from the kitchen made him raise his head. Marnie wasn't anything like he'd thought. She was just as beautiful up close, but more interesting. She was also smart and nice. Really nice. He knew he'd stumbled a time or two, but she'd pretended not to notice. He'd even gone most of the dinner without being distracted by her breasts. But someone like her could never be interested in someone like him.

He'd had his first crush at fifteen. Unfortunately, she'd been a twenty-four-year-old grad student he'd tutored. She'd thought he was cute. When he'd tried to ask her out, she'd laughed so hard she'd choked on her soda. He'd tried to explain that while on the outside he was a teenager with bad skin and a voice that cracked, on the inside, he was very much a man. She'd still been giggling when she'd left.

He hadn't kissed a girl until he'd been eighteen, and she (a precocious fifteen-year-old with bleached hair and too much makeup) had informed him he was doing it all wrong. That had sent him to the library where he'd studied technique without actually being able to practice. His first attempt at a sexual experience had been two years later, with another student he'd been tutoring. The evening had gone well until he'd lost control and climaxed the second he'd touched her breasts. They'd both been fully dressed. She'd been disgusted and he'd been too embarrassed to attempt it again with her.

A series of disasters had followed, all of them leaving him feeling confused, cursed and still very much a virgin. As a last-ditch attempt to actually do the deed, he'd hired a hooker. While the young woman had been relatively attractive, she'd insisted on douching in the hotel room sink before getting into bed. The graphic reminder that she'd spent the previous hour with someone else and would be leaving his bed to ply her trade elsewhere had turned his desire to dust. He'd sent her away without bothering to even try.

So here he was, virgin Will Ramsey, living with the sexiest woman alive. Wanting her and knowing that anything he tried was destined to fail.

"Ready for dessert?" Marnie asked as she stepped out onto the porch. She carried a tray containing two plates.

Will rose to his feet and reached for it. At the same time she turned. His hand slid around her breast instead of the tray. They both jumped back. She shrieked, he swore and the dessert tray hit the wooden porch, banging loudly in the night as the two plates of pecan pie shattered.

His fingers burned where he'd accidentally touched her. Humiliation washed over him, making him wish he'd never agreed to dinner. What was the point? Nothing he did ever worked out right. The only place he avoided screwing up on a regular basis was at Tectronics.

"I'm sorry," he mumbled, hoping it was dark enough that she couldn't see the flush on his cheeks. "I didn't mean—"

"I know." Marnie folded her arms over her chest. "No big deal." She glanced down at the mess. "I probably shouldn't eat pecan pie anyway. Too many calories."

"I'll help you clean up," he offered.

"No. I can do it."

They stared at each other. Will looked away first.

"I'm going back to the office," he said, moving toward the stairs.

Marnie's eyes widened in surprised. "But it's Friday night."

"I have a lot to do."

He had to walk past her to leave. But instead of moving aside, she touched his arm, freezing him in place as surely as if she'd turned him into ice.

"I know what the problem is," she murmured, not quite meeting his gaze. She dropped her arm to her side. "It's me. I'm too much of . . . everything, I guess." She cleared her throat. "George used to warn me about that. He said he was older and comfortable with women, but younger men would be confused and intimidated. I'm a lot more than this body, Will. I'm also pretty alone in the world. I thought maybe, if nothing else, we could try to be friends."

He heard the words but didn't believe them. Marnie lonely? Wouldn't a woman like her have every man in the county panting at her doorstep?

Then he thought about the past week. Whenever he came home, she was here alone. She didn't have live-in servants, or a big family. He thought about his solitary life—his one-bedroom apartment, his self-help books that didn't seem to be working. She'd made a confession to him; he decided to do the same.

"I'm not real good with people," he said, pushing up his glasses. "I don't mean to get it wrong. That just sort of happens on its own. It's not that I don't want to be friends, but I always mess it up somehow." He jerked his head toward her chest. "Like I just did."

She smiled. An honest-to-God smile that made him want her more than he'd wanted anything in his life. And not just in bed, he thought with some surprise. He wanted to sit on the bench on this porch and talk all night. He didn't care if they never touched at all.

"Will, it was an accident. When you have something as big as these sticking out, things like that are bound to happen. Believe me, I know the difference between an unintended bump and a free feel."

He blushed again, but this time it didn't seem so bad.

"Friends?" she asked.

He nodded.

She held out her hand. When he took it, she raised herself on tiptoe and lightly kissed his cheek. Fiery desire filled him, but it was as much for an emotional connection as anything else.

"Tell you what," she said when she'd stepped back. "If you won't run off to work, I'll let you help me clean up this mess. Then I'll cut us each another piece of pecan pie and we can play Trivial Pursuit. I have the new edition, although I should probably warn you that I kick butt."

He was afraid of making another mistake, but he was more afraid of being alone. So despite his history, he bent down and collected the broken glass.

"Actually I do very well at that game," he said.

She crouched next to him. "Honey, 'very well' doesn't even come close. I'm willing to put my money where my mouth is. Ten bucks says I win."

He grinned. "You're on."

Chapter
13

$\mathcal{S}$aturday morning Jonathan arrived at the Ladies' Auxiliary meeting hall less than ten minutes before the press conference started. What he wanted was to see Taylor. In the past three days he'd actually—almost— missed her. He who didn't let himself get close enough to miss anyone.

But instead of a gorgeous honey-blonde from his past, he ran directly into Katrina.

"I wanted to ask where you ran off to, but I already know," Katrina said, blocking his way. "How did the shows go?"

"Great. The spot ratings were high, the feedback encouraging." He had, in fact, received rave reviews. His agent was doing the happy dance. The syndication suits had given him another pep talk on the importance of winning the contest. Jonathan found himself on the verge of getting everything he wanted.

Katrina pouted slightly. "I wish you'd told me where

you were going. I could have come with you. Offered you some private coaching."

The purr in her voice was more predatory than seductive. Jonathan smiled pleasantly and lightly squeezed her hand. "Katrina, you're way more woman than I could handle. Thanks for thinking of me, but I'm not prepared to be one more notch in your garter. I'm a sensitive kind of guy."

She smiled. "I would think you would be more than up to the task."

"You flatter me."

Horrified was a better word, but why make trouble? He disentangled himself from her touch and headed for the front of the room, all the while searching for Taylor. He spotted her talking to someone from the media. When she saw him, she excused herself and headed his way.

"I want you to know that I checked your reasons for standing me up last night," she said lightly, although he thought he saw something troubled lurking in her eyes. "There really was a wild storm circling through the middle part of the country both Thursday and Friday."

"Tell me about it," Jonathan said. "My flight to Dallas was canceled. I got as far as Phoenix, where I had to spend the night in the airport. I barely made it in time this morning." He glanced around the rapidly filling room. "Looks like we're going to have a big crowd."

"We are."

Taylor took his arm and led him to the side of the room. She wore her hair loose today. The soft curls flattered her pretty face.

He'd missed her. He'd missed talking with her and

arguing with her. He wanted to say it was all about sex, but he knew that if someone had offered him a couple of hours in her presence with the restriction that they couldn't touch, he would have agreed in a heartbeat.

"I'm sorry I was delayed last night," he said, his voice sounding husky. Okay, maybe he'd been exaggerating about the sex not being important.

"Me, too." She suddenly looked nervous. "Look, I really need to talk to you. I wanted to explain everything last night, but what with your flight being canceled and all..." She shrugged, then glanced around the room. "Jonathan, I'm sorry. I've been waiting for the right time and this isn't it."

"I'm intrigued. What's the problem?"

"Let's go," her mother said as she walked by. "You two better head up to the stage and prepare to meet your adoring fans."

Taylor sighed. "She's right. We'll do this after the press conference."

He wondered what could be bothering her. As they walked to the stage, he watched her frown deepen. Attempting to lighten her mood before she had to face the media he said, "I think I've figured out what it is."

She glanced at him. "Really?"

He nodded. "You're desperate to rekindle our sexual flame. Now my first instinct is to play hard to get, but I might go easy on you."

A smile turned up the corners of her mouth.

He leaned close. "I heard on the news last night that one of your couples withdrew from the competition. Looks like that questionnaire might not be as perfect as you thought."

"Neither are you." She stepped up onto the stage.

He chuckled.

A folder sat on the podium. She opened it, then handed him a single sheet of paper. "Since you were out of town, I took the liberty of writing a prepared statement."

He scanned it. "I'm impressed. You even admit to being behind in the contest."

She glared at him. "What I admit to is that we've both had a couple withdraw."

"Sounds good to me." He handed her back the paper, then watched as she moved to the microphone.

"Good morning," she said.

The room quieted as the members of the press took their seats.

"The latest information on our contest is being handed around," she continued.

Jonathan noticed that Taylor was much more comfortable with this press conference than with the first one. Her need to speak with him in private piqued his curiosity. Was there a problem at home? Had something happened with her book deal?

He wasn't going to get the answer without her, so he turned his attention to what she was saying.

"As Dr. Kirby has been gadding about pursuing a second career in television, I took the liberty of preparing our statement for today. Let me start by saying that I'm winning."

Several reporters laughed. Jonathan noticed Katrina wasn't one of them.

Taylor sighed. "Okay, maybe winning is the wrong term. So far we've had two couples drop out. One was matched using Dr. Kirby's theories, the other through my questionnaire. I'm assuming the latter is because of a computer glitch, which I'm having investigated."

There was more laughter. Taylor glanced at him and smiled. He winked. She was a hell of a woman. It almost made him wonder how he'd been able to walk away from her seventeen years ago.

"We're continuing to meet with all our couples as we ease our way through the process," she continued. "I've never worked in a situation like this and it's been a fascinating learning experience. I'm sure Dr. Kirby would agree."

He nodded. His career path had taken him away from private practice years ago. But now that he'd been through a few sessions, he was finding the work appealing. There was something to be said for one-on-one contact.

"Hey, Dr. Kirby, is she any good?" one of the reporters yelled.

"Actually, she's damned impressive," he admitted. "I've enjoyed watching how she interacts with the couples. We have different styles, but they seem to complement each other. So far no one is threatening to sue us."

Taylor finished the rest of the statement, then asked if there were any questions.

"Have you looked over Dr. McGuire's questionnaire?" one reporter asked. "If so, what do you think of it?"

"I've seen it," Jonathan admitted, moving to the microphone. Taylor stepped back to let him in. "I understand her point of wanting to know as much as possible about each other before committing to marriage. I don't agree with it, but I understand it."

"Dr. McGuire, what is it like to work with Jonathan Kirby?"

This question came from Katrina, who'd maneuvered her way to the front of the room. Taylor approached the microphone.

"He's a very gifted therapist," she said easily. "Between his seminars and his books, he's touched hundreds of thousands of lives. Obviously I'm learning a lot."

Several more questions filled the air. Jonathan answered them one at a time. Taylor stayed close enough to add her comments from time to time. Things were wrapping up when the rear door of the hall opened.

A young woman stepped into the room. She was tall and slender, with medium brown hair down to the middle of her back. When she waved at him, he frowned. He didn't remember meeting her and she didn't look old enough to be one of the participants. It was only when she mouthed, "Hi, Mom," that he realized she'd been waving at Taylor.

"Your daughter?" he asked, speaking softly so the microphone couldn't pick up his words.

But Taylor didn't respond. Instead she stared at the young woman as if she had materialized out of thin air. "Linnie said she was going to the outlet mall with her friends," Taylor said to no one in particular, looking as if she'd just seen her daughter's ghost instead of a living, breathing young woman.

Surprised by her reaction, he glanced back at the girl who was approaching the stage. She wore shorts and a purple T-shirt. When she smiled, he recognized Taylor's smile, and Linda's. It seemed that all the McGuire women were—

He mentally hiccupped. Taylor's daughter? The girl in front of him wasn't the thirteen-year-old he'd assumed her to be. She was at least . . .

Jonathan heard someone ask him a question, but he couldn't answer. He could only stare at the girl as she moved closer and closer. There was something about the curve of her chin, the way her eyes were shaped. Something familiar—

Linda brushed past him. "I think that's enough for today," she said brightly into the microphone. "We'll have another press conference in a few days."

He looked at Taylor. She'd turned the color of chalk. His expression narrowed. "What the hell is going on?"

A half-dozen cameras flashed, questions exploded. Jonathan ignored them all and stared at the mother of his child.

Taylor watched the understanding dawn on Jonathan's face. Her stomach felt as if she'd been stepped on by an elephant. She wanted to both faint and throw up, and she only had herself to blame. Telling herself that Linnie wasn't supposed to be here didn't help matters.

Without answering his question, she grabbed his arm and led him toward the small room in the rear. The floor seemed to ripple as she walked, making her wonder if fainting really was a possibility. She hoped not. Although it would be a distraction, she figured she needed to have this conversation as soon as possible.

When the door was firmly closed, Taylor leaned against it and stared at Jonathan. She didn't know what he was thinking, which was probably a good thing. He looked furious.

If only Linnie hadn't come to the press conference, she thought, then reminded herself that none of this was her daughter's fault. Linnie had arrived home the previous afternoon, her flight beating the thunderstorms by a couple of hours. The second Taylor had seen her, she'd known that she'd been completely irresponsible in putting off telling Jonathan the truth.

Taylor swallowed a couple of times before speaking. "Obviously we need to talk."

Jonathan glared at her, then paced around the table to the opposite wall. "Is she—" He spun to face her. "Your daughter—how old is she?"

"I'll answer the question you're not asking. Yes, Linnie is your child."

He froze in place, staring at her, not speaking, just watching.

"Look, this is a shock. You're upset, you're confused, and you have a lot of questions. You're probably mad as hell. I don't blame you." She rubbed her temples. "Geez, this is such a mess. I'm sorry. I've thought a lot about telling you and I've been waiting to find the perfect time and the right words. I just this second realized that there would never be a perfect time. There are no right words."

He didn't say anything. He stared at her as if she were the devil incarnate. Taylor rubbed her arms. "Jonathan, I don't know what to say. You're furious. Okay. I can deal with that. But let me make it clear that while you can take out your temper on me, you can't be mad at Linnie. I don't want her hurt. She doesn't know anything about her father. Once you and I come to terms, we'll figure out how to tell her. But right now this is between you and me."

"Come to terms?" he repeated, his voice so cold that she shivered. "How the hell am I supposed to come to terms with this? I have a daughter. She's what, sixteen? You never told me." He sucked in a breath. "Why the hell didn't you tell me?"

"I tried. That's why I wanted to see you last night."

He slammed his fist on the table in the center of the room. "Not now. Before. You've had her entire life to pick up the phone and tell me. I had the right to know."

She didn't back down from the fury she saw in his dark eyes. Instead she raised her chin slightly.

"I can't agree with you on that one. Some days I think I should have told you, but other times I know I did the right thing."

He loomed over her. "The hell you did. You were pregnant and didn't tell me. You kept my daughter from me all these years." He took a step back and swore. "A child. I have a child." He raised his hands, then dropped them to his sides. "I don't know what to say."

"Jonathan, it's not as simple as you're making it out to be. I got pregnant a long time ago. Do you remember what it was like? You didn't want to be with me anymore. When I turned eighteen, I thought we were going to finally get married and be together forever. But that wasn't what you wanted. You were ending things. I didn't even know I was pregnant until I got home. Did you really want me to call you then and say, 'I know you thought the relationship was over, but just kidding'?"

She was speaking. Jonathan could see her lips moving and hear the words, but he didn't understand them. He couldn't understand anything except that he had a child. A teenager.

How could he have not known? Why hadn't he guessed or felt something? Wasn't there supposed to be a nearly mystical connection between parents and children?

"You had no right," he told her. "You made the decision for me."

"I was trying to do what was best for both of us. You didn't want me. Can you honestly tell me you would have been happy about finding out that I was pregnant?"

"Yes."

"Oh, please. You were on scholarship, just starting on your master's. A baby would have screwed up your entire life. So what would have happened? You would have done the right thing and married me? Then where would we have been?"

"I don't give a damn about us. I would have known my child."

He turned his back on her and circled the room. A thousand thoughts flashed through his head. Rage poured through him—a primal emotion unlike anything he'd experienced before. He wanted Taylor punished for what she'd done.

"You were wrong to keep her from me," he growled.

Taylor flinched and opened her mouth but before she could speak, there was a knock on the door. Linda stuck her head inside.

"You two have people waiting," she said, her expression wary. She glanced at each of them. "Never mind. I'll go cancel the appointments."

Appointments? Damn. Their sessions. They had at

least two scheduled right after the press conference. Jonathan shook his head, trying to clear his thoughts.

Taylor turned to her mother. "It would be better if they came at another time."

"No," Jonathan said sharply. "We'll see them now." He glared at Taylor. "You and I can finish this business later."

Linda stepped out and shut the door. Taylor drew in a deep breath. "What about Linnie? I don't want her frightened by this. We have to come to an understanding and figure out how we're going to tell her."

"Suddenly I'm part of the decision process?" he asked sarcastically. "Gee, thanks."

"Jonathan, don't."

"Don't what? Don't be pissed off because you kept my daughter from me for all this time? Don't blame you for what you did?" He walked toward the door. "We're in agreement on one thing. I don't think Linnie should pay for what you did wrong. So don't worry. I'm not going to blurt out the truth. As much as I don't want to, I agree that we have to discuss this together and present a united front. Be grateful that your daughter is buying you some time and more understanding than you deserve."

Grace turned off the television when the press conference ended. "Dr. McGuire and Dr. Kirby seem like nice young people."

Nelson grinned at her. "They're both in their thirties, Grace. There was a time when you would have thought that was old."

"Oh, you mean back when dinosaurs roamed the earth?"

"Was it so long ago? I would have thought just around the time of the woolly mammoth."

She chuckled, appreciating the teasing. Nelson teased her all the time. He also complimented her, held open doors for her and generally made her feel very special. Now, as he stroked Alexander, he sniffed the air.

"Is that pie I smell?" he asked, his blue eyes twinkling with delight.

"Maybe."

"Grace, you spoil me. You know I love your pie. I might even have to have seconds."

She wanted to smile back at him, say something teasing, but she couldn't. Her chest was too tight. "I like spoiling you," was the best she could manage.

Nelson was a good man, she thought happily as he picked up his newspaper and began to read. She returned her attention to the sweater she was knitting. The room was quiet, except for the sound of Alexander's purr.

Some of the pressure in her chest eased. Maybe, just maybe, God was going to let her get it right this time. Wouldn't that be a miracle?

Chapter
14

Rio shifted awkwardly in his seat. He really hated these sessions with the therapists. What did they know about him and his life? Or his marriage?

"Rio?" Dr. McGuire probed gently. "What do you want from Chris?"

He glared at her, then turned his attention to his ex-wife. Chris wore a T-shirt and jeans. Her long, dark curly hair hung down her back. She looked sexy and completely unapproachable. His least favorite combination. And speaking of sexy . . .

"She never wants sex," he said before he could stop himself. "Not just now," he amended, when Chris shot him a stunned look. "Before, when we were married. No matter what I said or did she was always too tired or too busy or too mad."

Chris turned in her seat and glared at him. "You want to know why I avoided being physical with you?" Anger laced her voice. "I'll tell you," she continued, not waiting for an answer. "Because you never gave me what I wanted. You never listened, you never helped. So there was no way I was going to give you what you wanted."

Her words stung. "Why'd you have to punish me that way?" he asked. "Why was sex a weapon? Why didn't you want it, too?"

"Chris and Rio," Dr. McGuire interrupted gently. "Please use 'I' sentences. They will help you focus and keep the other person from feeling attacked."

Yeah right. Didn't the lady doctor get it? He *wanted* Chris to feel attacked. He wanted her to feel damn bad for all that she'd done to him.

When he didn't respond, Dr. McGuire leaned toward him. "Rio, how did Chris's actions make you feel? Were you angry? Did you feel rejected?"

He squirmed in his seat, wishing he were anywhere but here. Why the hell had he thought the contest was a good idea? It was Saturday. He could have been racing or driving to Dallas to be with his kids. Instead he was stuck in this office, talking to strangers about why his ex-wife had never wanted to make love with him.

He glanced around the small office. He and Chris sat in club chairs. Across a low coffee table, the two psychologists stared at him. So what was the penalty for just walking out?

"I don't know about you, Rio," Jonathan Kirby said, leaning forward in his seat, "but I always hate it when the woman in my life doesn't want to make love with me. I end up feeling like I don't matter to her. I start to think she's more interested in my bringing home a paycheck or fixing the car. That she wants my money and what I can do for her, but that she isn't interested in me as a person. When she doesn't want to get close physically, I wonder if she cares about me at all."

Rio straightened. "Yeah. You're right."

Jonathan nodded. "When I want to make love and she doesn't, I don't get to hold her and feel all those good feelings that come from being close. I don't get to express my emotions, because for us guys, sex is usually the easiest way to tell our partner we love her."

It was as if a weight had been lifted off Rio's shoulders. He turned to Chris. "What he said."

His ex-wife stared at him. "I never thought of you as just a paycheck."

Probably because she made more than he did, he thought glumly. "Okay, maybe, but I never felt like I mattered. I was in the doghouse all the time. Then you'd tell me we couldn't do it and that left me with nothing."

"I understand that," Chris said. "But when you—" She glanced at Dr. McGuire and sighed. "When *I* talk and talk and feel as if I'm not being heard, I get frustrated. I felt as if the only time you paid attention to me was when you wanted to get laid. I wanted to be noticed the rest of the time, too."

Chris finished talking. Rio didn't know what to say to that. It was easy to snuggle up next to her when he wanted to slip into the bedroom with her, but the rest of the time, he just didn't think about it. He glanced at Jonathan, but the doctor wasn't looking at him. Instead he was staring at the table, a troubled expression on his face.

"Doc?"

Jonathan started. "I'm sorry, Rio. Do you want to respond to what Chris said?"

"I was kinda hoping you'd do it for me."

Jonathan smiled. "I just wanted to get things started before. Now you're on your own."

Rio nodded. Both psychologists seemed a little distracted this morning.

"Okay," he said slowly. "I get the whole ignoring part. You used to tell me that you wanted me to hug you and stuff when it wasn't about sex. That you wanted to be close physically without having to worry that I'd grope you."

Chris nodded. "That's right."

"So what about the way you always yelled at me?" He held up a hand before Dr. McGuire could interrupt. "I know—'I' sentences. I got yelled at a lot. When I helped around the house, I was told I was doing it wrong or that she'd rather do it herself. I didn't buy the right tomato sauce or I fed the kids the wrong thing for lunch. Finally, I just stopped trying."

When he finished he was rather pleased with himself for getting that all out. Chris clutched the arms of her chair.

"Was I really that much of a bitch?"

"Sometimes. You have a lot of rules."

Chris nodded. "I know. I'm not sure why. Maybe because I like being right and you being wrong."

"Marriage isn't about competition," Dr. McGuire said. She smiled. "What about being on the same team? You could try working together for a change."

Chris shook her head. "I can't always trust him to keep his word."

Dr. McGuire glanced at him. "Rio? Is that true? Do you promise things and then forget to follow through?"

"Sometimes. Things happen."

"You can't expect Chris to trust you if you're not trustworthy. Sometimes women control the little things because they feel so out of control about the big things."

He glanced at Jonathan, but once again he had the sense the other man wasn't fully participating in the conversation.

"How about if I don't make any promises I can't keep?" Rio asked.

Chris looked uncomfortable. "It's easy to say I'll give you a second chance in the trust department, but I'm afraid."

"How about starting with something small?" Dr. McGuire suggested. "You're both right. Rio needs a chance to prove himself and Chris needs time to build up her ability to trust."

"I'll think about it," Chris promised.

Dr. McGuire glanced at Jonathan, then said it was a good place to end their session. They all shook hands and Chris and Rio left.

Rio held the door open for Chris, then followed her out onto the street.

"What'd you think about our session?" Rio asked, shrugging on his jacket.

"I don't know. I kept feeling like they were distracted or something."

"Me, too." He shoved his hands into his jeans pockets. "But I thought a couple of the ideas were really good. I'd like you to trust me more."

She stared at him. "I didn't stop wanting sex to punish you," she said. "I was just so mad all the time."

"I know. I didn't make it easy."

They both looked away. What he really wanted to say was that he was sorry because now he'd lost the right to touch her and he desperately wanted to feel her warm body next to him. Not just because he wanted to make love with her, although he did, but because they'd always fit together. He missed the scent of her and the way they'd always slept tangled up together. They never did that anymore. He slept in their bed the nights Chris was working, but when she was home, he slept on the sofa.

He gave her a quick smile. "So, now what?"

"You want to get some lunch or something?"

He really wanted the "or something" but he knew this wasn't the time. Dr. McGuire had been right. If he wanted to earn back Chris's trust, he was going to have to do it one step at a time.

"Lunch sounds great."

Jonathan arrived at Taylor's house promptly at six that evening. Their discussion after their sessions had ended with the agreement that he would meet Linnie this evening without telling her who he was. Then he and Taylor would strategize about the best way to explain how he'd come to be in her life after all this time. If he didn't kill Taylor first.

He couldn't remember ever being this angry. Every time he thought about what she'd done, how she'd *lied* to him for years. He wanted to find a way to wound her as deeply as she'd wounded him. He couldn't believe the last couple of weeks. All their oh-so-friendly conversations. The teasing. The kissing. He swore again. He'd been an idiot.

He rang the doorbell, then waited for the sound of footsteps. Taylor opened the door and tried to smile, but her lips barely turned up at the corners. She looked nervous and guilty, which made him feel better.

"Come on in," she said stepping back. "My mom is making lasagna, which is Linnie's favorite. And salad. I know. Not a guy food, but this *is* a houseful of women. Oh, and a few of Linnie's friends are coming over after dinner. They're all going upstairs to watch movies together and do their nails. I always forget how much teenage girls giggle until they're in the same room and the sound echoes through the house."

She paused for breath, then smoothed the front of her skirt before closing the door behind him. "Sorry. I'm babbling."

She wore a fitted red sweater over a narrow black skirt. Sometime in the afternoon, she'd tamed her hair into its usual sleek style. Makeup accentuated her features, making her eyes seem bigger. For the first time since he'd seen her on the set of *Psychology in the News*, he thought she appeared fragile.

"You don't have to look so panicked," he told her. "I'm not going to kill you in your own home."

"I suppose that's something. I must remember never to leave the house." She tried for a smile and failed.

"Do you blame me for being pissed off?" he asked.

"No. I don't actually blame either of us. A sentiment you don't share."

"You're right about that."

The sound of someone coming downstairs interrupted them. Jonathan realized he didn't know what

Taylor had told her daughter about him. For all he knew, Linnie thought her father was dead.

Then she was standing in front of him, smiling, and he could only stare at her, trying to memorize her beautiful face.

"I'm Linnie," the teenager said, holding out her hand. "You're Dr. Kirby, right? I saw you at the press conference today."

Her mouth was full, the shape more like his than Taylor's. Big blue eyes studied him. She was taller than her mother and had an air of maturity about her. Yet she was still painfully young. Jonathan winced when he thought of all she still had to go through. Teenage years were hell.

"Nice to meet you, Linnie," he said, shaking her hand and releasing her, unable to believe this was really happening. "Please call me Jonathan."

Linnie's smile turned into a grin. "Sure. So is my mom going to win this contest or are you?"

"So far it's a tie."

Linnie moved to her mother and linked arms with her. "I've read over Mom's thesis and it makes a lot of sense to me. I guess I'll have to read one of your books before I can decide who I think is right."

Taylor patted her daughter's arm. "You, young lady, don't get a vote." She motioned toward the dining room. "I think dinner is about ready. Let's go on in."

Linnie glanced at her watch. "Everyone should be here in an hour. Is that enough time?"

Jonathan wanted to say that it wasn't. He was eager to spend as much time as he could with Linnie and get to know her. He'd already missed too much—the transition from toddler to child and child to teenager. He wanted to turn back time and claim every moment he'd missed. She'd grown up without knowing he was alive. How was that possible?

Taylor glanced at him and he had the impression that she could read his mind. She shrugged an apology.

"An hour should be fine," she said, leading them into the dining room.

Linda was already there, setting out plates of salad. She greeted him and motioned for him to sit at the head of the table.

"We only let good-looking men sit there," she said in a mock whisper.

He saw the sympathy in her eyes and suddenly knew why she'd asked him about children the last time he'd been here.

"I ate here once before and you didn't put me there," he reminded her, trying to act normal when all he wanted was to get the world to stop turning for a while. Just until he got his equilibrium back.

Linda winked. "Maybe you weren't so good-looking then."

Linnie giggled. "Grandma, are you flirting with Jonathan?"

Linda touched her fingertips to her chest. "Not me. I'm just an old woman."

"You *are* flirting. Wow. What else happened while I was gone?"

"Nothing very interesting," Taylor said, sitting on Jonathan's left and indicating that her daughter should sit on his right.

Linda left the dining room, then returned with a large casserole dish of lasagna. Taylor handed him a bottle of red wine to open. Linnie poured them each a glass of ice water.

"Our Linnie is a counselor at a camp for deaf children in Virginia," Linda said as she served the lasagna. "Tell Jonathan about it, dear."

Linnie tossed her head, sending her brown hair flying over her shoulder. "I don't think he'd find it very interesting, Grandma."

"I *would* like to hear all about it," Jonathan said honestly. "Do you miss being home?"

"Sometimes." She wrinkled her nose. "But it's a great opportunity. My sign language is really improving." She grinned and leaned toward him. "But what Grandma didn't explain was that it's an all-girls camp. And I go to an all-girls school. Can you believe it? I barely know what boys look like."

She passed Jonathan a plate of lasagna, then reached for the garlic rolls. "It's kinda weird not to have guys around, but I'm getting used to it. In a way it's nice not to have to worry about being too smart. And I was teasing before. We see them—boys, I mean. At things like dances or sporting events. It's kinda cool to hang out with guys that way, although a lot of them are really full of themselves."

She straightened in her chair and squared her shoulders. "Randolph Prescott the forty-second," she mimicked in a grave voice. "My great-great-great-grandparents invented fire."

Jonathan chuckled. "Are they all pretentious?"

"No. Some of them are nerds and those are the ones I like best. They're kinda quiet and shy, but once you get them talking, they're pretty interesting."

"What are your favorite subjects in school?" he asked.

"Math and languages. But I don't know what I'd do with *that* in college."

"Are there any special boys?" Taylor asked, then took a bite of her salad.

Linnie rolled her eyes. "Mo-om, you always ask me that." She returned her attention to Jonathan. "Mom worries about me being responsible where boys are concerned. She had me when she was really young and she doesn't want me getting pregnant for a long time." Color stained Linnie's cheeks. "As if."

Jonathan poured each of the adults a glass of wine. He picked up his fork. "You didn't answer the question."

Linnie frowned, then laughed. "Okay. No. I don't have anyone special. I've barely kissed a boy. Geez. Why is everyone so interested in my love life? Make that *lack* of love life."

"I'm nosy," Jonathan teased. "I don't know what their excuses are."

Linnie laughed. "So you're a psychologist, right? Like my mom?"

"Jonathan's a little out of my league," Taylor said. "He's been practicing for a lot longer. He's written what, thirty books?"

He nodded. "About that. Actually, I don't have a private practice anymore. I mostly write and lecture. A few times a year I have weekend seminars."

Linnie chewed, then swallowed. "I think I've seen you on television. That show Mom watches."

"*Psychology in the News,*" Taylor clarified.

The conversation shifted to the contest. Linnie was bright and opinionated, but not in a rude way. She teased both her mother and grandmother, asked him questions and generally charmed the group. He saw sparks of Taylor in her, and a lot of himself. Her interest in math, for one. The way she tilted her head, the gesture she made when she didn't believe what she was being told. He wanted to protest when all too quickly the doorbell rang and her friends arrived. They hadn't had nearly enough time together.

But Linnie was already pushing back her chair. "I'll get that," she said as she rose to her feet. "It was really nice to meet you," she told him, then left the room.

Linda followed her. "Those girls are always hungry. I better go see how many of them want dessert."

When they were alone, Taylor set down her fork. "You didn't touch your dinner."

He glanced at his full plate. "I'm sure it was excellent." Unexpected anger returned to rush through him. He turned toward her. "I'll never forgive you for this," he said in a low voice so Linnie and her friends wouldn't hear him. "How dare you keep her from me? I had every right to know about her existence. I would have wanted to be a part of her life."

Taylor didn't flinch from his harsh tone. "Easy enough to say now," she reminded him. "You were the one trying so hard to end the relationship seventeen years ago. You'd made it clear you didn't want anything to do with me."

"We're not talking about you. This is about my daughter."

"I'll never believe you would have willingly given up everything you ever wanted to take care of her. Being the best was always too important."

He leaned close and glared at her. "That's convenient. Now you never have to take responsibility for what you did."

He had the satisfaction of seeing her flush. "I do take responsibility. I agonized over that decision. Don't you think I wanted us to be a family? Do you think I liked raising her by myself?"

"I think you liked it just fine. You got to be Saint Taylor, while I was just the bastard who knocked you up."

Her eyes widened. For a second he thought she was going to cry, but instead she pressed her fingertips to her mouth and swallowed.

"I was a kid, Jonathan. When I ran off with you, I was two months younger than Linnie is now. Don't you dare tell me I should have done better. You were nineteen when we met and twenty-one when I left you. Why didn't you act like a grown-up?"

Taylor had been Linnie's age? He thought of the charming young woman who had sat next to him at dinner and was stunned. If someone like him tried to do that to Linnie—take her away, disrupt her life—he'd kill him. He would rip him apart with his bare hands. Not that he would concede the point to Taylor.

"What part of my behavior wasn't mature?" he asked. "When I honestly confessed that my feelings had changed? Or wasn't I supposed to ever end it? Is that my real sin? That I dared to fall out of love with you?"

She tossed her napkin onto the table. "Fine. This is all my fault. You were so incredibly perfect. Every act could be considered a model of optimum behavior.

I'm so sorry that the rest of us can't match your glorious perfection. It must be damned annoying to have to live in such a crappy world with lousy people who can't get it right. There! Are you happy now? Heaven forbid we should work on the problem or try to find a solution when it's so much more satisfying to assign blame."

She rose and stalked out of the dining room.

Linda appeared in the kitchen door. "You're having quite a day."

He shook his head. "I guess you're next. While I think Taylor was out of line, I know I deserve whatever you have to say."

She crossed to the table and sat down three chairs away. "There was a time when I wanted you killed," she admitted. "Or at the very least, thrown in jail. Do you know why I didn't do it?"

"Sure. Taylor threatened to run away if you did. She said you'd never find her again."

Linda nodded. "You can't know what that felt like. In a few years, when you've come to know and love Linnie as we do, you'll begin to understand all the pain I went through. My daughter and I had been so close for so many years. Then she met you and nothing else mattered." Blue-gray eyes stared into his soul. "She loved you with all her heart."

He nodded. "I know that."

"So if you believe she loved you that much, why would you think she did anything but make what she considered the best decision possible for you when she found out she was pregnant?"

"Don't cloud the issue with facts," he said with a

lightness he didn't feel. Staying angry with Taylor was the only way to stay in control of the situation.

"Taylor is Linnie's mother. If you don't come to terms with her, you'll never have a relationship with her daughter. Don't let your anger and pride destroy what you've only just found."

Chapter
15

*M*arnie sighed with contentment as she reached for the dice. A fire crackled in the fireplace, a glass of brandy sat on the coffee table in front of her and a very cute guy in glasses lounged next to her. Not bad for a Saturday night.

She tossed the dice, then counted forward and did a little shimmy in her seat. "I believe I need that one," she said, thrusting the box of questions at Will.

He pushed up his glasses as he took a card. "I'd hoped that by switching to the Millennium Edition I'd even the odds."

She leaned toward him and smiled. "But you were wrong, weren't you? At least we're not still playing for money."

He gently pushed at her shoulder, easing her back onto her side of the sofa. "Quit trying to read the answers," he said, covering the back of the card.

She gasped and placed the back of her hand on her forehead. "Are you accusing me of cheating, sir?

Me? A demure flower in the garden that is Southern womanhood?"

Her play-acting was rewarded by a slow grin. "Marnie, you're a lot of things, but demure isn't one of them."

She felt a shiver go through her when she heard the confidence in his voice. They'd come a long way in just a week. They'd sat up playing Trivial Pursuit five nights out of the past nine. He'd dined with her twice and had even stopped to chat before leaving for work on both Thursday and Friday mornings. Not that she was keeping track.

He picked up his brandy. "This is a great room, Marnie."

She glanced around at the French doors, the bookshelves and the fireplace large enough to house a family of four. "I like it, too," she admitted. "At least in here my voice doesn't echo the way it does in some of the rooms. I swear, it took me nearly a week to find my way around this place when George first brought me here."

Will put down both the question card and the brandy, then leaned into the corner with his arm draped along the back of the sofa. "You didn't grow up in a place like this?"

"Honey, I grew up in a trailer. Granted it was a double-wide, which was a big deal where I came from." She smiled. "The first time I saw this place, I thought it was a hotel."

"Tell me about growing up."

"Because it's something you haven't done yet?"

One corner of his mouth twitched, but he didn't actually smile. Even so, she knew he liked her teasing. She could tell by the laughter in his hazel eyes. Oh my, who would have thought she could fall so hard for a guy wearing glasses? In the past week she'd discovered that he was basically a sweet man who didn't have a clue about people in general or women in particular. She didn't know why some other woman hadn't snatched him up, but she wasn't about to question her good fortune.

"I have three sisters. I'm the second from the bottom, as my father used to say. We fought every day of our lives. Since leaving home I've found we can have perfect relationships as long as we're never in the same room."

"You speak on the phone?"

"Every week. About two years ago, we lost our heads and agreed to go home for Christmas." She shuddered at the memory. "It was so horrible, we didn't speak for at least three months after. We're just now starting to recover from the experience." She laughed. "Some people are not meant to be in the same room."

"You left home after high school, right?" he asked. "You said that you moved to Houston and put yourself through beauty school."

"That's me." She glanced down at her nails. Tonight she had painted little roses on them. "I remember hearing an interview with Dolly Parton once. She talked about growing up in a tiny town where the most glamorous women were the local prostitutes. She always thought they were so beautiful with their trashy clothes and makeup. When she grew up, she wanted to look just like them." She shrugged. "I guess I have a little bit of that in me, too. I try for elegant, but it never quite ends up that way."

"I think you're very beautiful," he said with an

earnestness that made her heart skip a beat. "And elegant."

"You do?"

He nodded.

My, but it seems a tad warm in the room, she thought as she cleared her throat. "Yes, well, it's something I wrestle with. I never know what to wear. It's a girl thing."

"You're definitely a girl."

He put his fingers over hers. He actually touched her! His large hand dwarfed hers, making her feel small and delicate . . . something that didn't happen very often.

"W-will?" She nearly groaned. Great. The man touched her hand and she started stuttering.

He smiled. A slow, sexy, male smile she'd never seen on him before. Her crush had turned into genuine liking. While she was scared to death at the thought of another man in her life, she wasn't about to turn her back on the first one who had interested her since George's passing.

"You're nothing like I thought you'd be," he said quietly.

Was it her imagination or had the man moved closer? And why didn't he kiss her? Couldn't he see she wanted him to? Marnie thought about making the first move, but sensed it would be a mistake. Instead she waited, not daring to hold her breath for fear she would faint.

Finally, after what felt like fifteen *hours,* he slid toward her. The hand that had been on the back of the sofa gently touched her shoulder. The fingers over hers tightened slightly. She raised her head and prepared for the brush of his lips against hers. Excitement fluttered in her stomach.

He moved closer and closer until she could feel his

breath on her face. Then nothing. He just sort of hovered there. Marnie thought she was going to scream. She waited—anxious and frustrated and aroused. Finally, when she couldn't wait any longer she bridged the final inch or so and pressed her mouth to his.

Unfortunately he'd decided to move as well and they collided with more force than was comfortable. She yelped softly and turned her head. Their noses bumped. Somehow she'd pulled one of her hands free of his touch and without realizing it, she caught the corner of his glasses on her finger, nearly jerking them off his head. Their knees knocked together painfully as they both withdrew. Will shot back to his corner of the sofa.

Marnie wanted to die. Could her first kiss—make that attempted kiss—in four years have gone worse?

"That went badly," she said, trying for humor. "I guess I'm out of practice."

When Will didn't say anything, Marnie looked at him. He was staring at her with the strangest expression on his face.

"You think this was *your* fault?" he finally asked.

"I don't think it was anyone's fault. I think we need to practice." *Hopefully with each other,* she thought.

He looked like he was going to bolt. Her heart tightened in her chest. Then he smiled.

"I'd like that," he said.

"More practice?"

"Absolutely."

"Good. Me, too."

He rose and reached down to help her to her feet. When she was standing, he tentatively put a hand on her waist and drew her close to him.

He was tall enough that she had to tilt her head to meet his gaze. His lean, runner's body was hard to her soft, and very masculine. He leaned toward her, then stopped.

"Wait," he said and slipped off his glasses.

Without the lenses to conceal them, his irises appeared more blue than green. She saw flecks of gold and brown as well. Heat radiated out from him and as she leaned a little closer, something hard brushed against her belly. The proof of his arousal made her go all gooey inside.

His mouth settled on hers. This time they managed to avoid bumping or crashing together. Instead there was only a warm, sweet pressure on her lips, and a heat that made her feel sexy, feminine, and safe.

For several heartbeats, he didn't do anything else. Marnie waited patiently, enjoying the way her breasts nestled into his hard chest and the gentle squeeze of his hand on her waist. Then he moved his mouth, brushing back and forth, as if discovering her. His free hand cupped the back of her head and his fingers tangled in her hair.

There was nothing smooth or practiced about his touch. He didn't seem to have a style with women, or a routine he favored. But the awkwardness felt good. Oddly, it comforted her, allowing her to relax. If he wasn't some kind of Lothario in disguise, she wouldn't be expected to be a femme fatale. Normal was very comforting.

She shifted a little closer, wanting to feel the pressure of his arousal. His hard muscles begged to be explored, so she trailed her fingers down his back, feeling skin shift beneath her touch. Slowly, almost as if he wasn't sure he was supposed to be doing this, his lips parted. She felt the brush of his tongue on her lower lip.

Marnie expected to like being kissed by Will. She welcomed the almost forgotten sensation of pressure between her legs as her body swelled and dampened. She'd hoped that they would find each other attractive and that his kiss would make her blood heat and pulse.

She hadn't expected to go up in flames.

The second his tongue touched her lower lip, she wanted to sob. Need crashed through her, making her cling to him to keep from falling. She couldn't open her mouth fast enough. When he slipped inside and stroked her tongue with his, she had to hold on in a whimper of pure ecstasy.

She longed to grab his hands and place them on her full curves, begging him to touch her there. That part of her, so long asleep, came painfully awake. The tingly, prickling sensation was as arousing as it was uncomfortable. She could feel the dampness of her panties. One thrust, she thought hazily. One deep thrust and she would be lost forever.

Her hips pulsed against him. She shifted, trying to place her sensitive center along the length of him. Will deepened the kiss, plunging into her, mimicking the act of love. One of his hands dropped to her rear, pushing her up against him more. She gasped as her heat made contact with him.

And then he was gone. Marnie didn't get it right away. One second they'd been clinging to each other, kissing with a passion she couldn't remember ever experiencing, the next she was barely able to stand on her own. She sank onto the sofa.

"I didn't expect that," he said, as he walked to the fireplace and leaned heavily against the mantel.

"Me, either."

"I'm sorry if I got carried away."

"You did," she murmured. "You were great."

"You, too. You really know how to kiss."

She blushed.

They stared at each other. It was one of those awkward moments. Marnie couldn't think of anything to say that wasn't completely stupid. What she really wanted to do was take off all her clothes and beg him to have his way with her. She doubted that would be very wise or successful. Will obviously preferred to take things slowly.

"I, ah . . ." He straightened. "I guess I should say good night."

She nodded because her throat was suddenly too tight for her to speak.

"See you tomorrow," he said.

She nodded again.

And then he was gone. Marnie was left staring at the place where he'd been, feeling her body still burning, wondering if what had just happened had been an exciting revelation or a cruel twist of fate.

Jonathan's cell phone rang around nine on Sunday morning. At first he thought it was Taylor. While he didn't want to speak with her, he knew there were dozens of unresolved issues between them. The mature response would be to answer the call. Then he remembered that she didn't know his cell-phone number and hit the "talk" button.

"Kirby," he said.

"Jonathan, it's Irene. I didn't think Marriageville was big enough to hide in, but I've been trying to reach you since late Friday. I have some feedback on your shows."

His mind was slow to understand what she was saying. *Shows? Oh—the talk shows.* His potential deal with the syndication people. His trip to New York and Los Angeles seemed to have happened in a different lifetime.

He paced to the window and stared out at the town. "What did they say?"

"It's good news. They thought you were terrific. Which means I'm going to ask for more money."

"I'm all in favor of that."

Irene talked for several minutes about the various opportunities and what would be expected of him if he agreed to the show. He barely listened.

"I have another intriguing piece of news," she said. "Your editor called. It seems that they're interested in Taylor McGuire's book. Bidding has been getting more intense. The rumor is that the offers are around five hundred thousand dollars."

So Taylor was going to get everything she wanted. A book sale with a large advance, along with enough publicity to ease her onto the best-seller list.

His rage flared to life, burning inside of him. He still couldn't believe how she'd screwed him, keeping Linnie from him.

"What if I don't want them to buy her?" he asked.

Irene hesitated. "Jonathan, your publisher doesn't

want to lose you, but they're not going to be comfortable taking orders from one of their authors."

"What if I know something?"

"Like what?"

He didn't answer. He knew the business. If he even hinted that Taylor's research was questionable, that some of the ideas weren't her own, the interest in her would disappear like so much mist on a sunny day. He could destroy her with a single lie.

"Jonathan?"

He shook his head. "Forget it. Just let me know what happens."

Early Sunday afternoon Taylor knocked on Jonathan's hotel room door. The previous evening, he'd left without them coming to some kind of a decision about how to handle things with Linnie. She was only in town for a week, so they had to get their act together before their daughter left to go back to school.

She leaned against the hallway wall. *Their* daughter. Linnie was theirs. For so many years she'd thought of her child as hers alone, but that wasn't right. She was Jonathan's as well.

The door opened and the man in question stared at her. After finally getting used to having Jonathan in town, she was suddenly facing a stranger. She didn't know the cold-eyed man in front of her.

"Hi," she said, straightening away from the wall. "Thanks for agreeing to see me."

He stepped back to allow her to enter his suite. "What choice did I have? You're holding all the cards."

Her stomach tightened. "You're not going to make

this easy for me, are you? No matter what I say, you're the victim."

His expression stayed angry. "It's pretty hard to work up sympathy for you under the circumstances."

He wore jeans, scuffed boots and a short-sleeved shirt. Not the suits she was used to seeing on him. The jeans were worn, fading at the seams by his hips and crotch. He was the best-looking man she'd ever been involved with—the only one she'd ever loved and if he had his way, she would be hit by a truck on her way home. Or maybe he would consider that too easy a punishment for her crime.

"We have to come to some kind of understanding," she said firmly as she sat on the sofa. "About Linnie. You can hate me all you want, but the bottom line is we're going to have to work together on this and present a united front. Linnie's not stupid. If we're fighting, she'll figure it out."

Jonathan sat across from her and leaned forward, resting his elbows on his knees. "I don't know what to say to you. I'm furious. The feeling goes past reason, all the way down to the gut. I listened to what you said last night. Your mother made a couple of good points as well, defending you. I hear the words, I understand what they mean and it doesn't matter a damn." He raised his head and stared at her.

Taylor looked back, unable to come up with any response. She'd spent much of the previous night trying to imagine this conversation. But knowing he was angry and facing the emotion was two different things.

"I'm sorry," she said. Her throat tightened. "I can't—" She realized then that there was absolutely nothing to say.

She rose to her feet and headed for the door. Jonathan came after her, slamming his hand against the door, preventing her from leaving.

"You're not getting off so easily," he growled. "Not like you did the last time."

Tears burned in her eyes. She blinked them away. "Do you really think it was easy?" she asked. "You threw me out of your life. You told me to pack up and go home. You never wanted to see me again. I loved you so much I thought I was going to die."

"That has nothing to do with this."

"It has everything to do with it. I didn't even know I was pregnant until a month later. I didn't know what to do. Once I knew about the baby, I picked up the phone to call you and tell you dozens of times. Then I would remember how you'd wanted out of our relationship. One day I decided you had the right to know. So I called. Rita answered."

His dark gaze bore into her. She stared back, unflinching. She had nothing to hide.

"I hung up," she said. "I told myself if you ever phoned me, I would tell you the truth. But you didn't."

"So this is my fault?"

"No. I'll accept responsibility. I'm telling you what happened. I knew you wouldn't want me and I genuinely believed a baby would only mess up your rise to the top."

He turned away and swore. She watched him pace to the window and back, his body stiff, his gaze icy. His anger and confusion circled around her, making her want to bolt again. But she stood her ground. They had to come to terms with the past and figure out how to handle this . . . for Linnie's sake.

Jonathan wanted to rage against the unfairness of it all. He still wanted Taylor punished and wanted her to pay. But more than that, he wanted time back. He wanted the chance to decide for himself. He wanted his daughter.

"Have a seat," he said quietly. "You're right about us presenting a united front. Let's talk about it."

Taylor eyed him suspiciously. "Why are you suddenly willing to be cooperative?"

"Because I don't have a choice. Linnie is more important than both of us."

Taylor returned to the sofa. Every movement of her body spoke of her reluctance. She sat, then drew in a deep breath. He watched the strength flow into her as she dug deep for the resolve necessary to carry her through.

"You're right," she told him. "We have to think about Linnie. Where do you want to start?"

"What does she know about me?" he asked.

"That her father was someone I had a relationship with for a couple of years. She knows that I was deeply in love with you and that I ran away to be with you." She shrugged. "I explained that we broke up because I wanted to get married and you wanted to move on, that I didn't know I was pregnant until later and that my decision to not tell you about her was based on my belief that you already had made plans for your life and that you didn't deserve me messing that up."

He raised his eyebrows. "Wouldn't it have been easier to make me the bad guy?"

"Probably, but that's not what happened and I'm not that much of a bitch." She pressed her lips together.

"Jonathan, I always thought I did the right thing in keeping my pregnancy from you. Maybe there was some subconscious desire to be the martyr. I don't know. Now, with hindsight, I'm not so sure about what I did." She raised her hands, palms out, and shrugged, then dropped her hands to her lap. "I can't change what happened. I'm sorry."

He wanted to tell her that wasn't good enough. But there wasn't any point.

"Did she want to know about me?" he asked.

"Absolutely. We had some fairly difficult times because I wanted to wait until she was eighteen to tell her. She didn't agree with my timetable."

So Linnie had wanted to find him and Taylor had prevented her. The anger returned and it took every ounce of willpower to push it down.

"Why didn't you give her my name?"

"I didn't know if you'd want her." Her steady gaze met his. "I followed your career, Jonathan. I read your books, I watched your various interviews. I heard about your marriage and subsequent divorce. I was trying to figure out who you were and if you would be interested in your daughter. I was never sure."

"You could have asked me."

"Once I did that, there would be no going back."

"This contest really screwed up your plan."

"Tell me about it. I didn't know what to do. But the more I got to know you, the more I liked the man you'd come to be. I knew you'd be a good father to Linnie."

"Who left you in charge?" he asked angrily. "You had no right to decide if I would be a good father or not. She's my child, too."

"It's not that simple."

"Not now, but it should have been." He stood and walked to the window. He stared down at the town where his child had grown up.

"I'd prefer to be there when you tell her," Taylor said. "It's going to be a shock."

"For all of us." His first instinct was to refuse her request, then he reminded himself that he didn't know Linnie and she didn't know him. She might get frightened.

"We'll tell her together," he said.

"For what it's worth, she's going to be thrilled with you," Taylor said.

Jonathan glanced at her. "Why do you say that?"

For the first time since walking into his suite, Taylor smiled. "Gee, I don't know. Maybe because you're handsome, successful, charming and I'm guessing fairly well-off. What's not to like?"

He didn't respond. In some ways he couldn't believe this was happening. "When?" he asked.

"She's visiting friends today and will probably spend the night. How about tomorrow evening?"

"All right."

"Anything else?" she asked.

He shook his head.

She stood and this time he didn't stop her. When she reached the door, she paused to look at him.

"I *am* sorry," she said softly. "I know that doesn't matter, but it's true."

Chapter
16

$\mathcal{G}$race carefully scooped the two poached eggs onto crisp toast and added a tomato garnish to the plate. She told herself she was being silly, taking so much time over breakfast, but she couldn't help herself. She enjoyed cooking for Nelson. He never failed to thank her for her efforts. Once or twice he'd even let slip that his late wife hadn't been much interested in cooking. That information had spurred Grace on even more than his praise.

She knew she was acting foolish. There wasn't any competition between her and Nelson's late wife. There wasn't a competition with anyone. He was in her life for a month and she didn't allow herself to think past that time. She should simply enjoy his company and stop trying to impress him.

But she couldn't help herself. She liked making Nelson smile. Maybe this wasn't all that different from the flowers he'd brought her two days before. She looked at the mixed bouquet she'd placed in her only vase and had placed in the center of the kitchen table. The flowers' soft scent and beautiful colors made her feel all fluttery inside every time she noticed them.

She picked up the plate she'd warmed and carried it to the table. As she leaned forward to set it at Nelson's place, Alexander wound his way around her ankles.

It was something he'd done a thousand times before. Something she was used to. But for some reason, his action startled her. She shrieked and jumped back. At the same instant, she let go of the plate. It teetered on the edge of the table, then slid toward Nelson's seat. She watched helplessly as food tumbled onto his chair. The plate bounced once, then hit the floor. The sound of shattering china filled the room.

Grace stared in horror at the mess. She couldn't possibly clean up everything and make another breakfast in time. Panic filled her. Panic and fear. She heard rapid footsteps as Nelson hurried to see what had happened.

"Grace! Are you all right?"

Instinctively, she shrank from him. She half turned away so that when he hit her, the blow would fall on her shoulder or back.

"I'm sorry," she whispered. "I'm sorry. I'll clean it right up. I'm sorry."

"Grace, don't apologize. It was an accident."

She heard the words. He sounded kind, but she knew better than to believe him. He wanted her to turn toward him. Then he would hit her. Then he would—

"How often did Alan hit you?" he asked flatly.

Shame poured through her. Heat flared on her cheeks and she wanted to curl up and die. It was her fault. It had always been her fault. Alan had told her so many times.

"Grace?"

Nelson moved toward her. When he took her arm, she flinched, but instead of striking her, he simply led her over to a chair and urged her to sit down. He crouched at her feet.

"Tell me," he insisted softly. "How long did he make your life hell?"

Shocked by his unexpected language, she found herself staring at him before she could stop herself. Once she'd gazed into his eyes, she found she couldn't look away. Not while he looked at her with such compassion and understanding. Tears burned but she blinked them away.

"Five years," she whispered, compelled to tell him the truth. "He'd always been difficult. He drank a lot. I thought it was my fault, that if I was a better wife, he wouldn't have been so mean. He told me I deserved his anger because I'd been unable to give him children and because I was worthless. I believed him."

Nelson shook his head slowly. "You know better now, don't you?"

"Most of the time." She swallowed. "About five years before he died, he lost his job. Then the drinking got worse and he started—" She made a vague motion. "The beatings were never bad. I went to a shelter once, but when I saw all those young women with their horrible bruises and broken bones, I knew that what I had to endure wasn't all that awful. So I came home."

"I'm sorry." Nelson lightly touched her hand. "I'm so sorry. I know God expects more of me, but I have never been able to forgive those who use physical punishment to make themselves feel like men."

"You don't understand," she said, knowing she had

to confess her greatest sin to him. "I was happy when he died."

"Of course you were. Why wouldn't you want a man like him dead? I'm happy, too. And if he wasn't already gone, I'd be tempted to take care of him myself."

His fierce words should have frightened her, but they didn't. Instead, for the first time since she could remember, her heart felt light, as if it could flutter away.

"I will never hurt you," Nelson told her.

She hesitated, then spoke from her soul. "I believe you."

He glanced at the mess on the other side of the table. "Why don't we clean it up together. Afterwards, I'll fix *you* breakfast for a change."

She couldn't believe it. Fix a meal for her?

"Do you know how?" she asked before she could stop herself.

He laughed. "I guess you're going to have to wait and find out."

Taylor tried to act normal as she stood in the living room of the house where she and her daughter had grown up. She hadn't been able to eat anything at dinner and the little she'd had for lunch sat heavily in her stomach. She couldn't remember ever being this nervous before. Jonathan didn't seem to be doing much better as he paced back and forth.

"What if she decides I'm not the one she wants as her dad?" he asked, then looked as if he wanted to call back the question.

Taylor remembered growing up without a father. She would have sold her soul to have a man as wonderful as Jonathan want to claim her as his own.

"You don't have to worry. Linnie is going to be thrilled." Taylor was much more concerned about her daughter being resentful toward her.

She heard footsteps overhead. Linnie had been on the phone with a girlfriend when Jonathan had arrived. Taylor had asked her to hurry down as soon as she was finished. Now her daughter raced down the carpeted steps and flew into the living room.

"I'm here," she said, her long hair pulled back into a braid, her eyes bright with curiosity. "What's up?"

Her gaze settled on the two of them standing in the center of the room. With a small gasp, she pressed one hand to her chest.

"I know! I know!" She spun in a circle on the hardwood floor. "You two have fallen madly in love and you're getting married. Oh, Mom, this is so cool."

Despite the fact that she wasn't drinking anything, Taylor nearly choked. She didn't dare glance at Jonathan, who was no doubt equally shocked.

"No, Linnie. That's not it at all." Taylor took her hand and led her to the sofa. "Have a seat. We need to talk."

Linnie did as she requested, then wrinkled her nose. "When you say 'let's talk' it's never good news. But I can't remember doing anything wrong." She eyed Jonathan, who hovered by the coffee table but didn't actually take a seat. "It's gotta be pretty bad if you're bringing in another psychologist."

"What?" Taylor shook her head. "No. It's not anything like that. You're not in trouble. Everything is great. And confusing."

She angled toward her daughter, studying the face she'd memorized the first hour after Linnie had been born. She saw the blending of features—the shape of his mouth, her skin color. Their genes had somehow created this perfect, wonderful child.

Taylor glanced at Jonathan, who shoved his hands into his slacks pockets and shrugged as if to say he was at a loss, too. Linnie waited expectantly.

She took her daughter's hand and squeezed it. "Linnie, I've tried hard to be honest with you. You know that when I was your age, I ran off to live with a boy. I was young and foolish and it seemed like a good idea at the time."

Linnie pulled her hand free and rolled her eyes. "Mom, I know this, okay? I'm not dating anyone, let alone thinking about running off. You don't have to worry about me."

Despite her tension, Taylor couldn't help smiling. "I know, Linnie. My point was more about me than you. I decided not to tell him about you because I thought if he didn't want a relationship with me, he might not want to be burdened with a child, either. I was afraid he would insist on doing the right thing and I didn't want to trap him. But by doing that, I took away his choice. He never got to say if he wanted to be a part of your life or not."

Her daughter stiffened. She slowly turned her head to look at Jonathan, then returned her attention to Taylor. Her eyes widened. "Mom?"

Taylor nodded. "Jonathan is the boy I ran off with when I was your age. He didn't find out about you until a couple of days ago. He's your father."

Jonathan stared at his daughter, and Linnie stared back. Taylor wanted to say something brilliant that would make the situation better for both of them, but her mind didn't cooperate. Silence filled the room, stretching and bending until she thought they might all be crushed by the endless quiet.

Linnie spoke first. "I thought about this happening a lot of times. I used to try and picture my dad and wonder what I'd say and do when I met him. The thing is, I could never decide. Now that it's really happening, I don't have any great ideas." She offered Jonathan a tentative, frightened smile. "Do you?"

He moved a couple of steps closer and shook his head. "I'm clueless. I guess we're both in shock."

Taylor rose and motioned for Jonathan to take her seat. She settled on the coffee table, facing both of them.

"This is awkward for all of us," she said. "So I suggest we take it slow. Get to know each other as a group. We'll start out as friends and see what happens after that. What do you say?"

"Seems like a plan."

Jonathan's voice was light, but Taylor knew he had to be wrestling with a thousand emotions inside.

"I agree," Linnie said, then laughed. "Wow. A dad. That's weird, but in a good way."

"Gee, thanks." He smiled at her. "Do you have any questions you'd like to ask me?"

Linnie tilted her head as she thought. "You really didn't know about me? I mean you never sensed something was missing from your life?"

"No." Jonathan leaned toward her. "I wish I had figured it out all on my own and come looking for you, but I didn't know. I'm sorry."

"It's okay. I just used to wonder, back when I was little, I mean, why my dad didn't know I was out there. Kinda dumb, huh?"

"Not at all. I would have wondered the same thing in your position."

He gave her a reassuring smile. Linnie seemed to relax a little. Taylor allowed herself to take a deep breath. Maybe this all *was* going to work out for the three of them.

Linnie glanced at her, then back at Jonathan. "Are you mad at my mom for not telling you?"

Taylor gave a small laugh that might have sounded a tad strangled. "Gee, Linnie, cut right to the heart of it, why don't you?"

"You always told me to be honest," her daughter reminded her. "You kept a secret from him for a long time." She fingered the end of her braid. "I think most guys would be pretty fried about the whole situation. But the thing is, she was really young when it happened. You have to remember that."

Linnie spoke with an earnestness that nearly brought tears to Taylor's eyes. Her wonderful, funny, incredibly grown-up daughter was trying to protect her mother.

"We were both young," Jonathan admitted. "As for being angry—" he looked at Taylor "—I'm working on it."

"Wow, this is so confusing," Linnie said.

"I'm sad that it took me so long to find out about you, though," he told Linnie. "I wish I could have known you when you were young."

"I was a pretty great kid," Linnie said with a grin. "Everybody adored me."

Despite her swirling emotions, Taylor couldn't help chuckling. "Do you want me to tell him about the time you broke the front window? Or when you set fire to the kitchen?"

Linnie winced. "No. I think those are stories that should be shared another time, Mom." Her expression turned serious. "Do you blame Mom and Grandma for keeping us apart?"

"Do you?" Jonathan asked.

Linnie sighed. "Sometimes I'd get really angry about not knowing who my father was. I'd be a brat about getting Mom to tell me."

Jonathan tensed, but didn't say anything. Taylor held her breath. If he was going to lose it, this would be the time.

The silence stretched between them. Linnie broke it first.

"I've always wanted a dad, but now that you're here, it's really strange."

"For all of us," Taylor said.

Jonathan lightly touched his daughter's hand. "I would like to get to know you, Linnie. But only as much as you're comfortable with. I don't want to push things too fast."

She looked at him from under her lashes. "I'd like that."

"How about dinner tomorrow?"

Linnie glanced at Taylor. "Is that okay with you?"

Part of Taylor was thrilled that this first meeting was going so well. She wanted Jonathan and Linnie to have a close father–daughter relationship. Linnie could use a male role model in her life. But a small emptiness inside of her cried out. She wasn't ready to share her daughter with anyone. Not yet. Taylor knew her emotions were purely selfish and she did her best to repress them.

"I think dinner is a nice way for you two to get to know each other."

Linnie's eyes widened. "You're not coming with us?"

"I think it would be better for just the two of you to be together. You'll be forced to talk to fill those uncomfortable silences, which means you'll have a chance to get to know each other."

"You make it sound so pleasant," Jonathan said dryly.

"You know what I mean."

"I do." He rose to his feet. "I don't want to overstay my welcome. I'll see you tomorrow, Linnie."

Taylor stood. "I can see you out."

He shook his head. "I know the way. I think you're needed elsewhere."

He tilted his chin toward Linnie, who sat looking completely stunned.

"Thanks," Taylor murmured quietly so her daughter wouldn't hear. "You could have made me pay."

"Not at her expense."

Her heart squeezed and in that moment, she knew that she'd lost something very precious with Jonathan. The spark, the attraction between them, had been burned away by his anger.

With a final wave, he headed for the front door. Linnie and Taylor both called out their good-byes, then Taylor moved to sit next to her daughter.

"How are you doing?" she asked.

Instead of answering, Linnie burst into tears. Taylor pulled her close.

"I know," she whispered, rocking her daughter, wishing she had the power to make it all better. "This is scary and exciting and complicated, all at the same time."

"He's really my dad."

"I know."

Linnie raised her head. Tears trickled down her cheeks. "Don't be mad, Mom, but I really wish you'd told him before."

Taylor nodded even as the comment cut through her like a honed blade. She deserved the blame. At least Linnie was still speaking to her. "I'm sorry," she said, fighting tears of her own. "Maybe I was wrong, Linnie. I didn't know what else to do. And this is the situation we have now. We have to deal with it."

"The McGuire women are known for their strength," her mother said.

Taylor looked up and saw she had entered the living room. Her mother sat on the other side of Linnie and wrapped her arms around both of them.

"Grandma, I met my dad."

"I know, sweetie." She kissed the top of her granddaughter's head. "He seems like a decent enough man. But as for wishing it had been different, we can't change the past. Don't forget I'm as much to blame as your mother. And I'm older than both of you. From where I'm sitting, I think we did the best we could."

Taylor met her mother's steady gaze. While she appreciated the vote of confidence, she knew that nothing was going to change her daughter's mind . . . or Jonathan's.

"We'll be okay," Taylor promised them both and hoped she was telling the truth.

Her mother squeezed them both. "What changes are afoot. It's not just going to be us girls anymore."

Chapter
17

*T*he next evening Jonathan and Linnie walked toward his car. Jonathan tried to act casual, as if he did this sort of thing all the time. Linnie gave him a tight smile as they paused in front of his rented Ford.

"Are you hungry?" he asked.

She shrugged. "I know we talked about having dinner, but I don't think I can eat. I'm really nervous." She ducked her head. "Dumb, huh?"

"No. I'm nervous, too. How about if we go for a walk first, and see if we can work up our appetite?"

"Okay."

They turned toward the street and walked down to the sidewalk.

"How was your day?" he asked as they made a left. He let Linnie lead the way, figuring this was her town and she would know where they were going.

"Fun. A couple of my friends are in town for the summer, so we're hanging out together while I'm home. We went shopping." Linnie glanced at him and wrinkled her nose. "I don't have to buy much because at school we wear uniforms. They're kinda weird looking, but at least everyone looks equally weird."

"Is it good to be home?" He felt stupid asking all these questions but didn't know another way to get to know her.

"I like it, even though I feel funny about being here. A week isn't enough time to get used to being back, you know?"

He nodded.

"But I really like camp and I love my school. I worked hard to get the scholarship. Academically, I'm way ahead of my friends. Next year I'll be taking college courses. The thing is, I don't have a clue about what to study. I mean, sometimes I think about being a doctor and other times I think it's too gross. Plus I really love studying languages. But I also like math. I keep going back to engineering—but what if everyone is way too smart?"

"You seem pretty smart to me."

"Thanks." She flashed him a genuine smile. "I try to study and stuff. With math, it's easy for me. But sometimes I'd like to be in a regular high school. Just be like everyone else. But Mom was really worried about me making the same mistakes she did."

They'd been walking through the graceful residential neighborhood. As she spoke, Linnie shook her head. "Sorry," she murmured. "I didn't mean that to sound bad."

"It's all right. I know what you meant. Looking back, I can't believe I encouraged a sixteen-year-old girl to run off and live with me."

Linnie glanced at him out of the corner of her eye. "Mom says you were really hot."

He chuckled. "Hard to imagine what with me being so old now, right?"

"Well . . ." She studied him critically. "You're not *so* old." She lowered her voice. "Mom still thinks you're hot, but she also thinks you're really mad at her, so she's not going to tell you that."

Jonathan didn't know what to do with the information. "Hot, huh?"

Linnie gave him a teasing smile. "Uh-huh."

He stumbled to a stop. In that second, with that particular smile curving her lips, his daughter looked exactly as Taylor had when he'd first met her. He felt as if he'd been slapped up the side of his head by a blow from his past.

So young, he thought, still stunned. *Practically a baby.* Yet that innocent girl had left her entire world to be with him. Taylor, who had never even arrived home five minutes after curfew, had broken her mother's heart to follow him.

"You okay?" Linnie asked.

"Fine." They continued walking. "You must miss your friends when you're gone," he said.

"I do. We keep in touch with e-mail. Plus I have school friends I miss when I'm home. I guess life is never perfect."

They reached the corner. There was a small park across the street. "Want to sit over there?" Linnie asked.

"Sure," Jonathan said, checking for traffic before stepping out into the road. His daughter followed.

His daughter. He was still having trouble believing

that all this was real. He wanted to find out everything about her, ask her questions until he knew all her habits, her preferences. He felt as if he had a lifetime to make up for—and in a way, he did. Which made him furious with Taylor. Yet for the first time since learning the truth, a small voice whispered she might not be so much to blame.

They settled on a bench under a grove of pecan trees. Linnie wore shorts and a blue T-shirt. She sat cross-legged on the bench, facing him. Her long hair had been fastened in a ponytail that hung down her back. She looked impossibly pretty and far too young to be going off to school on her own. Once again she reminded him of her mother at that age.

"So, do you like being a psychologist?" she asked.

"Yes."

"But you don't have a private practice, like Mom. How come?"

"I didn't plan to spend my time writing books and teaching seminars. It evolved."

Which was almost the truth. He'd started out with a private practice. Eventually he'd become successful enough to want a larger audience.

"But now, during the contest, you're seeing couples, right? Don't you and my mom talk to them and stuff?"

He smiled. "Mostly 'and stuff.' "

She chuckled. "You know what I mean. You two tell them what to do so they can be happy."

"If only it were that simple." He thought about that morning's sessions. "We saw an older couple today. He's a retired minister and she's a housewife. Each of them was married before and each lost his or her spouse." His good mood faded as he recalled the haunted look in the woman's eyes when she'd spoken about her late husband. "They seem to be doing well."

"So are you winning?"

"I don't know. We've each lost a couple when they dropped out. So right now we're tied. I doubt we'll have a winner until the month is over."

"Are they all in it for the million dollars?"

"Most of them. Not that older couple I just mentioned. I think they were both lonely and saw this as an opportunity to have someone to care about. But it *is* a million dollars."

"Would you live with someone for a month for a million dollars?"

"Is that a trick question?"

"No. I just wondered." Linnie rested her elbow on her knee and her chin on her hand. "Why don't you agree with my mom's theory? Don't you think people should be alike when they get married?"

"I think some characteristics in common are important," he hedged. "Your mom has a lot of great ideas."

Humor danced in Linnie's eyes. "You're just saying that because you don't want me mad at you."

"It crossed my mind that you'd defend her, so I'm trying to be diplomatic."

"That's nice. Thanks." She studied him. "I haven't read your books or anything. I guess I will now. I read my mom's thesis, though, and I thought it was pretty good. She's really patient, which is probably a requirement of the job, right? Which is one reason I do *not* want to study psychology. I would totally blow up the first time someone annoyed me. But not Mom. We used to have these really big fights about you."

"You didn't know me."

"Not you, Jonathan Kirby. Just my dad. I really wanted her to tell me who you were, but she wouldn't. She said that when I was eighteen, I would have to make the decision to get in touch with you myself. As an adult. I didn't think she should make me wait."

He heard the confusion in her voice and fought against the need to join her in her crusade against Taylor. He, too, wished they'd met sooner.

"Are you angry with her?" he asked, telling himself it was more important to play impartial witness than injured party. Whatever his feelings for Taylor, he wasn't about to hurt Linnie.

She wrinkled her nose. "Sometimes. I used to scream at her and threaten to run away. You know, kid stuff."

A pain cut through his heart. As if she were so grown-up now, he thought sadly. "Do you think she was right to keep the information from you?"

"I don't know." Linnie stared at him. "Do you?"

"I don't have an answer for that. I'm angry and frustrated because I lost so many years with you. Years I can never get back." He wanted to say more, but didn't. There was no point in burning bridges. And with a fairness he was surprised to feel, he was forced to admit, "I'm not sure I would have handled things well if she'd told me back when she was pregnant."

"Because you'd already told her it was over between you?"

"That's part of it. I don't want to see her side in this,

but I know she had to make difficult choices. Once she'd made them, she wouldn't waver."

Linnie nodded. "Mom can be really stubborn. She calls it determined because that sounds better, but as Grandma says, it's just plain bullheaded."

His anger battled with the realization that Taylor might have been doing the best she could at the time. He didn't *want* to see her side of things. She'd been wrong. She'd betrayed him and kept Linnie from him. He wanted her punished.

No, he thought sadly. What he wanted was the one thing he couldn't have—time turned back.

"Do you have any brothers or sisters?" Linnie asked.

"Sorry, you are aunt- and uncle-less. No cousins either, at least not on my side."

Linnie sighed. "Mom's either. We're all only children, which is kind of a bummer. Are your parents still alive?"

"No. My dad passed away a long time ago and my mom died a few years back."

"I'm sorry."

"Me, too. They would have really liked you."

"How did you fall in love with my mom?" Linnie asked.

The unexpected question caught him flat-footed. Jonathan mentally stumbled, trying to come up with an answer that would please a most likely romantic sixteen-year-old girl.

"It was a long time ago," he said, sidestepping the inquiry.

Linnie wasn't impressed. "She was your first real girlfriend, wasn't she? I can't believe you forgot what it was like to be in love with her."

Jonathan leaned back against the bench. Taylor *had* been his first real girlfriend. He'd never thought of her in those terms before. She'd been an important piece of his past. The one person he'd known that he'd loved.

Love. It had been so easy back then—before being the best had been the most important part of his life.

"It was love at first sight?" Linnie asked.

"We were young and we were in Paris," he told her.

"That's not an answer."

"Actually it is. You're going to have to trust me on that."

Linnie shifted, pulling her knees to her chest. "Mom says you were backpacking and she was in color guard with her high school band."

He nodded. "We met at a café. She was beautiful and laughing. I remember sitting by myself, watching her with her friends. I wanted to share the joke."

"Then she looked up and saw you and lost her heart," Linnie filled in with the air of someone reciting a favorite story. "It's very romantic."

"We were crazy about each other," he admitted, remembering how they'd tried to spend every second together. Between her schedule and her chaperons, it hadn't been easy, but they'd stolen away as often as they could.

The memories seemed better this time around, he thought with some surprise. He found himself feeling nostalgic about that time in his life.

"Once we got back to the States, we were desperate to find a way to be together. I was a scholarship student at Harvard."

"So Mom ran off to be with you." She sighed. "Just like a fairy tale."

"I don't think she thought so when she was holding down two jobs."

Linnie stared at him. "What?"

"Your mom was only sixteen. She didn't have any skills, not even a high school diploma. She could only get work in retail stores or fast-food. They didn't pay a lot. I had some living expenses covered through my scholarship money, but an apartment cost a lot more than a dorm room."

"You made her work?"

"I didn't make her. It was a joint decision."

Linnie didn't look convinced. "Right. She wanted to do it and you didn't stop her?"

Jonathan realized he wasn't going to come out the hero on this one. "I had a scholarship. I had to maintain my grade point average or I'd lose the money. I worked part time, but I couldn't make enough to support us."

Linnie shook her head. "It sounded a whole lot more romantic before I knew what really happened."

"We were young."

"No wonder Mom always talks about making smart choices. I didn't know about the two jobs. That's not romantic at all."

Her blunt assessment of Taylor's life with him made him squirm. This conversation wasn't going the way he'd planned.

Linnie stared at him. "I never knew why my mom didn't get married. I don't think it's because of her past with you. I mean I don't think she hated that time. She always talks about how special it was." She shrugged. "I used to think she didn't want to marry someone because of me. But my grandma always said I had nothing to do with it. And I've been away at school for nearly a year and she's still not involved with anyone."

She paused, looking expectant.

Jonathan raised his hands in a gesture of surrender. "Don't look at me. I don't have any answers."

Linnie grinned. "No deep, dark secrets to explain why Dr. Taylor McGuire never again found true happiness in love?"

"Not even one. She's a smart, capable, beautiful woman. Any man would be lucky to have her."

Linnie studied him. "So you still like her?"

He nodded because Linnie expected a positive response. And maybe because the situation had suddenly become a little less black-and-white than he'd thought.

"I think she likes you, too."

"I'm glad. After all, we're working together."

Linnie shifted and dropped her feet to the ground. "I'm hungry. Do you still want to go get dinner?"

"Yeah, I do."

She smiled at him. This time he didn't see anyone but his daughter. His chest tightened as he read the acceptance in her eyes.

Chapter
18

"Come in," Taylor called when she heard the knock on her bedroom door. She was lying on her bed, pretending to read. The truth was, she hadn't turned a page in the past hour. Instead, she'd been listening for her daughter's return and worrying desperately that her first evening with her father hadn't gone well . . . or that it had gone *too* well.

Linnie bounced into the room, grinning happily. She skipped to her mother's bed and flopped onto the foot of the mattress.

"We had a nice time," she announced, sprawling over the bedspread.

"I'm glad. Where'd you go for dinner?"

"That new burger place. The Texas Grill. But first we went for a walk and talked."

Taylor studied her daughter, trying to read what she was thinking, looking for signs of discomfort and stress. "Was it okay being with him?"

"Yeah." Linnie rolled onto her side, facing her

mother. "It was really weird at first. Like we didn't know what to say. I mean, he's my dad but I don't know him. I was afraid I wouldn't like him or that he wouldn't like me."

"But you do like him?"

"Yeah." She smiled. "He's not bad, for an old guy."

Taylor held in a grin. "Jonathan will be so thrilled by your high praise."

"Oh, Mom. You know what I mean. It's not like I think he's cute or anything. Wouldn't that be twisted? But he's nice. And I think he likes me."

"Of course he does. You're charming which, by the way, you get from him."

"Maybe I get it from you."

If only, Taylor thought. "Honey, I'm a lot of things, but charming isn't one of them. So what all did you talk about?"

Linnie obliged her. "Different stuff. He told me about meeting you in Paris and that when you were living together you like, worked *two* jobs."

It seemed a lifetime ago. "I guess I did. I was young and in love. It didn't seem so bad at the time."

"Yeah, but you were working while he was going to school."

"It happens."

Linnie snorted. "Not to me. I'm not putting some guy through college just so he can dump me afterward. Besides, I plan to be the one on scholarship so my boyfriends can take care of *my* needs."

"It's a good plan," Taylor said, her heart filled with love as she gazed at her child. "The problem is most boyfriends aren't into the whole catering thing. Not the way women are. Women have a nesting instinct. It can get in the way of good sense."

"Maybe."

Linnie didn't sound convinced. She pushed herself into a sitting position and pulled on the scrunchie holding her ponytail in place. "You know, he said he likes you."

Taylor wondered if he'd been telling the truth. "That's nice. Anything else?"

"Mo-om. He likes you. Doesn't that mean something?"

"It means that we're friends. I'm glad. Now that he knows about you, he's going to be a part of our lives. Far better for all of us if we can get along. It makes life more pleasant."

"Don't you want more than pleasant?" Her daughter combed her fingers through her hair and sighed in frustration. "Don't you have even one romantic bone in your whole body? Grandma told me she thought Jonathan was pretty hot and you think so, too."

Linnie paused expectantly, but Taylor didn't rise to the bait. After a moment of silence, her daughter sighed, then continued.

"I mean, think about it. It's been seventeen years. You're different now, but still attracted to each other."

Suddenly the pieces of the puzzle clicked into place. Taylor leaned forward and touched Linnie's arm.

"I'm sorry," she said softly. "I should have seen this coming. You're so grown-up most of the time that I forget you're still my baby girl."

Linnie looked disgusted. "What does *that* have to do with anything? I'm sixteen, Mom. Not a baby."

"I don't mean you're still an infant, but you are still my child. Wanting your parents to get back together, or in this case, get together at all, is a very natural response to the situation."

"I guess it beats an unnatural response," Linnie muttered.

"Honey, I like Jonathan. He's very intelligent and good at what he does." He was also, as Linnie had said, hot, but Taylor wasn't about to admit that. The man hated her guts. "We're not going to get together. We'll have a relationship as your parents, but it won't be a romantic one."

"Why not?"

"Because we have two different lives."

"Not so different. You're not even trying. What if he's fabulous? What if he's the man you've been waiting for all your life? What if the reason you never married anyone else is that no one could make you feel the way Jonathan did all those years ago? Think what you'd be missing by dismissing him."

Tears filled Linnie's eyes. Taylor gathered her close and hugged her.

"Can't we all just be a family?" Linnie whispered.

Taylor rocked her gently, wishing there was a way to make this better. She knew that Linnie's emotions were on a roller coaster. In time she would calm down. But that didn't ease Taylor's guilt or her own pain. Nor did it erase her longing. Because she wasn't just fighting Linnie's fantasies on the subject of Jonathan Kirby— she was also wrestling with her own.

The last of the couples left at four-fifty on Tuesday. Jonathan looked down at his notes. They'd had a full day of appointments, including one with Chris and Rio Harbaugh—the divorced couple. Something kept nagging at the back of his mind. Something that he'd been thinking about while they'd been talking.

"Jonathan? Are you still here on earth?"

He glanced up and saw Taylor gazing at him expectantly. From her expression, she'd been talking for several minutes.

"Sorry. I was trying to remember something I'd read. For Chris and Rio."

Taylor leaned back in her chair and sighed. "Yeah. I really wish we could help them more. I don't feel like we're making a lot of progress there."

"I want to check out a few things. Don't give up hope."

She tucked a loose strand of hair behind her ear. "I'm sure they'll appreciate your willingness to go the extra distance."

He was about to make a joke that getting back into therapy had forced him to rediscover his humanity, when he realized that the statement was neither funny nor false. He'd been away from the one-on-one connection with patients for so long that he'd forgotten what it was like. During the fifty-minute session no one cared how many books he'd written or if his timing was on or off. The couple in question wanted to talk about themselves. They wanted to share problems and get solutions. It was a part of his career he'd forgotten even existed.

"Well, hell," he muttered.

"What?"

"Nothing." He hesitated. "I was thinking that I haven't had a private practice in so long that I'd forgotten there were rewards in watching someone go through the process of healing."

"Not to mention what it does for us as therapists. I know there have been dozens of times when patients have helped me see my life more—" She broke off and turned away. "Sorry."

"Don't apologize. I was listening."

"But you don't want me to—" She made a vague gesture with her hands. "While we've managed to get through the last couple of days by being extremely civil to each other, we've avoided anything close to an actual conversation. I didn't think you wanted that to change."

Jonathan picked up a pen and tapped it lightly on the desk. "It's not easy, Taylor. I have a lot of unresolved emotions." *Talk about an understatement,* he thought grimly.

"That sounds so psychologically mature," she said. "What I think you really mean is that you want to rip my heart out with your bare hands and then tap-dance on it."

He glanced at her. "I hadn't thought of it in those terms."

She gave him a tentative smile. "Not the tap-dancing type?"

He was surprised to find he didn't want to snap at her. "It's the shoes. They make me look like I have duck feet."

Her smile faded. "I'm sorry," she said softly. "Oh, Jonathan, I never meant for you and Linnie to get hurt. We could go round and round about why I did what I did and why you did what you did, but the bottom line is you lost sixteen years with your daughter."

"I know."

But seventeen years ago, Taylor had been so much like Linnie—except possibly not so grown-up. He could feel his anger fading away, leaving only loss.

"My agent called," he said quietly, staring at the table. "She said my publisher had made an offer of half a million for your project." He continued to tap the pen. "It crossed my mind that with one sentence, I could destroy your writing career before it even began."

"Did you?" Her voice didn't give away her feelings.

"No. I hated that I considered it."

"I understand. You felt betrayed. I suppose I did betray you. I'm sorry."

He studied her. Pain and regret darkened her eyes. Her hair was in curls this afternoon, probably because it was raining again. She wore pink. A soft looking pink suit with a cream-colored sweater under her jacket. His gaze settled on the swell of her breasts and in that moment he knew that all the anger he possessed hadn't been enough to destroy his desire.

"Hell of a situation," he muttered.

"Maybe we need therapy."

Despite the swirling emotions inside, he grinned. "Only if I pick the therapist."

"Right. You'll choose a friend who'll say I'm completely at fault."

"Exactly."

Taylor sighed. "On a more serious note, I want you to know I won't get in the way of your relationship with Linnie."

"The thought never occurred to me."

"Thanks."

She began collecting her papers. He grabbed half the files. "I'll write up these notes," he said.

"But you have your book deadline."

"I want to help." Which was oddly true. He couldn't remember the last time he'd had to deal with case notes. Still, participating felt right.

He remembered something.

"I received a call from one of the national women's magazines," he said. "They want us to write an article on the real differences between men and women, and how to make a marriage successful. I agreed. We should probably set up a time to outline the article."

She stared at him. "Why?"

"An appointment generally makes things easier."

"No. Why did you agree? Your career is way beyond…" Her voice trailed off. "You must have agreed before…"

He knew what she meant. Before he knew about Linnie. He shrugged.

"You should tell them no."

"Maybe I don't want to."

She looked as surprised as he felt by the words.

"But you hate me," she said.

"No, I don't."

He didn't know what he felt. For years, his life had been simple. He wanted to be the best, which meant career first, second and third in his life. Now . . .

"It's your call," he said. "It'll give you a lot of exposure."

"I know."

"You should say yes. Don't be a martyr."

"How about if I say thanks and ask you to pick the night."

"That works, too."

"You couldn't be more wrong about all of this," Taylor said two nights later, tossing Jonathan's notes back toward him. She'd been trying to be diplomatic, but the man was making her insane.

He grabbed the papers as they slid across the polished dining room table in his hotel room suite. "Not that you have an opinion."

"Of course I have an opinion, and in this case, I'm completely right. It's important that men and women try to find some common ground. As you pointed out when we were on *Psychology in the News,* men and women are fundamentally different."

"So you're saying you agree with me?"

Taylor groaned. The man was being deliberately difficult. He'd been annoyingly cheerful all day during their appointments with the contestants. Now, when they were supposed to be spending their evening working on their magazine article, he was baiting her.

"I agree with you on some things," she said. "Not on opposites attracting. Actually, I take that back. Opposites can be attracted to each other, but that attraction doesn't guarantee a successful marriage."

"It's not just opposites attracting," he reminded her. "There's also a powerful element of sexual attraction." He paused just long enough to make her heart rate double. "Between the hypothetical couples, of course."

"Of course."

He wasn't talking about them, she reminded herself. There was no *them,* at least not in any romantic or sexual sense. She didn't want there to be—although Jonathan had an annoying habit of lighting her on fire on a regular basis.

"Back to the matter at hand," she said.

"Had we left it?"

She ignored him. "No one can predict which relationships are going to be successful," she stated. "All we can do is attempt to weigh the odds in favor of the couples. I think an agreement about style within a marriage helps, as do similar beliefs in areas of finances, child-rearing and religion."

"You think too much, and once again you're ignoring sex."

She ignored *him.* "I know that a traditional marriage begins with two fundamentally different people. In terms of getting their needs met, men nearly always come out ahead."

"And that's bad, how?"

She wanted to throw something at him. "If you don't want to write the article, say so."

"I want to write it. I was thinking maybe we could do a 'he said, she said' format. You can talk statistics and bore everyone to death while I—"

She cut him off. "Let me guess. While you talk trash."

He grinned.

They sat across from each other at the dining room table. Overhead light illuminated flecks of gold in Jonathan's dark hair. He looked relaxed and at the same time, dangerous.

She raised her hands in a gesture of surrender.

"Okay—you win. I don't understand the game anymore. Are you still mad at me, or what?"

He shrugged. "I'm dealing with it."

Ambivalence made sense to her. "Thanks for suggesting the article. If we ever write it, the exposure will help me a lot."

He nodded. "So why are you resisting the sex angle? It sells."

She blinked at him. "But that's so—I mean deliberately writing an article to titillate the reader." She blinked again. "No wonder you've had thirty best sellers. That's really smart."

"Agreed. Now let's start over. Give me an opening line that will interest our readers."

Taylor hesitated. For one thing, it was difficult to be creative on demand. For another, sex was dangerous territory, at least for her well-being.

"Okay, how's this? Do you know why women fake orgasms?"

That got his attention. His gaze sharpened. "I'd love to know."

She leaned toward him, placing her hands on the table and smiling slowly. "Because men fake foreplay. They want the goal, not the journey. But without the journey, women lose interest in the goal. It's a microcosm for all that's wrong between the sexes."

"Excellent." He opened his laptop and began typing. "Go on."

"The more men want sex, the more they push and the harder the woman pushes back. It's like with Chris and Rio, but don't use their names."

They looked at each other.

"Case studies," they said together.

"We could break down each entry," Jonathan said. "Do in-depth interviews and follow-ups. It's enough material for a book."

Excitement coursed through her. "It's great. The article could be chapter one."

He rose and walked to the phone. "I'm going to order in coffee. I think we'll be at this for a while."

While he was on the phone, Taylor stood, crossed to the window and stared out over the town. Beyond the splash of lights was the darkness of open land. When had Marriageville gotten so small? Had it always been this way or had she just noticed? Linnie wasn't going to be like her. Linnie would have bigger dreams that took her beyond the confines of this little town. Book idea or not, Jonathan would be leaving as well.

Jonathan, who was now bound to her by the knowledge of his child.

"Linnie said the two of you had plans to get together before she heads back to school," she said when he hung up.

"Tomorrow night. We're also going to stay in touch through e-mail."

Taylor nodded. Linnie had mentioned as much at dinner the previous evening. "She said you'd talked about her visiting you in New York this summer."

She sensed Jonathan moving toward her but kept her gaze fixed firmly on the horizon.

"I was going to mention that to you myself," he said, sounding much closer. "She and I haven't worked out any of the details. My apartment in the city has three bedrooms. You're welcome to come with her, if you'd like, or send Linda along." He paused. "I'm assuming here. Are you going to say she can't visit me?"

"Of course not."

An ache started in her chest. She knew it was heart-pain, but not the medical kind. Linnie was no longer just *her* little girl. She now belonged to Jonathan, too. No matter what happened in the future, things would never be the same. In good times and bad, Linnie would want to share things with her father.

"Why didn't you ever marry?"

Jonathan's question surprised her. She turned to face him, only to find he stood in the shadows of the room, close behind her, but not so close that they could touch. She found herself wanting to touch him. "Would you believe that no one ever asked?"

"No."

She shrugged. "Okay, I never met anyone I wanted to say yes to."

"You wanted to marry me."

"I know." She'd loved him as she'd never loved any other man. In seventeen years, no one else had come close to touching her heart.

"I was really young," she said, fearful that wasn't the entire truth.

She returned her attention to the window. Dear God, there had to be a reason she hadn't loved anyone since Jonathan. She'd been really busy. Linnie had taken a lot of her time. Not to mention the fact that there weren't many single men in Marriageville. Yeah, that was it. Lack of opportunity. She refused to believe she'd never stopped loving Jonathan.

"Enough about me," she said with a brightness she didn't feel. "You married once. Why not again?"

"Easy answer. My career."

"Your money won't keep you warm at night."

He smiled sadly. "You're right." He moved closer and touched her cheek. "I'm sorry I dumped you. From how great you've turned out, it was a stupid move on my part."

She laughed. "Oh, sure. You're sorry because of what *you* missed out on. Not because of my feelings."

"Hey, I'm a guy."

They both laughed. Then the laughter faded. In the space of a heartbeat, she grew hyper-aware of his nearness and the heat from his body.

They had so many unresolved issues between them, she told herself frantically. Room service would be delivering coffee any second. Yet when Jonathan moved toward her, rather than stepping away, she slipped into his embrace. She didn't have a choice. Suddenly his arms were around her and his mouth was on hers, a soft, sweet pressure and taste. She wanted him, needed him. Nothing in her life had ever been so important.

He seemed to feel the same intensity because his kiss deepened immediately. His tongue swept past her parted lips, entering her, teasing her, mating with her. She had the vague thought that it had been like this before—back when they were young and foolish and thought only of each other. She recalled nights and days spent making love over and over until they could only sleep in each other's arms to gather strength to begin it all again.

This was what she'd been waiting for, she thought hazily as his large hands moved up and down her back. The feeling of being swept away. Overwhelmed by passion, she had no choice but to respond, wanting him to take her to that place they could only go together.

The past, their problems, all faded. Trembling filled her. She clung to him so that she wouldn't collapse. He was strong and steady in her rapidly spinning world. He angled his head slightly so that he could deepen the kiss. She welcomed him with little strokes of delight. She reached one hand behind his head so that she could slip her fingers through the silky locks of his hair. Her breasts nestled against his chest, finding the place they'd once been so comfortable. He reached down to her rear, cupping her curves, drawing her against him. The apex of her thighs rested on the hard ridge of his desire.

More memories swamped her. Of the first time she'd seen him naked. How she'd been afraid and he'd been so gentle and understanding. He'd allowed her to look her fill until she'd felt ready to touch him. He'd been young and more than ready. A few strokes of her hand had made him explode, spilling onto her thighs with no warning. After a heartbeat of shock, they'd both started to laugh. Jonathan had cleaned her, all the while filling in the details that her health classes and her stilted conversations with her mother had failed to make clear.

Then they'd made love slowly, tenderly. Now as she flexed against him, she remembered that first time. The strange sensation of a man actually entering her body. The way her insides had hurt, even though there hadn't been any blood. The expression on his face when he'd climaxed and the care he'd taken afterward, touching her until she, too, had experienced her first release.

The memories filled her, making her want to cling to him now. She wanted to speak the words so they could share the feelings. His hands settled on her waist and moved higher. She caught her breath in anticipation of his fingers on her breasts, and when he touched her there, she thought she might faint from the pleasure of it all.

He cupped her curves the way he always had. From below, supporting their weight, his thumbs brushing over her nipples. Their kiss became more playful as he nipped her lower lip, then nibbled along her jawline.

Heat radiated up to her stomach and down her legs. Dampness collected as her body wept in anticipation of its conquest. She wanted him. Worse, she needed him.

He licked her neck, even as he kept touching her breasts. She felt herself weakening. One of her hands slipped to his shoulder and down his chest. She knew the ultimate destination. She also knew that if she touched him, she was lost.

She stepped back. "It's too soon," she said.

Passion darkened his eyes, but he didn't disagree.

"Maybe we should work on the book another time," she suggested.

He shrugged.

Taylor collected her belongings and headed for the door. She couldn't figure out if leaving was smart or if she'd just lost something she would regret for the rest of her life.

Chapter
19

*T*aylor wasn't sure what she was supposed to say "the morning after," so she didn't say anything as she walked into the office she temporarily shared with Jonathan. He was already there, looking handsome and rested, while she felt about as appealing as something a cat had gacked up after a particularly rough night.

She had spent most of the predawn hours telling herself that she was smarter than this. Why would she willingly get all hot and heavy with a man who had already dumped her once and would be moving on?

"Good morning," she said, doing her darnedest to sound professionally cool and detached.

"Taylor."

He was practically grinning like a Cheshire cat. It was only when she'd plopped her butt into her chair that she noticed the spray of flowers on the credenza behind them. Brilliant pink starburst lilies nestled next to white roses.

"From an admirer?" she asked, thinking that if they

were from Katrina, she would have thought leather whips more the reporter's style.

"No."

It was only after he spoke that she noticed her name on the card. Her name . . . and his name. She swallowed.

"You bought me flowers? Why?"

"They're a peace offering," he said.

"Thank you." She touched the soft petals of the closest lily.

He rose and walked to the coffeepot on the small table at the side of the room. After filling his mug, he poured a second one for her and brought it back to her. Then, instead of sitting back in his chair, he settled on the corner of her desk.

"I read your thesis last night."

She wasn't sure if that was good or bad. She settled on neutral. "Oh?"

"It was good."

"You sound surprised."

"I'm not. I expected it to be a thoughtful discussion of your theory, which it was."

Talk about a noncommittal response. Didn't he want to tell her that he'd really enjoyed it and that she was brilliant? Or at least that she looked really good in her hunter green wrap dress?

"What made you want to read it now?" she asked instead.

"You got to me last night," he told her. "I couldn't sleep after you left. Something about all that coffee, not to mention my blood being stuck south of where it belonged."

He paused just long enough for her to blush at the memory of the passion they'd shared.

"When I knew I couldn't sleep, I picked up your thesis."

"Because you thought it would make you drowsy?" she demanded. "There's high praise."

"Aren't we touchy this morning? No, I picked it up because I was curious. I thought by reading your work I would understand you better."

Taylor squirmed on her seat as if she couldn't decide whether or not she wanted him to understand her.

"Why does it matter?"

"You're Linnie's mother. To understand you is to understand her. Plus we're working together."

She tried not to be disappointed by his response. "Right, Linnie and work." What else would it be? Why would she be foolish enough to hope for more?

Before she could figure that out for herself, the door to the reception area opened and she heard voices in the waiting room.

"Show time," Jonathan said, taking his seat.

Marnie and Taylor slid into their usual booth in Wilbur's Diner. Taylor felt weary down to her bones and it was only noon.

After Lorraine took their order, Marnie planted her elbows on the table. "Taylor, you're a great friend and I say this with all the love in my heart, but you look awful. Aren't you sleeping?"

"I'm fine."

It was a flat-out lie, but Taylor didn't know how much she was willing to confess to her friend. As she didn't understand the mess that was her life, she didn't think she could do a very good job of explaining it.

"I've been dying to call you but I didn't know what your schedule was," Marnie said. "So tell me what happened with Jonathan?"

Lorraine returned with their drinks. Taylor unwrapped her straw. "He knows about Linnie."

Marnie raised her eyebrows. "That's news. When did you tell him and how big was the explosion?"

"Over the weekend. He figured it out when he saw her at the press conference. At first I thought he was going to kill me, but now he'd probably just settle for a maiming. He met Linnie that night, without her knowing who he was, then we told her together a couple of nights later."

"What does she think of all this?"

"She's thrilled. She's always wanted a father, and Jonathan's a pretty great one to have." Taylor leaned back in her chair. "He was furious with me, which is understandable; however, he seems to be on the road to forgiving me. We're thinking about writing a book together, which wouldn't be so bad if he weren't so damned charming."

"Why is his charm a complication?" Marnie asked. "I would think it would make dealing with him more pleasant."

"It's not that simple."

"Because you loved him once and you don't want to love him again?"

Taylor nearly choked on her water. "I'll admit to being crazy, but I'm not stupid." She thought about the kiss the previous night. "Well, I try not to be."

"So you don't love him?"

"No," she said firmly, refusing to remember the revelation of the previous evening. "I don't."

"But you could."

"What is love without trust or forgiveness? He blames me for everything."

Marnie smiled. "Is this where I point out you just mentioned a couple of reasons why he wouldn't love you but not why you wouldn't love him. Curious."

Taylor shook her head. "I refuse to be sucked into a conversation about my love life, mostly because I don't have one. Let's change the subject. How are things at your house?"

Marnie surprised her by looking away and flushing. "Fine. Good, really." Her expression softened. "Will is real nice. I was concerned because all I knew about him was that he's smart and not involved with anyone. But he could have been a complete jerk or insensitive."

"I take it he's neither of those things."

"No. He's very special. Kind of quiet at first, and shy, but we've spent enough time together that we're getting more comfortable with each other." Marnie raised her head and smiled sadly. "In a way being around him makes me miss George more because they're both good men. But Will is different enough that I don't get confused about who I'm with. I just don't want to get my heart broken."

Taylor was surprised. "Is that really a danger?"

"I hope not."

Lorraine appeared with their lunches. As she settled Marnie's bacon and mushroom burger in front of her, Taylor picked at her salad. She wanted to tell Marnie to protect her heart at all costs. That it could easily be stolen away before she noticed. Then she realized that might also be very good advice for herself.

Will slipped *The Joy of Sex* back into the glove compartment of his car. He'd read the entire book from cover to cover and he was still confused. The hell of it was all the theory in the world wasn't going to help him. What he needed was practical experience.

He had a brief thought that he could try hiring another hooker, but the previous experience had been so hideous, he didn't think he could go through with it. Besides, he didn't want to do it with anyone but Marnie.

Just thinking her name was enough to get him aroused. No news there. Maybe he should have kissed her again, he thought. He'd wanted to, but there hadn't been a good opportunity. If he'd had more experience, he might have been comfortable simply going up to her and pulling her into his arms. And if he was seven-feet-six, he'd be playing professional basketball.

He groaned, then started the engine of his truck. The situation was hopeless. Liking Marnie only made him more nervous. He might as well forget it. He was never going to have sex—not with her, at least. He should be grateful that they were friends.

"Big money!" the contestant shrieked as the wheel clattered to a stop in front of her flashing arrow.

"Six hundred," the handsome game host said.

"I'd like an 'N' please."

Grace absently patted Alexander as she watched her favorite game show. Nelson sat next to her on the sofa, the cat between them. As Nelson turned the pages of his newspaper, Grace studied the puzzle.

An "N" wouldn't help, she thought. Sure enough, there was a beep from the screen and the next contestant reached for the wheel.

"I really enjoyed dinner," Nelson said.

Grace glanced at him. "You had mentioned before you liked my meatloaf."

He smiled at her. "I do. It's perfect. And that gravy. I don't know what your secret is, but you could sell that in the grocery store and make a lot of money."

Pleasure filled her. No matter how small a service she performed for Nelson, he always noticed and always thanked her. He was so gentle and patient. When she'd found out he would rather read his newspapers than watch television, she'd offered to put a reading light in the living room. But he'd said he preferred to be in here with her. That the noise from the TV didn't bother him.

She continued to stroke her cat as she returned her attention to the puzzle. *Maybe a "D" would help,* she thought.

Then an unexpected warmth sent every coherent thought from her head. Something strong and large settled on the back of her hand. Alexander slipped out from under her palm and jumped off the sofa, leaving Grace with her fingers pressed into the nubby fabric and Nelson's hand resting on hers.

She didn't look at him, not even when he turned her wrist so that he could lace his fingers between hers.

"Grace?"

She was afraid. So very afraid. The growing gladness in her heart was unfamiliar and fragile. She liked and admired Nelson. She found herself dreading the end of the month when he would leave her small life and she would once more be an old woman living alone with a cat.

"Grace, please look at me."

Slowly she turned her head to find his blue eyes fixed on her. "I've thought you were very pretty from the first moment I met you."

She blinked in surprise. "Me?"

He smiled. "Who else would I be talking to right now?" He leaned forward and kissed her on the mouth. A soft, tender kiss that left her breathless.

Her free hand fluttered at her side. She wanted to protest that they were too old and she wasn't the sort of woman men wanted. Her husband had told her that often enough.

"Grace?"

She saw something flare to life in his eyes. Something even she could recognize.

"Unless you'd rather watch your show."

There was a note of teasing in his voice, but also the promise of understanding. This was a big step for her. Perhaps she didn't want to change the nature of their relationship. His kindness told her that he would understand.

Silently, she picked up the remote and turned off the television. Then she allowed Nelson to draw her to her feet, and together they slowly walked from the room.

Chapter 20

*M*arnie pulled on her yellow sundress and stretched to reach the zipper. She and Will had dinner plans at an actual restaurant tonight. Since they hadn't been out yet together, she felt as if this was their first-ever date. To make things even better, he'd been the one to invite *her!*

When she'd finished with the zipper, she stepped in front of the mirror to check her appearance. She'd left her hair loose, brushing out as much curl as she could. The dress was sleeveless, but not the least bit low-cut, and the hem ended a mere two inches above her knee.

Once she'd looked at herself from as many angles as possible and had decided that this was the best combination of conservative and pretty, she stepped into her high-heeled sandals and reached for a simple pair of gold hoops. She was so nervous, her fingers shook slightly. She wanted tonight to go well. She also wanted Will to kiss her again, but while she had some control over the first issue, she had none over the second.

After blotting her lipstick, Marnie squared her

shoulders and headed for her bedroom door. She couldn't decide if she should have a glass of wine. Sometimes it relaxed her, but she wasn't much of a drinker. She stepped into the hall. If she—

Her mind and body both came to a dead stop. Will had just stepped out of his room. The man was gorgeous. From the top of his still-damp hair down to his freshly shined shoes. She'd only ever seen him in jeans, running shorts or his business casual clothes. Tonight he'd dressed in a dark suit, white shirt, and red power tie. He looked like a tycoon. He turned and saw her, then smiled self-consciously.

"Hi," he said. "You look nice."

She swallowed. Speaking seemed impossible. So did breathing and that was probably a more pressing issue. Still there was nothing she could do but stand there, gaping like a fish.

"Will. You're prime CEO material," she said.

He cleared his throat, then pushed up his glasses. "I wasn't sure if the suit was too formal. The restaurant doesn't have a strict dress code, but I thought it would be a nice change."

"It is." Not that she didn't appreciate seeing him in running shorts and a T-shirt. "I should probably change into something dressier."

She made a move toward her bedroom door, but he shook his head to stop her. Crossing the distance between them, he reached out and touched her shoulder.

"Don't change anything. You're perfect."

Had any other man made the same comment, she would have assumed it was a line. But this was Will and he didn't do lines. In her chest, her heart fluttered slightly, making her long to step into his embrace. She wanted to open her bedroom door, too, but this time for a different reason. Instead of changing clothes, she wanted to invite him inside so that they could make love.

If only.

"Marnie?"

"What?"

"Tell me what you're thinking."

The request was unexpected—and shocking. Instantly she blushed. "Nothing."

Will put his hand on her shoulder and rubbed his thumb against her bare skin. "Are you sure? I thought I saw—" He dropped his hand to his side. "Never mind. I'm sure I was wrong."

But he was looking at her the way a man looks at a woman he wants. She might not have had experience with anyone but George, but she was reasonably sure she and Will were thinking the same thoughts. So why didn't one of them do something about it?

"You make me crazy," she murmured, then gathered up all her courage, leaned forward and pressed her mouth to his.

The results were instantaneous. He groaned low in his throat, parting her lips and thrusting inside of her. His arms came around her, hauling her close. She could feel the strength of him, not to mention the tension of his arousal. That hard ridge pressing against her stomach was as gratifying as it was exciting.

His tongue circled and danced with hers. She clutched at his shoulders, as much pulling him close as holding on as the world tilted around them. She was as hungry as he, kissing him back, needing everything he had to give her.

A nearly forgotten ache flared to life between her legs. She felt herself going from damp to wet in the space of a heartbeat. *So much for needing to be ready,* she thought, torn between passion and humor. If he pushed her up against the wall and took her, she wouldn't do a thing to stop him.

Unfortunately, he didn't. Instead he pulled back and leaned his forehead against hers. Their breathing was labored. The heat flaring between them made her glad she wasn't wearing all that much.

"We have reservations," he said, his hands resting on her waist.

"Are you talking about the restaurant or emotional issues?"

He smiled slightly. "Dinner."

"Ah. So you're very hungry?"

She'd thought he might tease her, or kiss her. Instead he stepped back and looked at her. Without speaking.

Silence filled the hallway. Marnie waited. Will avoided her gaze, instead studying the wallpaper beside her. There was something odd about his stance, something almost tentative.

"Will?" she asked, wondering if she'd made a horrible mistake. "Should I have not kissed you? Are you angry?"

His gaze flew to hers. "No. It was great. Better than great. You're incredibly beautiful and sexy and smart. Why wouldn't I want you kissing me?"

She exhaled in relief. That was something. "Then I

don't understand. I think you like me. I had a couple of clues that you want me."

He averted his gaze again. "Yes, well, that's fairly obvious."

Was it her? Was it . . . "Is it because this is George's house?"

She had his attention again. "What does that have to do with anything?"

"I don't know. I was just asking. I, ah, I wouldn't mind if we skipped the restaurant and ate in. Later."

He stared at her as if she were speaking Gaelic.

Something was really wrong. She could feel it with every fiber of her being. But what?

"Is it my room? Are you concerned about ghosts in the bed? All the furniture is new. I replaced it a couple of years ago. Or we could go to your room."

He shook his head but didn't speak. Marnie felt her confidence draining away. "Okay, fine. We don't have to do this. Do you still want to go to dinner?"

He took a step toward her. "The thing is, Marnie, I'm really lousy at this. I do want…" He cleared his throat. "That is, if you're asking me if I want to make love with you, there's nothing I've ever wanted more. I've dreamed about it, and not just when I'm asleep. I think you're amazing. But you're also so far out of my league that we might as well be from different galaxies. I know I'm going to screw up the whole thing. I don't want to, but it's going to happen."

He was nervous! She felt as if she'd just been given a reprieve. Nervous she could handle.

"We'll be fine," she promised.

She opened the door to her bedroom and led the

way inside. Will hesitated, then followed. When she closed the door behind him, she turned to study the room, trying to see it from his point of view.

The bed was too small—only a queen-size mattress against one long wall in a vast open area. She'd tried grouping furniture to fill floor space, placing a love seat and two chairs in front of the fireplace, and a desk by the window. The colors were all restful blues with yellow accents.

She took Will's hand and pulled him toward the bed. After she'd stepped out of her shoes, she put her hands on his chest, under his suit jacket.

"You look so good in this, I really hate to take it off, but we all have to make sacrifices."

She expected him to smile at her humor, but he only stared at her as if he'd never seen her before. His unrelenting gaze made her nervous, so she ignored it as she slid off his jacket and put the garment over the back of a chair. Then she paused to give him time to make the next move.

He didn't.

"Will?" Her uncertainty returned. "Am I making you do something you don't want to do?"

"No!" He turned away. "Dammit, Marnie. Don't you get it? I don't know what to do. I don't know what you want or—"

She got it then. Of course. He was a bit of a nerd and probably hadn't been with a lot of women. No doubt his usual type was a bookish brain, not some big-breasted, big-haired vamp. Or so he thought. She wondered what he would say if he knew the truth about her and her limited experience with men.

"What I want is you," she said, touching his arm so that he turned back to her. "Just you. I want to be in your arms, with you holding me."

While she spoke, she unfastened his tie and pulled it free. Then, with him watching her, she slid down the zipper on the back of her dress, then shrugged out of the garment. It fell to the floor, leaving her in an ivory bra and matching bikini panties.

Will's mouth actually dropped open. His obvious pleasure in her body gratified her. When his gaze fixed on her breasts and didn't budge, she figured it would be safer for everyone if she was lying down when he unfastened her bra. To that end, she stepped toward the bed.

"Why don't you take off a layer or two and join me," she said, pulling back the covers and sliding between the sheets.

He was out of his shoes, socks, trousers and shirt nearly before she'd slid across the mattress. He'd moved so fast, she hadn't had any time to admire his body, now clad only in briefs. But that would happen later, she told herself as he moved next to her, pulling the covers to his waist. He set his glasses on the nightstand.

She reached up and rested her hand on the back of his neck, then drew him toward her. "Do you really want me to tell you what I want?"

"Absolutely. In detail."

She chuckled. "All right. Touch me everywhere. But go slowly."

She reached behind her and unhooked herself, then tossed it aside and rolled onto her back. Will didn't move for the longest time, instead he just looked, as if he'd never seen a woman's bare breasts before.

She would have thought that she would feel self-conscious about the whole experience, but she found she liked him looking at her. There was something reverent in his expression. He reached out with one hand, hovering above her generous curves. A shiver of anticipation filled her. Heat grew and flared everywhere in her body.

But he didn't touch. Not yet. His fingers curled, as if preparing themselves to embrace her. Finally, when she couldn't stand it anymore, she put her hand on top of his and brought it down until they connected.

Pleasure filled her. He was warm and strong and tender as he cupped her curves. His thumb brushed across her tight nipple and she breathed his name.

"You like that?"

She opened eyes she hadn't realized she'd closed. "More than I could ever explain."

The man really listened, she thought, as he touched her. He moved slowly, so slowly she went mad in the best way possible. He explored every inch of her right breast before moving to her left. He lightly rubbed her nipples, teasing them with his fingertips, before circling his palm against them. *There was something to be said for a man into the details,* she thought contentedly as desire pulsed through her.

She reached up and wrapped her arms around his neck, drawing him close. They kissed, a perfect, deep wonderful kiss of tongues and lips. Her breasts nestled against his bare chest, her nipples flattening in a way that made her gasp. One of his long legs slipped between hers. She waited for his hand to slide over her belly, heading lower, but he didn't touch her at all.

Hoping to encourage him, she raised her leg slightly so her thigh pressed against his erection. She rubbed against him.

Suddenly he stiffened. His body convulsed against hers. Before she could figure out what had happened, he sat up in bed and swore.

If there was a God in heaven, He would be merciful and strike me dead right now, Will thought, too humiliated to move. He rested his elbows on his bare knees and dropped his head in his hands. He had to leave, he told himself. He had to just get up, grab his clothes and disappear from Marnie's life. Why the hell had he started something he knew he couldn't finish?

A harsh laugh escaped his lips. No, that he *could* finish. About twenty minutes before he was supposed to.

"Will?"

The bed shifted as Marnie moved. Will closed his eyes. He didn't want to see her incredible pale, full breasts or the tight pink nipples. He didn't want to remember what it had been like to touch her there and kiss her. He didn't deserve those memories. He was—

He started to rise to his feet, but she grabbed his arm, holding him in place.

"No, you don't," she told him. "Not until you tell me what on earth is going on."

He wanted to leave, but he knew that he owed her an explanation. Bracing himself against her contempt, he allowed himself to look at her.

And wanted to die. Because she was the most beautiful creature on all the earth. They were close enough so that he could see her, even without his glasses. Her loose hair tumbled down her back. Large green eyes pleaded with him. Her full mouth, red and swollen from their kisses, whispered his name. And her breasts. He forced himself not to look there.

"What happened?" she asked softly. "Tell me."

"Isn't it obvious?" He glanced down at his groin and the wet patch on the front of his briefs.

She followed his gaze, then caught her breath. "You came."

He braced himself for the castigation that was sure to follow her realization. It didn't matter that he'd heard it all before. Coming from Marnie it was going to hurt even more.

But instead of speaking, she stretched out on the bed and smiled at him. "Honey, that's the nicest thing to have happened to me in a long time."

He blinked at her. "You don't understand. I blew it."

"I suppose that could be a technical definition," she said teasingly. "I prefer to think of it as losing control with an incredibly sexy woman."

"Okay. How is that different?"

"Will! Don't you get it? You just gave me a huge compliment. We were touching and kissing and it was so exciting to you that you couldn't hold back."

She wasn't making sense. "But it's ruined now."

"Why?" She glanced down at his briefs. "I'm guessing that in a few minutes we can pick up where we started."

"You mean I can get it—"

"Yes," she said interrupting him.

"Sure."

"Then what's the problem?"

He wanted to believe her. Desperately. Her wide

eyes blazed with affection and desire. Nothing else. Nothing bad.

"Really?"

She stunned him by slipping off her panties. Which left her exactly naked. If he died now, he would die a happy man.

"Really," she said. "Now bare that adorable butt of yours and get over here."

"Yes, ma'am."

When he stretched out next to her, she took his hand and drew it down between her legs. "Touch me, Will. I'm already wet because of what you were doing."

Her erotic words were a distraction, right until he slipped his fingers between her damp curls and felt the swollen center of her. She felt amazing. So hot and slick. Remembering the diagrams from the sex books he'd read, he explored her, discovering her vagina, then moving up until he encountered a tiny nub buried just under the skin. As he stroked it, she gasped and clutched at him.

Her long legs stirred restlessly. Her eyes closed. He tried to recall all that he'd read about what women liked. Pages of text appeared in his brain but he couldn't focus enough to read them.

"Tell me what feels good," he said.

Marnie opened her eyes and stared at him. Then she smiled and placed her hand on top of his.

"Like this," she said, moving him around that sensitive spot.

He did as she'd illustrated, finding tremendous satisfaction in making her moan and squirm. As he watched her eyes close again and her head lean back as she experienced pleasure he'd created within her, he grew more confident. Different passages from the various sex books he'd read came back to him and he experimented with rhythms and pressure.

Soon she was panting. Color spread from her chest toward her face. Her fingers clutched at the mattress. Trying to keep his movements steady, he slipped one finger inside of her.

She screamed. Instantly her body contracted around his finger. Instinctively he thrust in and out of her as visible tremors rippled through her legs. She called out his name, begged him to never stop, then finally stilled and clung to him.

"See," she whispered against his chest. "I came without you inside of me, too."

A rush of feelings swept through him. Affection. Need. Gratitude. He'd actually done it. He'd made a woman climax.

Marnie leaned past him and opened her nightstand drawer. After pulling out a box of condoms, she handed it to him.

"There's this large object poking me in the leg. I think we should take him out for a test drive."

Will glanced down in surprise. He hadn't realized he was aroused again. Was this really going to finally happen?

Trying not to act too nervous, he fumbled with the protection and managed to get it on without ripping the latex or scarring himself. He knelt between Marnie's legs, not sure what he was supposed to do. Before he could try anything, she reached between them and touched him, guiding him forward.

He thrust his hips toward her, then felt himself entering her slick, tight passage. It was better than he'd imagined anything could be. She was hot and welcoming. Her arms came around him. He supposed he should kiss her or something but he couldn't do anything but feel her muscles tightening around him as he filled her completely.

He withdrew and pushed in again. Damn, this was incredible. Too good, he thought as the pressure built. He wanted to make it last, he wanted to—

His body took over, convulsing without warning, spilling himself into her in a spasm of orgasms that went on for what felt like hours. When he finally resurfaced, he felt instantly guilty.

"I'm sorry," he muttered. "I didn't mean—"

"Kiss me," she told him.

He did as she requested. First because he liked kissing her and second because it was a whole lot better than apologizing. The kisses deepened and got longer. He broke free so that he could nibble along her neck. When he started to pull out, she held him in place.

"Don't go. I think we have some real potential."

At her words, he felt himself getting hard again.

This time, he moved more slowly as he slipped in and out of her. He kissed her and then shifted so he could kneel between her legs and touch her breasts. He glanced down to watch himself moving in her, then saw the glistening place of her pleasure. Without thinking, he reached between them and touched her there. She gasped.

Their gazes locked as he continued to make love to

her, filling her, touching her, urging her on until she was the one who crashed first, losing herself to spasms that milked him into ecstasy.

Later, when they'd both caught their breath, Will couldn't stop grinning. He felt as if he'd conquered the world. Marnie curled up in his arms, her head resting on his shoulder.

"That was pretty amazing," she said, her breath soft against his bare skin.

Amazing? She thought he'd been amazing? He wanted to stand up and cheer. Hot damn!

He shifted so that she was on her back, and stared into her green eyes. "I want to do better next time."

She laughed. "I think doing it much better than that would kill me."

"No, I mean it. I want you to teach me everything you know."

"That would fit on a little bitty Post-it," she said with a smile.

Her long hair tumbled across the pillow. Her skin was still flushed from her release.

"You're so incredibly beautiful," he said, then kissed her mouth. "I can't believe I'm here with you."

"I agree." Her expression softened. "I thought you were pretty cute and smart, but that doesn't begin to describe you, does it?"

She'd thought he was cute? Him? He thought about his absent taste in clothes, his glasses, his cluelessness when it came to women. Happiness filled him. Maybe he did have a shot at getting this whole male–female thing right.

"I meant what I said," he told her. "I want to learn

everything. Teach me all the tricks and what you like best. What's the craziest thing you've ever done?"

Her smile faded. "Will, what are you talking about? You can't mean in bed."

"Sure. I want to hear about the other men." He hesitated, thinking that maybe he didn't want to hear *everything*. "Not the exact details, just what you did that you liked best."

She pushed him away and sat up, pulling the sheet with her so that she was covered to her throat. "What men?"

"All the guys you were with before you got married." He frowned, confused. "You're so beautiful and sexy. You must have dated a lot before you got married. Didn't you run around with rich men back then?"

She jerked as if he'd slapped her. Will knew instantly that he'd made a mistake, but he didn't know where. Was Marnie ashamed of her past?

"I'm sorry," he said quickly. "I didn't mean to pry. If you don't want to talk about it, we don't have to."

She continued to stare at him as if he'd become a stranger.

"I mean it, Marnie." He gave her a tentative smile, hoping to restore the good mood between them. "I'm not the least bit upset about what you did before. It doesn't matter to me. It was a long time ago."

Her gaze sharpened. "Gee, Will, that's really big of you. I'm impressed by your generosity. So let me get this straight. You want to hear all about my years as a whore?"

He pushed himself into a sitting position. Something was really wrong. "Marnie, I don't think you were a whore. I just thought . . ." His voice trailed off as he realized he wasn't sure what he could safely think.

She glared at him. "Not a whore, but very experienced, right?"

"Well . . ."

She pointed to the door. "Get the hell out of my bed."

He gaped at her, not sure which was more shocking—her obvious fury or her word choice.

"You swore," he said stupidly. "I've never heard you swear before."

She swung her hand toward him, slapping him hard on the cheek. "You're going to hear it again, you bastard. Get the hell out of my bed and out of my house. I never want to see you again."

Will stumbled to his feet and grabbed at his clothes. "I'm sorry," he said miserably, not able to believe how badly he'd blown it. "Marnie, let me explain."

But she didn't relent. Instead, she glared at him as he walked to the door.

"I'm sorry I ever met you," she said.

He turned to defend himself, but her expression told him there was no point. Slowly shaking his head, he walked out into the hallway and shut the door behind him.

Chapter 21

Chris checked the contents of the cooler a second time in as many minutes. God, she felt like a teenager—as nervous as she'd been on her first date with Rio. That felt like a lifetime ago.

He'd been so damned gorgeous. Men weren't supposed to be so good-looking, but he had been. And still was. Tall, muscled, blond. What was it about her and blond men? Most women went for dark and dangerous. Not her. Give her blond hair and blue eyes and she was a goner.

The kids were home for the weekend. She and Rio had talked about spending time together as a family, which explained her idea for the picnic.

Molly came into the kitchen, a worn stuffed puppy in her arms. "When's Daddy gonna be here?" she asked, eyeing the cooler. "I'm really, really hungry."

Chris checked the kitchen clock. Rio'd had to work for a couple of hours that afternoon. "Any second now, pumpkin. Go watch at the front window with your brother, okay?"

Molly nodded and disappeared the way she'd come. Chris paced. She was setting herself up, she thought grimly. The way she always had with Rio. Except . . . except this time things seemed different. He was helping out more around the house, showing up on time, even paying his child support. Amazingly, the counseling sessions seemed to be helping. What had started out as a way to try to win a million dollars might have some other benefits. She wasn't willing to say that they had a second chance together, but—

The sound of a car in the driveway broke through her thoughts.

"He's here! He's here!" Molly shrieked from the front room.

"Shut up, runt," Justin said. "Quit being a dork."

"I'm not a dork. You're a dork."

"Am not."

Chris headed toward the front of the house before the squabbling escalated. As she entered the living room, Rio walked through the front door.

After a couple of hours at the garage, he was dirty and sweaty, with stains on his blue shirt and grease spots on his jeans. Yet she found herself ignoring all that and instead watched the way he smiled when he saw his children. He bent at the waist and collected them in his arms.

"Where's Debbie?" he asked Justin.

The boy shrugged. "Playing Barbie at Kelly's house. Girls are dumb."

"You say that now, young man, but when you get

older, they're going to rule your world." He looked up, saw Chris and grinned. "Isn't that true?"

"No, but I wish it was. Things would have been pretty cool around here if I'd been in charge."

Rio laughed. His white teeth flashed against his tanned skin. She adored the shape of his face—the hollowed cheekbones and strong chin. And his mouth. Sometimes at night she dreamed about his mouth and the things he could do with it. She shivered slightly.

"Daddy, you gotta hurry," Molly said, tugging on his shirt. "Take your shower so we can have dinner."

He stood and pulled off his shirt. "You're going to have to eat without me, kiddo," he said, ruffling her hair. "I have tickets to a race tonight." He looked at Chris. "One of the guys at work couldn't make it. I wouldn't have taken them except we did our family time last night. I figured you'd want time with the kids by yourself tonight. I already called J.J. He's waiting for me."

She felt as if she were free-falling and when she hit the earth, it was going to hurt. Molly's face screwed up with confusion.

"But Daddy, we're going on a picnic. Mommy made all your favorites and I helped with the cake."

Rio glanced at all of them. "Hey, we can do this another time, right?"

Justin nodded slowly and walked out of the room. Molly stared at her father, tears filling her eyes. Chris wanted to scream. All the familiar feelings of anger and resentment crashed through her. She knew better than to plan something nice for Rio. In their marriage, no good deed went unpunished.

Unexpectedly, tears burned in her eyes, too. She

blinked them away and walked into the kitchen. She and the kids would enjoy their dinner without him. They'd learned to get along without him once, they could do it again.

"Chris?"

She walked to the cooler and began unloading food. "It doesn't matter, Rio. I should have called and discussed this with you instead of assuming you'd want to spend the evening with us. I know how important racing is to you. Go and have a good time."

She didn't dare look at him. Not when he was shirtless. She already felt too vulnerable and the sight of him was only going to make it harder to be mature.

He repeated her name. She lifted out the cake, secure in its Tupperware container.

"Just go, Rio," she said, her back still to him. "This always happens. I plan something nice and it gets ruined. I used to think it was your fault, but it isn't. It's just lousy luck and timing. Really. Go. It's okay."

"No, it isn't." He moved closer. She felt his presence behind her. "Tell me what you're thinking."

The question startled her so much, she turned around. "What?"

"Tell me what you're feeling. Are you angry?"

She stared at him. Her feelings? "I, ah, don't know." She thought for a second. "Sad, I guess."

"Because you wanted us to have a fun evening together?"

She nodded. "I guess I'm feeling lonely. Stupid."

He frowned. "Why stupid?"

I hadn't meant to say that one, she thought. "Because I don't know what we're doing. Are we playing house for a million dollars or are we screwing up lives? I miss my kids. I know they're better off staying with my mom but having them home makes me miss them even more. And it's hard having you here."

"I'm confused, too. I'm sorry. I should have called before making plans for tonight. I'd really rather go on a picnic with you guys than go to the races, but..."

"J.J.'s waiting." She finished the sentence for him. "You'd better hurry."

He hesitated, as if torn. Maybe he was battling inside, but she didn't doubt who would win. Which didn't stop the hurt when he turned away from her.

"I won't be late," he promised as he left.

"Okay."

The pain inside was familiar, but along with it was a new and powerful resolve. Rio wasn't going to change. If *she* wanted changes, they were up to her.

Sunday morning, in the dining room of the Royal Marriageville Hotel, Jonathan sat across from the two women who had recently invaded his life. Around them aging waiters cleared plates from those who had already visited the buffet. Jonathan found he was far more interested in his guests than in any brunch entrée.

Mother and daughter sat side by side. Taylor was elegant in a purple dress, her hair swept up. Linnie wore a white blouse tucked into a fawn-colored cotton skirt, her long hair loose and curly.

"You're grinning like a sheep," Taylor commented, picking up her mimosa and taking a sip.

"I never understood that expression," he admitted. "Do sheep grin?"

"They have charming smiles," she assured him. "And lovely teeth. I can't believe you've never noticed."

Linnie laughed. "She's always been like this, you know. But I can't figure out how to change her."

Jonathan let his gaze roam over Taylor's face. "Stubborn people can often be difficult."

Taylor sniffed. "I'm determined. There's a difference."

Linnie raised her eyebrows, but didn't respond to his statement. Instead she leaned toward him and lowered her voice. "There's a woman staring at us. Are you being stalked by a rabid fan?"

He looked in the direction she indicated and saw Katrina Melon dining with another reporter. When she saw him looking, she waved her fingers. He nodded.

"She's the host of *Psychology in the News*," he said. "No one special."

"She wants to be, though," Taylor said, sotto voce. "The slightly older Katrina has the hots for your father."

Linnie didn't look impressed. "So do you have a girlfriend now?" she asked.

Jonathan sipped his coffee. "No. Do you have a boyfriend?"

Linnie laughed. "Dad, we've talked about this. I see boys at dances and stuff, and as far as I'm concerned, that's plenty."

Dad. She'd said it before, but Jonathan didn't think he would ever get tired of hearing the word. "Just checking."

Linnie looked at her mother and rolled her eyes. "He's trying to trip me up. The thing is, I'm not lying."

"I know, sweetie. Men are inherently insecure."

Jonathan glanced at his daughter. "Ignore her."

Linnie laughed. "I will. For now. So you don't have a girlfriend, but you were married before, right?"

"Don't grill your father," Taylor said mildly as she cut into her omelet.

"Why not? I need to get to know him, right? So I have to ask questions."

"I don't mind," Jonathan said quickly. "Yes, Linnie, I was married before. Shelly's an attorney for a large firm in New York. We were married for three years. If you want to know what went wrong, I can't tell you because I don't know. We said and did all the right things and in the end, we didn't want to be together."

Linnie tilted her head to the side as she studied him. "Don't you think it's really interesting that neither you or Mom are married? I mean, it's probably just a coincidence, but a really interesting one."

"Subtle," Taylor said. "Very subtle."

Linnie didn't look the least bit remorseful. "You're the one who said it was perfectly normal for me to want a traditional family. At sixteen, I'm caught between the world of being an adult and a child. At least that's what you're always telling me. So the kid part of me wants my parents to be together. Why wouldn't I? I've never had a dad and a mom together before."

Jonathan didn't know what to say. He still fought with anger when he remembered what Taylor had done. He mourned for the lost time with his daughter. Yet he couldn't complain about the job Taylor had done, the way Linnie had been raised.

"Do you think there are any more cinnamon rolls?" Taylor asked, changing the subject for him. She flagged down a waiter and asked him to bring more to the table.

The conversation shifted from families to food to Linnie's return flight to camp.

"I'll be fine, Mom," their daughter said.

Taylor didn't look convinced. "I should have driven you to Dallas like I always do."

Linnie had a flight out of the Marriageville regional airport on a commuter plane. She would land in Dallas and board her direct flight to Virginia.

"Mo-om, I'm not a kid. You don't have to pin a name tag on me and worry that I won't find my way. Besides, Mr. Baker is going to be on the flight and his plane leaves Dallas way after mine. He said he'd make sure I got safely onto my flight."

"I know." Taylor bit her lower lip. "I'm worrying, but I can't help it."

"Try," Linnie said, rising. "I'm going back for another round at the buffet. Be right back."

Jonathan watched her go. "If it helps, I'm worried, too. But I think you made the right decision. She's plenty old enough to do this on her own."

"You're right. It's just hard." She toyed with her fork. "I'm sorry, Jonathan. The more I see the two of you together the more I realize I was wrong to keep her from you. You're a terrific father."

"That's pretty high praise after seeing me in action for a week."

"I still think it's true. You're really good to her, and for her."

If she was being honest, he decided he had to be the same. "I'm good *now* because I'm older and she's already grown-up. There's not a lot left for me to do. I can't swear that I would have handled the situation as well seventeen years ago."

She blinked in surprise. "Is that a concession?"

"An observation. I've spent the past seventeen years focused on my career. There wasn't room for anything else."

"I've always thought…" She cleared her throat, then smiled as the waiter delivered the extra cinnamon rolls. She took one and broke it in half. "I used to wonder if we would have made it. You know, if I'd told you about being pregnant and all."

"You're assuming I would have done the right thing and offered to marry you."

Her steady gaze met his. "There's not a doubt in my mind."

He liked her confidence in him. "Okay, I'll bite. Would we have made it?"

She nibbled on her sweet roll and chewed. When she'd swallowed, she shook her head. "No. We were too young, there was too much stacked against us. I've been thinking a lot about what went wrong in our relationship. The harder I clung to you, the more you pushed away. I stood in the way of your need to be successful. I doubt we would have lasted more than a couple of years."

He considered her frank assessment, then nodded. "I agree."

"The truth makes me sad," she admitted.

"I'm not sure what I feel," he told her. "Even if we'd divorced, I still would have had Linnie in my life."

She nodded.

He could see the pain in her eyes. She desperately wanted him to let the past go, all the while knowing it would take time for him to heal. By then, he would have long left Marriageville. Funny, he hadn't realized it, but the contest was nearly over. Soon he would be back in his regular life. He would have gained a daughter and lost Taylor. Again.

"We should probably change the subject," she said. "As long as we keep talking about *something*. The distraction keeps me from worrying about Linnie and her flight."

He glanced at his watch. They had to leave for the airport in half an hour. "Tell you what. After we get her on the plane here, we'll find something to do. Something that will keep you from thinking about her flight. Maybe a nice, long walk."

She glanced down at her clothes. "I'm not dressed for exercise. I'm wearing three-inch heels that hurt even when I'm sitting."

"No problem. I'll take you to your place to change, then we'll head to my hotel and I'll do the same. How does that sound? We can spend the day distracting each other."

She smiled. "That sounds nice. Thanks."

Marnie stood under the hot water of her shower. It was nearly noon on Sunday and she'd finally forced herself to get out of bed. She felt as if she'd been run over by a train. Her body ached, her eyes were swollen from crying, her head hurt. Worst of all, her heart had been broken.

All this time she'd been falling for a guy whose only interest had been getting it on with the local whore. Will was just like everyone else—interested in her body and not caring about her mind or her spirit. Not caring about *her*. She'd thought he was different, but she'd been wrong.

She turned off the water and stepped out into the bathroom. After drying off, she didn't bother with her usual regime of body lotion. She didn't even put on makeup. After halfheartedly rubbing on some sunscreen, she turned away from the mirror and walked to her closet where she dressed in shorts and a T-shirt.

She didn't understand how she'd made such a mistake. All those evenings they'd spent together had given her a chance to get to know him. Or so she'd thought. Hadn't they discussed their goals and dreams, their beliefs, what they liked and didn't like? Hadn't he teased her and been kind and gentle and attentive? Had it all been an act?

She knew what men thought about her. She'd been hearing it ever since she turned thirteen and woke up one morning with breasts. She'd gotten used to being judged and for the most part it didn't bother her. But Will was supposed to be special.

It hurt so much, she thought as she stepped into sandals, then returned to the bathroom to blow-dry her hair. When George had died, she hadn't felt anything for weeks. She'd welcomed the numbness, knowing it would end and when it had, she'd thought she was going to die. But she'd been prepared. This was different. Will's betrayal had caught her exposed and had dropped her to her knees with no warning.

Never again, she promised herself as she held the blow-dryer to her hair. As long as she lived, she would never trust a man again.

When she was finished in the bathroom, she walked

into the bedroom, grabbed her purse and keys, then headed toward the hall. She'd been in the house for far too long, canceling her appointments and not bothering to go to work. Now she needed to breathe fresh air and figure out a way to forget what had happened.

She walked down the stairs, noticing the complete silence of the house. Will had moved out Friday night. It was better with him gone, she told herself. She liked having the big house to herself. She'd made a real mistake inviting him here. She should—

A flicker of movement caught her attention. Marnie slowed on the stairs, but not in time to escape notice. Will sat on the small bench in the foyer. When he saw her, he stood and shoved his hands into his jeans front pockets.

"Don't run off," he said, his voice low and pleading. "Please, Marnie, I really need to talk to you."

Conflicting emotions passed through her. Anger. Hurt. Shame. She didn't know which was the most powerful, or what she was supposed to say. So she stayed silent.

"I'm sorry," he said at last. "I never meant to offend you."

"I hate to think what you would have said if that *had* been your plan all along."

He winced. "I know I was a complete bastard. I'm so bad at this sort of thing."

"If you mean making me feel like something you scraped off the bottom of your shoe, I'd say you did a fine job."

He took a step toward her. She hated that she actually noticed how good he looked in his jeans and white long-sleeved shirt. He was still the best-looking nerd she'd ever met.

The emotional battle ended as anger won. She didn't stop to acknowledge that she was as mad at the world's constant judgment of her as she was at him.

"For your information," she said as she walked to the bottom of the stairs then crossed the foyer. "I was a virgin when I met my late husband. I'd never been with anyone before and I haven't been with anyone since. Except you. And that was a mistake I'm going to do my best to forget."

"Marnie—"

She cut him off with a shake of her head. "I was so wrong about you. I thought because you were shy and quiet that you were really deep. But the truth is you don't talk because you don't have anything to say. You don't know squat about people and less than that about women. How dare you judge me on my appearance?"

"I was wrong," he said, looking anguished. "If you knew the truth about me—"

"What makes you think I'd care?"

He nodded. "You're right. I just wanted you to know that I'm sorry. I never meant to hurt you. I *did* judge you because of how you look. I couldn't imagine someone so beautiful wouldn't have been pursued by dozens of guys."

She planted her hands on her hips. "Did it ever occur to you that I might have the strength of character to say no?"

He ducked his head, which was answer enough.

"I'd never been with anyone else," he mumbled.

His single sentence erased every thought in her brain. "Excuse me?"

He looked at her. "I was a virgin, Marnie. Between being smart and going to college so young, and a series of really strange events, I never did it. I'd never made love. Then I met you and I knew you were the last person I could be with. Not—" He held up his hand. "Not because I thought you were a hooker, but because I thought you were incredible. What could you possibly see in a jerk like me? I don't deserve you. But when it seemed as if you might like me, even want me that way, I allowed myself to hope. Then when we started making love…"

He took a step toward her. "You were amazing. I'd imagined the experience a thousand times, and it was better than my best fantasies. Being with you was something I'll treasure for the rest of my life. I never, ever meant to hurt you."

Marnie tried to find comfort in his words. She supposed they were, in a way, a compliment. But all she could think was that he was thrilled that he finally got laid. She wanted to hear that she mattered to him. That *they* mattered. Instead he wanted to talk about how great the sex had been.

"I'm glad it was a life-changing experience," she said coldly as she walked past him. "I'll be sure to give you the first-timers' discount when I send you a bill."

Chapter
22

"Okay, my flight is on time and I'm boarding in about ten minutes," Linnie said cheerfully from Dallas. "I survived the flight from Marriageville to here. Are you going to panic until I call you from Virginia?"

Taylor smiled as she held her cell phone. "Oh, probably. I've always been very good at panicking."

"Are you hanging out with Dad?"

Taylor turned toward Jonathan's open bedroom door. He was inside, changing into casual clothes. They'd already stopped at her house where she'd replaced her dress with shorts and a shirt.

"Yes. We're going to panic together."

Linnie chuckled. "He's pretty cool, Mom. I like him."

"I like him, too," Taylor said softly, wishing she didn't.

"You know, this might be a second chance for you guys. You could think about that."

"I could," Taylor agreed, not wanting to admit she already had given it quite a bit of thought.

"Tell him hi and I'll talk to you both later, okay?"

"Bye, sweetie. I love you."

"Love you, too, Mom."

The phone line went dead. Taylor pushed the "end" button and tucked the phone back into her purse.

"Was that Linnie?" Jonathan asked as he came out of his bedroom.

Taylor tried not to stare, but it was difficult. He'd changed into jeans, but hadn't bothered to fasten the shirt he'd pulled on. She stared at his chest. Except for a few gray hairs replacing the brown ones, he didn't look all that different from seventeen years ago.

"What? Oh, yes. She's at the Dallas airport and her flight is about to board. She'll call us when she gets to camp."

She found herself talking to his chest, which was ridiculous, so she forced herself to raise her gaze to his face. A smile tugged at the corners of his mouth . . . as if he'd noticed the direction of her attention. *Darn the man.*

"Um, there are several lovely walking paths around town," she said, suddenly feeling nervous and taking a step back from him. "Through the park, of course. That's always nice. There's also a historic walking tour." She frowned. "Or is it 'an' historical tour? I can never remember about those pesky 'h' words."

"Pesky," he agreed, as he stepped closer. "We could take either tour." He was close enough to touch . . . which he did, placing his hands on her face and bending down to lightly kiss her. "Or we could stay in."

"Jonathan, stop!" She pushed him away even though she didn't want to. When he didn't move, she took a step back herself. "This is crazy. We're dealing with some serious emotional issues. A physical encounter would only complicate things."

She hated that she was being sensible. Why didn't the man just kiss her senseless and then ravish her?

"I want you," he breathed, kissing her again.

His lips were astonishingly gentle against hers, brushing back and forth, teasing her into responding. She groaned, trying to find the strength to resist. This was nothing more than a slippery slope to regret. But every fiber of her being longed for him.

"We have to stop," she said, although even she could hear that she sounded halfhearted at best. "Really, I . . ."

She meant to push him away, or at least put her hands on his shoulders to find the strength to turn and run. Instead she felt her palms against his bare chest. The hair there tickled slightly, in the most erotic way. Tickled and teased, all the sensations making her moan softly.

"Taylor," he breathed. "Want me."

"I do," she said and lost herself to him.

His mouth parted. Hers did the same. She welcomed him, savoring the sweet taste of him. He licked her lower lip, then slipped inside where he brushed against her, circling once, twice, lazy circles that made her squirm.

She slipped her arms around him so that she could rest her hands under his shirt, against his back. She pressed her fingers into the thick muscles there. He was so strong, so masculine. Her traitorous mind remembered what it had been like to make love with him. Images from the past blended with the present, until she couldn't distinguish one from the other. She could only know that this time it would be even better.

Jonathan withdrew enough to kiss her cheeks, her

forehead, then nibble along her jaw. "You're even better than I remember."

She sighed. "You talk a lot more than *I* remember."

He laughed, nipped on her earlobe, then sucked the tiny injury.

She pushed his hands away so she could tug off his shirt. Then she began unfastening her own blouse.

She shrugged out of the garment. Fortunately she'd put on one of her nicer bras so when his gaze settled on the lacy cream-colored cups hugging her breasts she didn't have to worry about tears or holes.

He reached for her, pulling her close. One of his hands dropped to her rear where he pulled her against himself so that she could feel his arousal. She pressed against him, suddenly weak with anticipation. His other hand reached for the fastener of her bra and flicked it open easily.

The air in the room felt cool against her bare skin. Her already taut nipples tightened even more. She was barely aware of shrugging out of her bra. When he brushed his thumbs against the tight peaks, she thought she was going to faint from the glory of his touch.

He bent down and kissed her sensitive skin, drawing her into his mouth and sucking. She gasped, clinging to him. Fire shot through her. Fire and a need that made her want to beg him to never stop. Why did it have to be better than before?

She clutched his shoulders with one hand and ran her fingers through his hair. *Cool silk,* she thought absently, as he moved to her other breast and made her gasp all over again.

Every inch of skin felt hypersensitized, she thought

hazily. A flick of his fingers on her breasts nearly brought her to her knees. She didn't want to think about what would happen when he touched her more intimately. On second thought . . . she did want to imagine that physical perfection.

Without warning, he shifted his arms, sliding one behind her thighs and the other across her back. He lifted her off her feet and drew her against his chest. Ever elegant, Taylor shrieked in protest, flailing her arms before turning toward him and grabbing him around the neck.

"What are you doing?" she demanded.

He grinned. "I would have thought that was obvious. I'm sweeping you off your feet and carrying you to my bedroom."

"I can walk."

He gave her a mock frown. "Didn't you used to be romantic?"

"I'm too heavy. You'll hurt yourself." Plus she didn't like the sensation of being carried. It was disconcerting.

"You're not that heavy. Besides—" He winked. "I work out. Can't you tell?"

Actually she could. He had plenty of muscles and no soft spots that she could see. But she wasn't about to feed his obviously overinflated ego. Still, when he bent down and set her gently on the mattress, she couldn't help being a little impressed.

He knelt on the floor beside her and brushed her hair from her face. "Taylor," he whispered softly. "I've missed you."

His tender words brought tears to her eyes. How she wanted to believe him. She blinked, determined not to give in to the emotion of the moment. "You haven't given me a moment's thought in the past seventeen years."

"I'd say at least a moment's worth. Maybe more. But being with you here has made me miss you."

He brushed her mouth with his, then deepened the kiss. One of his hands tangled in her hair, while the other caressed her breasts, touching and taunting until she was breathless. He moved lower, nibbling along her neck, then licking her nipples until she didn't care that she wasn't breathing. Between her legs, heat and anticipation pulsed in time with her rapid heartbeat. The insistent pressure made her want to force him to take her now. She held back, in part out of reticence and in part because the waiting would make it better.

He moved to the foot of the bed and drew off her sandals. She unfastened her shorts and he tugged them free. Her panties quickly followed. When he moved next to her on the mattress, she shifted to give him room. He slid close and wrapped his arms around her. One of his legs slipped between hers, the worn denim soft against her bare skin.

He brushed his hand against her belly, making her catch her breath in anticipation. She parted her legs, hoping he would get the hint. He did. But instead of slipping his fingers into her waiting heat, he shifted his whole body, moving between her legs, then bending low to kiss her into a frenzy.

The first touch of lips and tongue nearly sent her over the edge. She didn't want to think about how long it had been and how much her body needed this intimate contact. But it was so much more than that. Jonathan had been the man to teach her this incredible pleasure. He'd patiently explored her body, discovering uncharted points of ecstasy, what made her laugh and moan and cry out his name. He'd been able to push her over the edge with a few well-placed flicks of his tongue. And he hadn't forgotten a thing.

He began slowly, licking all of her, dipping his tongue into that place he would enter later. He easily found the tiny bundle of nerves and reintroduced himself with a soul-stirring kiss that made her legs tremble. She drew back her knees and grasped the bedspread in her hands. It was too good, too intense. She couldn't possibly survive what he planned to do.

He obviously didn't care. She found herself begging, although instead of asking him to stop, she implored him to go on forever. She rocked her head from side to side, tried to catch her breath, all the while he rubbed and circled and even sucked that one sensitive place. Pressure grew. Her muscles tightened in anticipation. She felt her body get hotter and hotter until flames licked at the bottoms of her feet.

She wanted to hold back, to attempt some semblance of control, but it wasn't possible. Even as she grasped for a few ragged shreds of dignity, he slowly slipped a finger deep inside of her. He pushed up, rubbing her point of pleasure from underneath as he caressed her with his tongue from above.

It was too much. She came with an incoherent cry of delight as spasms rippled through her. The orgasm went on and on, aided by Jonathan's light touch. He drew every ounce of it from her, leaving her sated and trembling.

"You do that better than anyone I know," he said, returning to her side.

"Do what?"

"Respond to me."

She snuggled close to him. "That's because you taught me what to like."

He chuckled. "And here I had always remembered it as you teaching me how to do that to a woman."

"You knew before you met me."

He touched her chin, forcing her to look at him. "Taylor, before you, there had been one girl my first year of college. It happened in the backseat of my car in about fifteen seconds."

"Really? You acted so confident."

"I was faking it. Besides, you seemed to be the one person on the planet who knew less than me. We learned together."

Had they? She remembered differently, but was pleased with his recollection. Now she recalled a few things of her own. She reached over and ran her fingernails lightly over his nipples. They puckered instantly and he groaned.

"Don't do that," he protested.

She didn't stop. "Why not?"

"Because you know what it does to me."

They were playing, but the teasing game had an element of poignancy. She *did* know what that particular caress did to him. She knew lots of things. They had a past, which shouldn't have made her sad, but it did. Perhaps because she suddenly wanted them to have more of a past. Her heart regretted all the lost years and the "what could have been."

She leaned over and kissed his belly, hiding her face until her emotions were under control. When she could once again smile at him, she trailed her fingers down to the front of his jeans.

"One of us is incredibly overdressed. I was thinking of letting you have your way with me, but if you don't take off your clothes, I'll think you're not interested."

He was naked in less than thirty seconds. "What were you saying?" he asked as he slid back onto the bed.

"Nothing."

She reached for him, but before she could touch the hardness of his arousal, he grabbed her wrist.

"Not this time," he said lightly.

She grinned. "Jonathan, are you having a control issue?" she teased.

"Yes, and it's damned humiliating at my age. But there's something about being with you." He stared into her eyes. "You're still beautiful, Taylor. More beautiful than before."

His compliment embarrassed her. "Honey, you don't need to use flattery. At this point, I'm pretty much a sure thing."

But he didn't smile. Instead he touched her cheek. "I mean it. You're lovely. And I want you."

His intensity chased away her humor. She nodded and waited while he pulled a box of condoms from his dresser and slipped one on. She almost made a joke about him being a very prepared boy scout, but his expression was too intense. She could read the fire of need in his eyes and it set up an answering spark deep inside of her.

He knelt between her thighs, then kissed her. She

felt him probing and automatically slipped a hand between them to guide him home.

Home. *Bad choice of words,* she thought as he filled her. Because it was all too familiar. The feel of him inside of her, the taste of him, the way he kissed. Past and present blurred until she didn't know what was real. Nor did it matter. Because with his first thrust, she felt herself carried toward paradise.

Again and again he moved in and out of her. It was perfect. No, better. It was incredible. His pace increased. He broke the kiss and stared into her eyes.

"Come for me," he whispered.

His erotic request sent her over the edge. She began to convulse around him. He groaned, holding on until she was nearly finished, then he stiffened and called out her name as he shuddered.

They found their way under the covers. Jonathan pulled her close, his arms around her. He dropped light kisses onto her forehead and cheeks.

"Pretty amazing," he said, then sighed with contentment.

"Amazing," Taylor echoed, still stunned by what had happened.

In the aftermath of their encounter, she found herself slowly returning to sanity. A single voice screamed inside her head. It got louder and louder, repeating the same question.

What the hell were you thinking?

There it was. The truth. She hadn't been thinking. She'd been feeling. She'd been getting lost in a gray area between what was and what had been.

She'd made love with Jonathan Kirby. Linnie's father, her, Taylor's, competition in their crazy contest. The man who had once broken her heart and if she was foolish enough to hand it over a second time, would break it again.

If?

The truth struck her with a blinding light. *Too late,* she thought frantically. Much too late. Somewhere in the past few weeks she had fallen for him.

"You're looking serious," Jonathan said, propping his head on his hand. "Second thoughts?"

"I passed them a long time ago." She forced herself to look at him. "Making love might not have been the best idea on the planet. Our situation was complicated enough before. Now what do we have?"

"Personally I have an overwhelming desire to take a quick nap, but that will pass."

He was teasing her. She could see it in the crinkling of his eyes.

"Do you really not think this was a big deal?" she asked.

"Of course it was. I just don't think it's the end of the world."

She knew it wasn't that. Of course he could be light-hearted—he hadn't just fallen in love with *her.* He was going to walk away from their time together with a few good memories and a new daughter. She was the one who would be left broken and bleeding.

"I have to go," she announced abruptly.

Jonathan sat up. "Don't run away, Taylor. It won't solve anything. Let's talk about this."

She stood and circled the bed, picking up clothing

as she went. "Women across America would sell their souls to hear the man in their life say those words. Jonathan, you're betraying the brotherhood."

"I'm trying to understand. What went wrong?"

"Nothing." She pulled on her panties and her bra, then stepped into her shorts. "I need some time to think about this."

"You're just going to go home, eat chocolate and tell yourself I'm a bastard."

She fastened her shirt. "I'll admit to the chocolate, but I don't think you're the bad guy. You haven't done anything wrong."

"Then why are you leaving?"

In other circumstances she would really think that he wanted her to stay. For a second she gave in to the fantasy of them spending the day together. They would stay in bed, making love over and over again, ordering room service to keep up their strength. Then they would talk. Maybe about the past, maybe about the book they wanted to do together.

The images tempted her, but self-preservation warned her to get away while she could. Maybe she could figure out a way to stop loving him before it was too late. She didn't want to spend the next seventeen years the way she'd spent the ones before—waiting for the only man she'd ever loved.

The unexpected insight nearly sent her to her knees. Taylor froze. She'd been waiting for Jonathan? No. That wasn't possible. She'd had a full life—she'd been busy. If she hadn't ever felt a spark for someone else, it was because . . . because . . .

"I have to go."

She shoved her feet into her sandals, grabbed her purse and headed for the door.

"Taylor, wait!"

She heard him slip out of bed and quickly stepped out into the hall. She had to get away. If she stayed, he would figure out something was wrong. Then he would pick at it until she confessed and then where would she be?

Taylor ran through the halls of the hotel. At least she didn't have to worry about getting home. Her car sat in the parking lot. She'd driven over to the hotel that morning when she and Linnie had joined Jonathan for brunch. It felt like a lifetime ago.

She got into her car, then rested her head against the steering wheel. She was shaking and felt nauseous. It was bad enough that she'd fallen for him again, but to realize that she'd spent the past seventeen years of her life waiting for him to show up was frightening. How could she have done it? How could she not have known she was doing it?

Her fingers were shaking as she put the key into the ignition. She had to get home, she told herself. Once there she could pull the covers over her head and pretend this had never happened, or at least try. Unfortunately, self-delusion had never been one of her strong points.

Taylor turned right out of the parking lot, taking back streets toward the main highway. At the next intersection, as she slowed for the stop sign, she saw a familiar car parked behind Marnie's Palace of Beauty. Taylor frowned. Marnie never worked on Sunday. She thought that was akin to blasphemy.

Curious and grateful for a distraction, Taylor turned

her car into the parking lot and pulled up next to the shiny BMW.

"Knock, knock," she called at the screen door in the back. She tried the handle and found it open. "Marnie? Are you here?"

"In my office."

Taylor walked down the hall and entered Marnie's office. Her friend sat behind her desk, several computer printouts in front of her.

"I'm going over my books," she said without looking up.

"Marnie? What's going on? You never work on Sunday."

Marnie sniffed, then raised her head. Taylor stared, not sure if she was more shocked by her friend's lack of makeup (which she'd never seen before) or the tears pooling in her eyes.

"Oh, Marnie."

Taylor walked to her friend and pulled her to her feet. Hugging her gently, she patted Marnie's back. "What happened?"

"He th-thought I was a whore," Marnie gasped between great sobs of pain. She pulled free of Taylor and reached for the box of tissues on her desk. "We made love Friday night. I thought it was special and that I mattered to him, but he didn't care about me at all. He just wanted to get laid. And then when it was over, he practically accused me of being a whore."

Taylor winced. When Marnie sat back in her chair, Taylor settled on a corner of the desk.

"Did he really say whore?"

"No, but he implied it. I hate him. I even swore."

Taylor knew how rare that was—like never.

"And I slapped him."

"He deserved it."

Marnie blew her nose, then tossed the tissue into the trash container by the wall. The plastic receptacle already overflowed with used tissues.

"I miss George," Marnie said miserably. "He cared about me—the me who laughs and cries and dreams. He thought I was smart and capable."

"I know this is hard and what Will did was very wrong."

Marnie glared at her. "If you take his side in this, I'll never speak to you again."

"I'm not taking his side."

Marnie sniffed. "You're using a reasonable tone of voice. You're not my therapist, Taylor."

"Okay." Taylor held up her hands. "Will was a real shit. But based on how you look and how people react to you, his assumption that you were sexually experienced isn't unreasonable."

"Taylor!"

"It's true, Marnie. Come on. Give the guy a break. You're stunning. Guys hit on you all the time. In your position, most men would be saying yes to every woman who asked, so it doesn't occur to them that you'd say no. Even though he made a horrible mistake and was a real jerk, the bottom line is he wasn't put off by your supposed past. That's small comfort."

Marnie held up her thumb and forefinger less than a hair's breadth apart. "Very small comfort." She grabbed another tissue. "He should have assumed better about me."

"I agree. So he was stupid. Is that news for the gender?"

Her teasing comment made Marnie smile. "I guess not."

"Besides, they can't read our minds, even when we want them to," Taylor continued. How long had it taken her to learn that particular lesson? All those months of waiting for Jonathan to figure out that she was pregnant and come back to her. It hadn't happened and she'd been crushed.

Marnie sighed. "I know everything you're saying is right. I just feel so gross. He tried to make it better by telling me that it was special for him, but that was a matter of too little, too late."

"What did he say?"

Marnie squirmed in her chair. "He sort of told me that he'd been a virgin."

Taylor stared at her. "What? He's got to be at least twenty-seven, twenty-eight?"

"I know. But that's what he said. Something about going to college really young and some other things he didn't explain." She shrugged. "So it was his first time."

"I can't believe it," Taylor said. A male virgin in his twenties. She thought that only happened with priests.

"I was mean about it," Marnie said, ducking her head. "I told him that when I sent him a bill I'd give him the first timers' discount."

Taylor winced. "He won't be getting it up for a while after that."

"You think?"

"Marnie, you know you terrify guys who are sexually active. What do you think it was like for a man like

Will to make love with you? I'm sure he was horrified at the thought of doing something wrong. He finally gets through the event, only to insult you. Wouldn't you feel awful if you were him?"

"I refuse to be sympathetic. For him it was just about the sex. He doesn't care about me."

"How do you know? He's probably been desperate to do it for fourteen years, and it finally happens. Of course he's going to talk about the physical, but that doesn't mean the emotional wasn't important. If you want to know how he feels, you're going to have to ask him."

"I don't care anymore."

"Liar."

Marnie glared at her. "Therapist."

Chapter

23

Taylor's improved mood lasted all of seventeen seconds after she got back into her car. By the time she'd driven home, her spirits had slumped back into the gutter and she was wondering why she'd ever thought she was the least bit intelligent. She'd messed up her life. She'd been pining for Jonathan for years, she'd made love with him knowing he would leave, and now she had to deal with that man forever because they had a child together.

If my patients could see me now, they'd run screaming in the opposite direction, she thought as she stepped into the house.

"Taylor?"

She turned toward the sound of her mother's voice and saw her walking out of the living room. She gave Taylor a concerned look.

"Are you all right, dear? Jonathan has called here twice in the past half-hour looking for you. He sounded worried."

"I can't imagine why he would be concerned," she lied. "I'm fine."

Her mother studied her. "Uh-huh. That is not an 'I'm fine' expression. Want to talk about it?"

Taylor set her purse on the small table in the entryway. "There's nothing to say. The contest will be over soon. Based on the ongoing sessions with the couples, it's going to be a tie. Ironic—all this effort and we tie."

Linda took her arm and led her into the living room. "Why don't we sit here so you can start at the beginning."

Taylor settled on the sofa where many life-altering conversations had occurred in the past few weeks. "There's no problem, really. Just a lot of changes." She looked at her mother. "I'm not holding out for the million-dollar book advance. As I said, it looks like we're going to tie. The last offer Alexi told me about was for seven hundred thousand dollars. That's more than enough. I'm going to take it."

Linda smiled. "Think they'll pay you in cash? I've never seen that much money before."

"Me, either." Taylor tried to ignore the pain in her chest and instead concentrated on the good news. "It'll make a big difference in our lives. We can get a new roof on the house. Get the whole place painted."

"You can even move out," Linda teased.

"What? Be a grown-up? Live on my own?" Taylor touched her mother's arm. "I wouldn't have made it without you. When I think about what it was like when Linnie was born—I was terrified. But you were my rock. All those times you could have reminded me that you'd tried to bring me home, to save me from myself. You never said 'I told you so.' "

Linda chuckled. "Honey, I was thinking it."

"I'll bet." Taylor leaned back into the sofa. "I can fund Linnie's college and your retirement. According to Alexi, I'm going to be traveling a lot, promoting the book, so I'll have to change my therapy schedule, but I think it can all be done."

"Your life is going to be very exciting."

Taylor nodded, because the alternative was to try to speak. And if she did that, she was going to cry. Despite her good fortune and improvement in circumstances, she'd never felt so empty and lost inside.

Linda's gray-blue eyes turned knowing. "Now do you want to tell me what's really going on?"

"I'm in love with Jonathan."

Taylor spoke the words aloud, let them settle around her in the quiet of the room. They felt...right.

"I think I've always been in love with him. There aren't words to describe my stupidity," she said.

Linda sighed. "I'm sure we could come up with a few."

Her mother's unexpected response made her laugh—in a gasping, strangled sort of way. "Mom— that's not real sympathetic."

"I know, Taylor. This isn't the time for sympathy. You knew he was a snake when you let him in the door."

Taylor stiffened. "How can you say that? He's your granddaughter's father. He's intelligent, well-educated and damned good at what he does. Linnie gets her charm from him, along with her abilities in math. He's funny, he's good-looking. He's going to be a great father." He was also terrific in bed, but what was the point of sharing that with her mother?

"Just checking," Linda said, patting her arm.

Taylor blinked at her. "Excuse me? I'm spilling my bleeding guts all over the floor and you're running a test?"

Her mother looked at her impatiently. "Explain the problem. You're in love with him. From your description, he seems to be a man worth loving. Why is that horrible?"

"He hates me. He's never going to forgive me for keeping Linnie from him. He got his way in everything and I'm the one who gets my soul ripped out again."

"The pity party was interesting when you were eighteen, but it's tedious now."

Taylor couldn't have been more shocked if her mother had slapped her. "Pity party?"

Linda shrugged. "I don't know what else to call it. Take a look at your life, Taylor. Your daughter is happy and successful. After years of counting pennies, you've just been handed financial freedom. Your career is about to take off and you've fallen in love."

"With a man who hates me."

"Hate is too strong a word," Linda told her. "He has a right to some time to adjust to the change in circumstances. In his shoes, we would both be just as furious and upset. Seventeen years ago, keeping the information from Jonathan seemed like a good idea. You were so hurt and I didn't want that boy in your life. Plus, there was a part of me that wanted to punish him for taking you away. So when you didn't know if you should tell him about Linnie, I encouraged you to keep the secret. Over the years I've often wondered if it was the best decision."

Taylor hadn't thought there were any more surprises left, but she'd been wrong. "Mom, you can't blame yourself. I chose what to do."

"Did you? You were young, Taylor." Her mother

shrugged. "It's over now. Jonathan owes me for stealing you away and I paid him back by keeping him from *his* daughter. I would say we're even." She looked at Taylor.

Taylor shifted uncomfortably. "I don't know." She thought about their recent passionate encounter. Had those moments been an insight into the state of his heart? Had he forgiven her?

"Last time Jonathan said he wanted out, you came running home. Are you going to give up without a fight again?"

Taylor stood and glared down at her mother. "That's so unfair. I didn't give up—he ended the relationship."

"How is that different? You preach strength and autonomy to your daughter, but what do you dream about in your heart? There have been men interested in you. Why didn't you marry one of them?"

Taylor planted her hands on her hips. "For the exact reason you never remarried. I wanted to feel the same love that I felt with Jonathan. Not more. It didn't have to be better or flashier or more passionate. I just wanted to be that emotionally engaged. I wanted to care as much. I wanted a love that made me feel content."

Her mother nodded. "Fair enough. Did you ever find it?"

All her anger drained away, leaving behind an empty heart. "Yes. This morning. With Jonathan."

"I'll ask my question again. Are you going to walk away from him? Or are you going to fight for what you want?" She rose and faced her daughter. "I've heard you talk about how the two of you wouldn't have made it. How do you know? You never tried. It's always been easier to dream about what you want than to go out and make it a reality." Her mother touched her cheek. "I've seen you succeed against impossible odds. Don't let this be the one time you're too afraid to go after what you want."

Her mother walked out of the room, leaving Taylor feeling as if she'd just gone ten rounds with a prizefighter. She slumped back on the sofa and closed her eyes. Her mind raced from subject to subject. Her mother's words echoed, most of them unpleasant truths. She wanted to protest that she hadn't backed away from making it work with Jonathan, but she had. Instead of staying and working it out, she'd run home. She'd taken his child and had punished him for not loving her enough. Yes, they'd both been young, but they'd also been unwilling to try.

The phone rang, startling her. She reached for it thinking that Linnie had arrived in Virginia, but just as she said "Hello," she glanced at her watch and realized it was too early.

"I wanted to check on you."

The sound of Jonathan's familiar voice made her blush. Hot embarrassment flooded through her. They'd made love and she'd run out on him because she couldn't face taking responsibility for her feelings. How mature was that?

"You're very thoughtful," she said, trying to sound normal. "I'm okay."

"You don't sound okay."

Her conversation with her mother along with her trip into the past had shattered her pride, not to mention protective barriers.

"I've been doing some inventory-taking. So far I haven't impressed myself with my past performances. You caught me in the middle of self-flagellation."

"Sounds kinky. Can I watch?"

Despite the ache inside, she chuckled softly. "It's not as attractive as it sounds."

"Want to talk about it?"

"Maybe. What do you charge by the hour?"

"Hey, I'd give you my professional discount. No charge."

"That's very generous." She closed her eyes and clutched the phone more tightly. "Jonathan, I'm sorry about Linnie."

"You've already apologized. We're dealing with it."

"I know I've said the words, but I have more insight now. I wanted to punish you for leaving me." She bit her lower lip. "I can't believe what I did to you. You're a good man and you deserved the chance to be her father. I took that away from you. There's nothing I can say or do to make it up. I wish I could. I would do anything to give you back that time."

Taylor opened her eyes, then wiped away the tears that spilled down her cheeks.

"I don't know what to say to that," he admitted.

"You don't have to say anything. I wanted to tell you how I felt."

"I'm sorry I couldn't be what you needed me to be," he said quietly.

"Thanks." She cleared her throat. "There's more. I'm calling my agent and accepting the book offer on the table."

"Taylor, why?"

"Because the offer is more amazing than anything I'd ever dreamed I would get."

"If you win, you could get more."

"This is enough. I don't expect you to understand but—"

"I do," he said, cutting her off. "There's more to life than being number one."

Despite everything she smiled. "You think?"

"I only wished I'd figured it out before."

She wondered if he was talking about all those years ago, when they'd been together.

"It's been quite a month," she told him.

"It's not over yet. Let me know when Linnie gets home, okay? Then I'll see you in the morning."

"Okay. Bye."

Jonathan put down the phone and stretched out on the bed. He could still smell the scent of their lovemaking, along with the sweet fragrance of Taylor's body lingering on the sheets.

As she'd said, it had been some kind of month. Five weeks ago he hadn't known he had a daughter and never thought about Taylor McGuire at all. He'd been entirely focused on his future. Now he had a child, he couldn't get Taylor out of his mind and following Oprah didn't seem quite so important.

Four days later Will still hadn't figured out how to fix things with Marnie. He knew there was a good chance that she would start throwing things when she saw him in her foyer. He also knew that he was crazy to think he could explain the situation to her—mostly because he didn't understand it himself. However, he did know one thing: that she was the best, most amazing person he'd ever met and he would rather die than have her hate him.

He heard her car door slam, then the sound of the garage door closing. He braced himself, trying to prepare his arguments, which was probably a waste of time. He didn't know how to talk about personal stuff. Now, if she needed her computer debugged, he was her man!

The click of high heels on the floor caught his attention. He tried not to let his jaw drop when he caught sight of her in a cropped T-shirt and shorts. She wore strappy sandals and there were little pink daisies painted on her toenails.

She came to a dead stop when she saw him. Her full lips straightened into a disapproving line and her eyebrows drew together.

"This is what I get for not taking my key back. What are you doing here?" she asked him, her voice low and cold.

He shuffled his feet and in an act of total desperation, held out a stack of papers. "I made a spreadsheet."

"Aren't we proud?"

She started to walk past him. He grabbed her arm to hold her in place.

"Marnie, please." He thrust the papers at her and waited until she grabbed them.

"Okay. You made a spreadsheet. I'm thrilled at your computer prowess. Next week maybe you can try a database for—" She glanced down at the papers. Her frown deepened. "What on earth?"

"I've listed all my dates," he said, leaning over her shoulder and pointing. "Who she was, how we met and what went wrong. I gave myself a positive score for what I did correctly, and a negative score for mistakes. This column references chapters in Dr. Kirby's book on

understanding women. Which I don't. This here is
what I later came up with as possible remedies for what
went wrong. Not that I could bring Fluffy back from
the dead."

Marnie looked at him, her eyes slightly glazed.
"Fluffy?"

"The cat." He pointed to the appropriate row. "She
died."

Marnie scanned the information. "Oh my. You were
in a bit of trouble there. You killed the family cat with a
poisonous plant?"

"Not on purpose."

She pointed to a score. "You gave yourself points for
bringing a gift, which I agree with. Of course that's off-
set by the negative points from killing the cat." The
corner of her mouth twitched. "I'm actually quite a fan
of cats, so I don't mean to laugh. It's just…"

Her voice trailed off as she studied the pages, flip-
ping slowly. There in laser print was his entire sad history of dating and his feeble attempts to have sex. He'd
even put in the part about the prostitute, down to how
he'd run out of her room, vowing he would rather die a
virgin than touch her.

When she finished, she stared at him. "You've had
quite a journey."

He shrugged. "I never meant to be so abnormal. It
just happened. I've read everything I could, Marnie,
but books aren't real life. I don't know how to be successful outside of work or a classroom situation." He
swallowed because he had her attention. He didn't
know what he was doing, but as he'd already blown his
chance with the only woman he'd ever fallen in love

with, he was left with an opportunity to apologize correctly. Her not hating him was his only goal.

"I never thought making love could be so amazing," he said slowly, staring into her green eyes and wishing he knew what she was thinking. Or maybe it was best that he didn't. "I never imagined I could feel like that, or be with someone like you."

She turned away. "I don't want to hear about being a good lay."

He grabbed her arm again, forcing her to face him. "Don't you dare say that, or think it. I do not consider you a lay. It was never like that. I screwed up. I said the wrong thing. Yes, I was convinced that someone so beautiful would have been hit on by every guy in America and I thought you had given in. That was wrong of me. But geez, Marnie. Take a look in the mirror. Is it such a surprising mistake to make?"

Tears filled her eyes. "I would never sell myself."

"I *know.* I made assumptions based on physical appearance and I know better than that. I've been judged all my life. I can't believe I was so stupid and thoughtless. The worst part isn't that I lost my chance with you, if I ever had one, but that I hurt you. I would never do that on purpose. I'm so sorry for how I made you feel."

A single tear trickled down her cheek. Will felt as if he'd been slugged. His insides ached and he felt helpless to heal her pain.

"I'm sorry," he whispered, lightly brushing away the tear. "Oh, Marnie, you're spectacular in every way. Sometimes it's hard to get past your face and your body, but even if it makes you mad, I have to tell you that I like who you are on the inside a lot more than who you are on the outside. While I can appreciate your beauty, it makes me nervous."

He tried to smile, but failed. God, he was screwing this up. "What I mean is I'd like you better if you were ugly."

The single sentence hung in the silence. He wished he had a gun so he could shoot himself right now. Just end it. Humiliation clawed at his throat as Marnie stared blankly.

"What?" she asked.

"I didn't mean that the way it came out," he said quickly. "What I'm trying to say is it wasn't about sex. It was about you. Being with you. Playing Trivial Pursuit and talking. Those evenings were the best of my life. You're kind and gentle and smart. I'm falling in love with you."

He released his hold on her arm and handed her the house key. "I'm going to go now."

He turned and headed for the front door. He'd parked around the side of the house so she wouldn't see his truck and leave without talking to him. Now he'd said everything he had to say and it was time to go back to the empty solitude of his life.

"Walking out on our problems doesn't solve them."

He heard the words and came to an abrupt stop. "What?" he asked, slowly turning back to her.

She shook his papers at him before dropping them onto the floor. "For someone who reads so much, you're not very smart."

"I know. It's a failing."

She closed the distance between them and stared at him. Nervously, he pushed up his glasses.

"I have some responsibility in this, too," she told him. "I was looking for a man as wonderful as George, and that's not going to happen."

Will felt as if she'd reached inside and ripped out his guts. Pain spilled from him. Of course. He should have known. Why would he have thought—

"The thing is," Marnie continued, "everyone is different. George had his ways of being wonderful and you have yours. I should have recognized that from the beginning."

Had he heard her correctly? "I'm . . . ah, wonderful?" he asked hesitantly.

"Sometimes you're a real jerk, but yes, you have qualities that are pretty excellent." She wrapped her arms around him. "I think maybe I got scared when we made love. It was really special and I overreacted to your assumptions. Later, when you wanted to talk about how great it had been, I was still hurt because I thought it was just about bodies to you."

He hugged her close. "It's not just about that. I swear. I'll take a lie detector test if you want."

She laughed. "I don't think that's necessary, but thanks for offering."

"I'd do anything for you, Marnie. I meant what I said. About my feelings."

She raised her head and looked at him. "You think maybe we could spend some time getting to know each other before we talk about that?"

"All I ask is that you give me a second chance."

She nodded and pressed her lips to his. Heat filled him instantly. Then she stepped back. "By the way, while we're confessing our secrets, I have one of my own."

The fear returned. He'd failed to please her in bed? They'd—

"Will! Stop panicking. All I want to tell you is that I rigged the contest."

"What?"

She sighed. "I went to see your buddy Mark. He arranged to have us matched up." She leaned her forehead against his chest. "I've had a crush on you for a long time, but you never seemed to notice me. I didn't know how else to get your attention without scaring you off."

"I . . ." He closed his mouth then tried again. "But you . . ." A crush? On him? Her?

She laughed and took his hand. "Hard to believe, but true. I thought you were sweet. After I got to know you, I was thrilled to find out I liked who you were on the inside."

He was still speechless. After a couple of seconds he noticed she was leading him upstairs.

Trying not to get his hopes up, he asked as casually as he could, "Where are we going?"

"To make love." She grinned. "I said we should get to know each other better. I guess I didn't mention that I wanted to do that naked. Besides, I've been cruising the Internet and I've found one or two things we might like to teach each other."

His heart filled with joy. Unable to help himself, he swung her up in his arms. "I meant what I said," he told her between kisses. "I'd feel this way if you were ugly."

"Words to warm a woman's heart."

He winced. "Did I say that wrong?"

"No," she whispered, then kissed him back. "You said everything exactly right."

Chapter 24

Chris got up and pulled on her robe. It was new—silk and the palest shade of lavender. Not exactly practical for the working single mom of three kids. Her body felt pleasantly tired, and not because she'd put in a long night. Instead, she and Rio had spent hours making love. Now she stared at her sleeping ex-husband and tried to figure out what they were doing.

His eyes fluttered open. "What are you thinking?"

Rio sat up in bed, not bothering to pull the sheet over him to cover his naked body. Chris allowed her gaze to linger. This morning he'd proved that he still knew how to push all her buttons. So where did that leave them?

She sat on the end of the bed and smiled at him. "Just about us . . . about this morning."

He grinned. "Pretty amazing for an old married couple, huh?"

"We're not married, Rio. We haven't been in a long time." She pulled the robe closer, knowing that its purchase meant that he wouldn't be paying her the full amount of child support she was due.

"You're great with the kids," she said slowly. "They adore you. I adore you."

He rubbed his jaw. "But?"

"I can't do this. You've let me down too many times for me to ever trust you again. I want it to be different," she said quickly. "Believe me, this past month has been such a learning process. For a while I thought maybe it would be okay." She touched his leg through the covers. "You still want to go out and race every chance you get. You're not doing it because you're trying to make me happy, but how long can that last? How long until you resent me for keeping you from what you love?"

"But I love you. I want to be with you."

She stared at him, not sure what to say. A part of her wanted to give in, but she couldn't. She was tired of being his mother, too. If she was going to be in a relationship, she wanted it to be with a partner.

"I'm not angry," she said. "I don't hate you or think less of you. But I don't want to be married to you."

He glanced away from her. "Are you still thinking of going to Dallas?"

She nodded.

"I didn't think I'd be able to change your mind," he said, still not looking at her. "Maybe I can find a job in Dallas, like you said. I need to be near my kids."

"They need you. I would really like it if you were close."

"Then that's what I'll do."

Impulsively, she reached for him. They held each other tightly. Chris felt tears on her cheeks.

"Tell me you love me," he whispered. "Just say it one last time."

"I love you, Rio."

She'd said the words a thousand times before. Maybe more. Something inside of her shifted as she spoke, and for the first time ever, the words were a lie.

"Have you thought about what you'd like to do with the money if you won?" Dr. McGuire asked.

Grace smiled at Nelson, who held her hand in his. He smiled back. "No, we haven't," he said. "If you think there's a chance we might, I guess we'll have to consider the matter."

A million dollars, Grace thought contentedly. If the Lord blessed them with the bounty, they would, as Nelson said, consider what to do. It would be discussed and her opinion would matter. As she did nearly every moment she was awake, she marveled at her good fortune. After all these years to finally find complete happiness with a man. She wouldn't have thought it possible.

Dr. McGuire pulled out a pad of paper. "Give it some thought. You two have as much chance as everyone else." She scanned the notes she'd made during their last session, then looked up at them.

"So, how's it going?"

"Just fine," Grace said.

"You're getting along?" Dr. Kirby asked. *He's a handsome man,* Grace thought, *although not as handsome as my Nelson.*

She nearly giggled. *My Nelson.* It was hard to believe she had the right to think of him that way. But she did.

He'd told her he loved her and she'd admitted her feelings as well.

"Oh, yes. Grace is a bit of a talker," Nelson said fondly. "She gets up and tells the Lord to start the day while I prefer to stay up late at night and sleep in."

Dr. McGuire frowned. "Does that create friction?"

"Not at all," Grace assured her. "I like puttering around the house in the morning. Nelson enjoys his time alone at night. We spend the afternoons together."

She was careful to avoid Nelson's teasing gaze. She was *not* about to share with the nice young doctors what exactly they did during most of their afternoons.

"We have our routine," Nelson said. "I read several newspapers a day, while Grace prefers television or a good mystery novel." He shrugged. "I never was much of a fiction reader myself."

"So you don't have much in common?" Dr. Kirby asked.

Nelson glanced at her. "Grace is the prettiest lady I've had the pleasure of sitting next to in all my days. As for having things in common, we both have deep faith, we go shopping together, we argue about our favorite flavors of ice cream. When we pray together, she does most of the talking. After hearing me preach for nearly forty years, I'm sure the Lord is grateful for the change."

Dr. McGuire shifted in her seat. "Yes, well, that's lovely. But I'm confused. Are you two staying together at the end of the month?"

Nelson raised Grace's hand and kissed it gently. "I hope so." He turned to her. "In fact, I had planned to propose this week."

Grace gasped in surprise. Her heart filled with so much love and joy, she knew she could never be sad again.

"Nelson?"

"I love you, Grace. I want to spend the rest of my life with you . . . if you'll have me."

"I'd be lost without you," she whispered. "I'm honored."

He kissed her on the mouth and returned his attention to the psychologists. "That should answer your question."

Dr. McGuire blinked. "It does."

Both she and Dr. Kirby looked stunned. Dr. Kirby raised his hands, as if he didn't understand either.

"We're in love," Grace said, trying to explain what to her was fairly obvious.

"Excuse me if this sounds rude," Dr. Kirby said. "But why?"

"Who knows?" Grace glanced at Nelson. "We're right for each other. We have been from the moment we met. It was magic. That's what love is. The magic is all around us, if we're willing to take a chance and believe."

The older couple left the office. They practically floated with happiness.

"Magic?" Jonathan said disbelievingly. "I'd agree to sexual attraction maybe, or even having a lot in common."

Taylor looked at him. "Gee, thanks for the footnote of approval of my theory."

"Are you saying you're not shocked?"

Taylor shook her head. "No. They caught me off

guard, too. I'll admit it." What she wouldn't admit was a feeling of envy. She wanted what they had. She wanted Jonathan with her for the rest of their lives.

She cleared her throat and forced her unrealistic hopes and dreams away. "So how do you think we're going to quantify the magic element?"

"Hell if I know." He stared at the closed door as if expecting them to return with the answer. Finally he turned his attention to her. "Do you believe in magic?"

She tried not to flush. "Of course not. I'm a trained psychologist. I understand the workings of the human mind and all the reasons . . ." She shrugged. "Okay, psychobabble aside, it's actually not a bad description for what happens when people fall in love."

Jonathan leaned back in his chair. "I've spent nearly fifteen years telling people how to have happier relationships. I've given seminars to thousands of people, gone on talk shows, written books. Are you telling me that it all comes down to magic? What about the biological attraction between a man and a woman? What about the societal pressures to produce children?"

"I think it's pretty unlikely Grace and Nelson are going to be reproducing," she teased.

"You've got a point."

"They fell in love."

"According to your theory, they shouldn't have."

She winced. "Great. Our senior citizens are proving your theory of sexual attraction. I suppose it's something to look forward to in my old age." Assuming she didn't spend it alone, pining for the one man she couldn't have.

Jonathan laughed. "I can't believe it. My entire professional career is crashing down around me."

"You're taking this too seriously."

He wasn't. Jonathan knew that he had fundamentally changed. He didn't know how much of it was the town, his daughter, or being with Taylor again. What had once been so important—his career—now didn't matter as much. He stood and crossed the room.

Love as magic. Was it possible?

"Who have you loved?" he asked, pacing toward the desk.

She stared at him as if he'd started speaking Latin. "Excuse me?"

"In your life, who have you loved?"

She shifted in her seat. "Why do you want to know?"

"I'm exploring the metaphysical question. Did you fall in love because of magic?"

She relaxed. "No. Because of the man."

"You see. They're crazy."

"Dr. Kirby, I believe you were the one who reminded *me* that we don't use words like that in our profession. Besides which, I'm not sure that Nelson and Grace are wrong. What about the women you've loved? Can you tell me the wheres and whys?"

He stared at her. The women he had loved? He could tell her about the women he'd dated and the women he'd slept with. He could talk about his ex-wife, although he no longer understood why he'd married her. But loved. Who had he loved?

Taylor. She'd been his first love. And then no one.

The revelation stopped him in mid-pace. No one? Not one other person? Linnie, of course. He would love his daughter, but that was different. How could he not have seen that truth before? Or had he ignored it because it got in the way of his need to be the best?

He turned and stared at Taylor. She frowned. "Jonathan, what's wrong?"

He'd assumed with the arrogance of youth that finding another relationship like the one he had with her would be simple. That he would love again, perhaps many times. Only he hadn't. All these years—what had he been looking for? Taylor?

Of course. Taylor. She was the one who made him believe in magic.

"Knock, knock!"

He looked up and saw Katrina entering the office. "Oh, good," she chirped. "You're both here."

Taylor stood. "We are and we're expecting a client in a couple of seconds."

The talk-show host cut her off with a flick of her wrist. "Not a client, dear. Contestants. We're here to film the exit interviews. Rumor has it the contest is going to be close. I want to capture every moment on film."

"You understand this is simply an exit interview," Katrina Melon said with an insincere smile. "It will in no way affect the outcome of the contest. Whether or not the two of you plan to stay together after today, you *are* entered in the drawing."

She leaned forward and assumed what Chris supposed was a sincere pose. It wasn't working.

"In the interest of science, it's important that you be completely honest with me," the television reporter said.

Rio grunted. "Yeah, sure."

Chris narrowed her gaze. She didn't like the well-groomed reporter with her fancy, expensive suit and her "oh, of course you can trust me" voice. She much preferred Dr. McGuire's down-to-earth nature.

Chris sought out Taylor's gaze. "Are you doing this with everyone?"

"Absolutely. Dr. Kirby and I are holding exit interviews, as Katrina said. However, they're not all being filmed. If you object to the camera crew, we can ask them to leave."

Chris looked at her husband, who shrugged at her as if to say it didn't matter.

"I guess it's all right," she told Dr. McGuire.

"Thanks." Dr. McGuire gave her a reassuring smile. "We need to know if you and Rio will be staying together as a couple. In addition, if you have any concerns about the process you've just been through, or are worried about what is going to happen to you afterward, Jonathan and I are available for counseling."

Dr. Kirby winked at Chris. "Taylor is forever giving away our services for free. Please, take advantage of that."

Katrina cleared her throat. "Shall we continue?"

She parted her lips in what Chris assumed was a smile, although her face didn't seem to be working right. Too much plastic surgery, she thought, feeling slightly better. She wasn't against a little nip and tuck, but trying to look twenty years younger was not only crazy, it was a recipe for medical disaster.

Katrina consulted her notes. "You two were matched via Taylor's questionnaire. Is that correct?"

"Yes," Chris said.

"Will you be continuing to see each other now that the contest is over?"

Chris hesitated, then shot Taylor an apologetic look. "No, but it's not her fault. Rio and I were divorced when we signed up for this. Every problem we have existed long before we met her. We were really interested in a chance at the money, not saving our marriage."

Taylor shook her head. "Chris, it's fine. You don't have to explain."

Katrina scribbled on her pad. "So despite being a nearly perfect match, you aren't happy together? Interesting."

Chris's hold on her temper slipped. "Look. Dr. McGuire is a really good therapist and if you try to say otherwise, you're going to look like an idiot."

Dr. Kirby winked at her. "I couldn't agree more."

Taylor laughed. "Gee, thanks, but I don't think Katrina is here to make anyone look bad. I'm sure she's just going to do her job and report fairly."

Katrina looked pained. "What else?"

Chris didn't believe the reporter for a second. She fumed, then realized there was nothing she could do. She had a house to pack and kids to move. It was time to get on with her life.

"So you'll be staying together?" Katrina asked.

Taylor was aware that the other woman was still making a play for Jonathan. She just wished Katrina wouldn't sound so gleeful every time he scored another couple for his side. So much for impartial reporting.

Marnie and Will sat across from them, both looking blissfully happy.

"We'll be seeing each other," Marnie said discreetly.

Taylor had to look away to keep from laughing. She

knew for a fact that the two of them were playing house in Marnie's big mansion. Based on the glow, she doubted they were sleeping in separate beds.

Katrina asked several more questions, wrote on her pad, then thanked the couple. Taylor rose with them. She and Marnie moved toward the door, while Will had a word with Jonathan.

"I hate her," Marnie whispered, pointing at Katrina. "Why's she being so mean to you?"

"She wants Jonathan."

"Tell her she can't have him." Marnie leaned closer. "Speaking of having, why don't the four of us go to dinner sometime? I've never been on a double date in my life and I think it would be fun."

Taylor didn't want to spoil her friend's good mood, so she spoke casually. "I believe that Jonathan is heading back to New York after the drawing tomorrow."

"You believe? Is this psychobabble or do you really not know."

Taylor shrugged. "I don't know. We haven't talked about it."

"Then you'd better. You can't be serious about letting that man get away."

"I don't know what's going to happen." Which was true. Taylor couldn't remember ever being this confused before.

"Take a chance," Marnie said. "Tell him how you feel. If you don't, you'll regret it for the rest of your life."

"What if I don't know how I feel?"

Marnie looked impatient. "Then you're lying to yourself, because it's written all over your face."

Her friend kissed her cheek, then left with Will. Taylor stared after them, envying their obvious happiness. Was Marnie right? Should she tell Jonathan how she felt? Was it too late for them? Chris and Rio hadn't made their second chance work. Could she and Jonathan?

Chapter
25

7he high school marching band turned the corner, the last notes of the wedding march fading into silence. Taylor winced. It was not a tune best played by an overly enthusiastic brass section made up of teenagers. Jonathan grimaced.

"Do they play that a lot?" he asked.

"I think this is a special occasion for them."

He laughed. They sat on folding chairs behind the podium set up in the main square. City officials were to their left, Katrina to their right.

"You love this place, don't you," he said, leaning close.

"Of course."

He nodded as if the information were not a surprise. "I think I'll miss it, too."

Taylor didn't want to think about him leaving. "You might come back from time to time to see Linnie," she said, trying to sound casual.

"Is that an invitation?"

Here it was, she told herself. The perfect opportunity to tell him how she felt.

"Jonathan, I—"

Katrina rose to her feet and approached the microphone. *Talk about timing,* Taylor thought glumly.

"Good afternoon, ladies and gentlemen," Katrina said. "I'm Katrina Melon and as this entire event was born on my show, it seems right that I should be here to wrap things up." She smiled and paused for applause.

"Now, about our contest. All of you who participated have been interviewed over the past few days. I must say I found your experiences fascinating. Both theories on relationships are extremely valid." She paused expectantly. "Which created the unforeseen circumstance of a tie. Both Dr. Kirby and Dr. McGuire have eleven couples who will stay together after the contest and nine who won't." She glanced at Taylor and Jonathan, glaring as if she blamed them personally for this anticlimactic moment.

"That being said, let's get on with finding a winner for the one million dollars."

Screams of delight filled the air. Taylor rose along with the rest of the dignitaries. Everyone clapped. Katrina picked up a large glass bowl filled with cards and motioned for Jonathan to join her.

"Are you ready?" she asked, then nodded at Jonathan. He pulled out a single card.

"Grace Anderson and Nelson Reed," he said into the microphone.

People turned frantically, trying to find the couple. Taylor struggled to put faces to the names, then laughed when she remembered the charming older couple who believed in magic.

Sure enough, as the crowd parted, she saw tall, white-haired Nelson leading Grace toward the stage. Both of them were laughing with delight. Taylor walked to Jonathan's side.

"It couldn't have happened to a nicer couple," she told him.

"Oh, I don't know. What about us?"

He was being cryptic. Worse, he was doing it in front of several hundred people.

Grace and Nelson made their way up the stairs. Nelson waved when he saw them. It took several minutes for them to reach the microphone and when they did, dozens of flashbulbs exploded in their faces.

"Oh my," Nelson said into the microphone. "I never thought I'd be a celebrity at this late date."

Everyone cheered. Taylor moved close to Grace. "Congratulations," she whispered.

The older woman patted her hand. "We owe our happiness to you and Dr. Kirby," she said. "If you hadn't come up with this contest, Nelson and I would never have met."

Taylor shook her head. "I think you owe your happiness all to yourselves."

Nelson cleared his throat and spoke into the microphone. "We never expected to win this money. However, at our exit interview, Dr. McGuire asked us what we would do if we won, so we've been talking it over." He drew Grace close and put his arm around her.

"This lovely woman has agreed to marry me."

Cheers erupted.

Nelson chuckled. "That's how I felt, too, when she said yes. So we're going to spend a little money on a small wedding, then a cruise. In addition, we'll be giving each of the other couples ten thousand dollars."

The roar that followed was deafening. Taylor saw several of the couples hugging and clapping. It was a most generous gesture.

Nelson held up his hands for quiet. "The remainder of the money is going to a very important cause. Grace and I will be donating it to the Marriageville women's shelter with the request that they pay closer attention to older battered wives. There's a great need out there."

Chris couldn't hear what Nelson Reed was saying anymore but that didn't make her any less happy. "Ten thousand dollars," she repeated. "I can't believe it."

"Me, either." Rio grinned like a little kid who's just discovered a candy mine in his backyard. "Do you know what we can do with that money?"

Her stomach tightened. Please God, don't let him start talking about a new race car. But before she could say anything, he touched her cheek.

"Don't sweat it, Chris. I thought we could use the money to pay off the car I trashed at the races, and the rest could finance the move to Dallas."

Relief filled her. "That would be great."

As she spoke, she found herself swept up in his arms and pulled close. "I'm sorry," he said into her ear. "This whole thing seemed like a good idea at the time."

"It *was* a good idea," she told him. "If we hadn't tried again we wouldn't have known if we would have made it." He released her and she stepped back. "I want you to be happy, Rio. I mean that."

He hugged her again. "You, too, Chris. You're the best thing that ever happened to me. Find some responsible guy and have the life you want."

Tears filled her eyes. Tears of relief and happiness. Maybe things were going to be all right now.

Marnie leaned against Will as Nelson Reed outlined his plans for the women's shelter donation. She'd always been a big supporter of the shelter, but they certainly could use more money. Maybe Grace and Nelson's generosity would make its way into the media, causing other people to give as well.

Speaking of money . . . "Will, you can take the ten thousand dollars for yourself," she said. "I don't need it."

He stiffened and for a second she thought she'd insulted him. "Shouldn't I have said that?" she asked.

"No, it's fine. It's just…" He cleared his throat.

She stepped back. "What is it? Are you in some kind of financial trouble?"

"No. Not at all. It's just—" He pushed up his glasses. "The thing is a few years ago I developed this software program. It allows Internet servers to talk to each other more quickly." He started into a technical description that made her eyes cross.

She grabbed him by the front of his shirt and tried to shake him. He didn't budge. "What is your point?" she asked when he stopped talking.

"Oh. That I licensed the software design."

She thought about the little she knew about software. Then she thought about Bill Gates. "Will? How much are you worth?"

He shrugged. "Ten million, give or take a few thousand." He blushed as he spoke.

She shrieked once, then wrapped her arms around him. "You, sir, get more perfect every day."

Jonathan watched as the older couple was congratulated by everyone on the stage. Katrina still looked angry enough to spit. She'd been hoping for something more exciting than a tie to boost her ratings and keep her in the limelight.

From his place on the stage, he could see the crowd collecting in the square. There was an ice cream cart across the street and a couple of kids riding their bikes. This town was unlike any place he'd ever seen. He didn't know if Marriageville was the reason he felt different inside, if it was meeting his daughter or if Taylor had transformed him. Or maybe he'd done it all by himself. Regardless, he wasn't the same man who had arrived here over a month ago. Being the best in his career no longer seemed so damned important. How much more money did he need? He was financially secure for the rest of his life, he enjoyed his work. Wasn't it time to climb a different mountain?

He saw Taylor being hugged by her mother, and he thought about how she'd done such a good job raising his daughter. She had dreams. Funny how seventeen years ago he'd never thought to ask what they were.

He headed for the microphone. "It's not a tie," he said loudly.

There was a gasp from the crowd. Katrina glared at

him. "What are you saying?" the talk-show host said, hurrying to his side. "What are you talking about?"

He ignored her. He even ignored the crowd. Instead he focused all his attention on the only woman who had ever touched his heart.

Taylor took a single step toward him, then paused. "Jonathan, what are you doing?"

"There was one other couple," he said into the microphone, still looking at her.

"The man had his priorities all screwed up, but the woman knew exactly what was right. He's learned a lot from her."

"You're making this up," Katrina said, trying to push him away from the microphone. The crowd had gone completely silent. "She's not worth it. Can't you just sleep with her and forget her?"

He covered the microphone with his hand and shrugged. "I did sleep with her. And I can't forget her."

Katrina glared at him, then stomped away. "Make a fool out of yourself," she announced as she went. "I don't care."

Jonathan ignored her and motioned for Taylor to join him. She approached hesitantly. He put an arm around her and pulled her close.

"As I was saying, there was one more couple," he said into the microphone. "I took Dr. McGuire's quiz and I found out that we're perfect for each other. Even if she tries to run me out of town, I'm not leaving, so we're going to be together a long time. That makes twelve couples for her and eleven for me. Dr. McGuire's the winner."

Taylor's head was spinning. She tried to catch her breath but couldn't. People yelled out questions, those on the stage were talking loudly, but she couldn't make out what anyone was saying. She looked at Jonathan.

"What are you doing? What about Oprah?"

He grinned. "She's a lovely woman and I doubt she'll care if my show follows hers or not." He touched her face. "I love you, Taylor. I always have. I got lost for a while, but now I'm home. You showed me I belong here, with you."

"But what about your career, your talk show?"

"What about you telling me you love me back?"

Tears filled her eyes. She threw herself into his arms. "I've loved you all my life. I've never loved anyone but you."

"That's kind of how I feel."

It was only when the crowd noise grew deafening that she realized the microphone had picked up everything they'd said. But she was too happy to be embarrassed.

"Marry me," he said, then kissed her before she could answer.

She pulled back long enough to whisper, "Yes," and the crowd went wild.

The two men from the television syndication company looked at each other. "Change of plans," the first one said. "We need them *both* on the show. Who the hell is Dr. McGuire's agent? Get him or her on the phone pronto. I want to make a deal."

Somewhere in the Virginia woods, Heather Allison stared at her best friend. "Look! Your parents are kissing."

Linnie clutched a pillow to her chest and tried not to hope too much. But there they were, kissing on national television. They looked pretty in love to her.

Happiness filled her. It seemed she was going to get her wish for a family after all.

Heather shrieked. "He's touching her butt!"

Linnie stared. Sure enough her father's hand had slid down to her mother's rear. She covered her face with the pillow and screamed. "It's one thing for them to fall in love and get married," she gasped. "But do they have to have sex, too? Gross!"